"Written with humour and wisdom and delightful abandon, *At Last Count* negotiates a way through this often unfathomable life with loveable, fallible characters and a story you won't soon forget."

— JANE FINLAY-YOUNG, AUTHOR OF *FROM BRUISED FELL*

"Full disclosure: I didn't understand the allure of birding until I read *At Last Count*. Paisley Ratchford is a beautifully drawn character who has endured much in her short life. She has OCD, the depiction of which is at once realistic, sensitive, and uplifting. I couldn't stop turning the pages as I followed Paisley's journey to confront her demons. Claire Ross Dunn masterfully weaves heartbreak and hope together through the prism of searching for the rarest bird of all, happiness."

— ZARQA NAWAZ, CREATOR OF *LITTLE MOSQUE ON THE PRAIRIE*,
AUTHOR OF *LAUGHING ALL THE WAY TO THE MOSQUE*
AND *JAMEELA GREEN RUINS EVERYTHING*

"Dunn has a way of making us laugh and cry in the same breath. She makes us think about the patterns we keep on retracing and the joy of taking flight."

— ABBY SHER, AUTHOR OF *AMEN, AMEN, AMEN: MEMOIR OF A
GIRL WHO COULDN'T STOP PRAYING (AMONG OTHER THINGS)*

"Claire Ross Dunn has written a beautiful novel! *At Last Count* is as touching and moving as anything by American bestseller Anne Tyler—that funny and heartbreaking chronicler of life's disasters and how we manage to move through them."

— ANTANAS SILEIKA, AUTHOR OF *PROVISIONALLY YOURS*

AT LAST COUNT

Claire Ross Dunn

Invisible Publishing
Halifax & Prince Edward County

For many years, in the sixties and then again forty years later, my in-laws lived on Amherst Island, in Lake Ontario, between Prince Edward County and Wolfe Island, near the city of Kingston. I was deeply inspired by the magic of the place and its wonderful, warm community. Nevertheless, the people and events depicted in *At Last Count* are entirely fictional. For the purposes of this story, some places have also been invented or altered in their description.

Library and Archives Canada Cataloguing in Publication
Title: At last count / Claire Ross Dunn.
Names: Dunn, Claire Ross, author.
Identifiers: Canadiana (print) 20220158517
              Canadiana (ebook) 20220158525
              ISBN 9781988784953 (softcover)
              ISBN 9781988784960 (HTML)

Classification: LCC PS8607.U5495 A8 2022 | DDC C813/.6—dc23

Edited by Leigh Nash
Cover and interior design by Megan Fildes | Typeset in Laurentian
With thanks to type designer Rod McDonald

Invisible Publishing is committed to protecting our natural environment. As part of our efforts, both the cover and interior of this book are printed on acid-free 100% post-consumer recycled fibres.

Printed and bound in Canada.

Invisible Publishing | Halifax & Prince Edward County
www.invisiblepublishing.com

Published with the generous assistance of the Canada Council for the Arts, the Ontario Arts Council, and the Government of Canada.

"I would say…to whomever needs to do all these things…thank you for keeping your hands washed, and for counting the cracks in the sidewalk, and for making sure the lights are off and the oven is off and the plugs are unplugged and the door is locked. And your work is done."

— ABBY SHER, INTERVIEW ON CBC RADIO ONE'S *TAPESTRY*

NOW

Paisley Ratchford was trying to open her apartment mailbox. Her fingers ached from the cold and weren't working. She stuck her hands between her generous thighs and clamped tight, just for a moment, to warm them up. The building was frigid. Month of March frigid.

She tried to open the mailbox again. Success. She pulled out a *Snapshot of Your Ontario* pamphlet from Premier Dalton McGuinty's office and slid it into the overflowing recycle bin. She found flyers from pizza and Chinese food joints and sifted through, adding the ones she already had to recycling, too. She would file the new ones alphabetically in an accordion file she had for just that purpose. Takeout was helpful when you weren't able to leave your apartment. You could order an Indian dinner for four from the India House on Sherbourne, for example—Paisley's favourite—and have it last the week. There was also this month's issue of *Birders International*, with a cover photo of a birder from the UK. He was standing in a marsh, his soaked shirt revealing his six-pack and, well, nipples. British water must be cold, thought Paisley. He was photographing a pair of critically endangered spoon-billed sandpipers (*Calidris pygmaea*), which the Wildfowl and Wetlands Trust reserve in Slimbridge, Gloucestershire, had brought over from the sandpipers' home in Russia's far east, to start a breeding program. The cover of *Birders International* promised a centrefold, but it wasn't clear if it was of the birder or the birds. Both were enticing. And there was yet another reminder from the building's management about the impending eviction.

How could she forget?

Paisley balanced the eviction notice on the ledge and put her hands back between her thighs, resisting the urge to tap out an eight.

1 2 3 4 5 6 7 8

Eight.

Eight is a composite number, with the divisors of one, two, and four.

A cool trick of eight: any number—no matter how big— is divisible by eight if its last three digits, taken as a number, are divisible by eight.

Eight is a pattern of which figure skaters are quite fond.

All spiders have eight legs. Octopuses have eight tentacles.

Eight is a lucky number in Chinese culture.

In humans, there are eight teeth in each quadrant of the mouth, and the eighth tooth is called the wisdom tooth.

Eight is the atomic number of oxygen—so, in one sense, the number eight is necessary to breathe.

Eight is double four. Four is the number of fingers on each hand, minus your thumb, which isn't a finger but a digit.

A digit is also a number.

Four is the number of taps you can make if you tap thumb to index finger, thumb to middle finger, thumb to ring finger, thumb to baby finger.

Each time you tap, you say the number under your breath: 1, 2, 3, 4.

Next time: 5, 6, 7, 8.

And on and on like that. Eight times over, if things are particularly bad.

As with most things in life, there is a spectrum to OCD, or obsessive-compulsive disorder. It can go from non-existent to mild to off-the-charts type stuff. Day to day, Paisley was in the mild-to-medium range, with bad episodes only happening once or twice a year, or when lightning of some sort struck. After a neighbour's grease fire a few years ago, Paisley's counting had been so bad, she hadn't left her apartment for weeks. But who could blame her? A grease fire was a dangerous thing. That would make anyone anxious.

No, things were manageable now—contained—had

been for a long time. Paisley rarely needed to worry about being caught counting. Back in the day, as a kid on Amherst Island, when she'd been widely known to count, one set of eight under her breath had generally kept things on the straight and narrow. Eight sets of eight were awkward and obvious but helped even more. More than eight sets because of some difficulty could put you into a place of further difficulty, not to mention the fact that all that counting was time-consuming.

This most recent eviction notice gave Paisley a desire for eights for the first time in a while. Because the outside of the envelope, in capital letters, declared: *IMPORTANT NEW INFORMATION ENCLOSED*. She stared at the envelope and picked at a cuticle on her thumb, tearing it down several layers with her teeth, not just the dry skin but the pink flesh beneath. It would hurt like hell later. Her nose, still covered with freckles at her age, was dripping from the cold. She stared down, past the old winter coat and all its pockets (ideal for winter birding), the same U of T sweatshirt hoodie and jeans she'd been wearing for the last week, to her fake Uggs, which were covered in salt stains. Between the dripping nose, the dirty boots, and the shredded cuticles, she must look like a mess. She felt like one. Being evicted was a disaster. She shook off the desire for counting and opened the notice right there.

THEN

The clock radio came on at seven: "Kiss on My List" by Daryl Hall and John Oates. Hall and Oates were massively good and medium cute. Paisley whipped on her clothes—a striped sailor T-shirt and faded denim pleated shorts—and wondered if she'd ever be kissed. Not that kissing was on her list, not at thirteen. Birds were on her list. Nevertheless, she knew kissing was something the kids did in haylofts all over the island—or the back beach, school dances, ferry dock, street dance, or the dry rock quarry—on Friday nights. Even if the rest of what they did was a mystery.

It was the last Saturday of July 1981. For the past thirty-two years, probably the next hundred and thirty-two, too, the last Saturday of July was the day of the annual St. Andrew's Presbyterian Church summer social. The whole house smelled of pies, which filled Paisley with a simple joy. She opened her brown-and-orange curtains and looked out the window. Not a cloud in the sky. Perfect.

She gave her thick, dark hair a quick brush, then tied it with a green hairbow, then untied it, then tied it again, bigger bow this time. She inspected herself in the mirror. She was nothing special—curvaceous like her mother, boobs and all, even at thirteen, but she'd blend into a crowd without any effort. You've got shoulders wider than a swimmer, her mother would say, thighs like a horse, front teeth like a cute little rabbit but a rabbit still, and enough hair on your head for two, don't you ever comb it? Paisley did, but it had a mind of its own. She wanted hair as glamorous as Farrah Fawcett's. Not a chance.

She grabbed a tin full of coins—allowance from the last four months. There would be so many things to buy at the summer social: cupcakes with butter frosting, used books galore, old *Tiger Beat* magazines, new-to-her clothes, treasures from the white elephant table. She couldn't wait.

Eudora Ratchford, or Eudie for short, stood barefoot in the kitchen amid a dusting of flour, rolling out pastry. Pies lined the counter, cooling.

"They smell sooooo good," cooed Paisley. "You're going to bake the most pies of everyone!"

Paisley slipped past her mother into a chair at the kitchen table and poured herself some cereal. I should resist, she thought, putting a handful back into the box. If I time it right, I can save my calories for a cupcake that would officially be breakfast, and then I can have another cupcake or pie and ice cream for lunch, and if I eat nothing else, I won't even come out heavier tomorrow. Eudie was always on Paisley about self-control and being the very best you could be. Watch your waistline, watch your p's and q's, watch how other people do things to fit in, watch your table manners. "Would you put your elbows on the table if you were dining with the Queen?" Eudie would ask. "No. I don't think so." Paisley wasn't so sure her mother thought like other islanders. But she tried her best to be perfect—even if, to her mother, Paisley's best didn't usually seem like enough.

"Where's Dad?" Paisley asked. Putting cereal back into the box was not as easy as getting it out.

"Where's Dad! Where's Dad, exactly! Where's Dad!" said Eudie, rolling, rolling. "I've been up since four baking pies, I have pies coming out of rude places, so that's exactly what I want to know. Where the hell is your father!"

With Eudie, a simple question always had the chance of backfiring. Sometimes things with Paisley's mother were just fine—fun, even. She was an interesting person, even Paisley could see that, and she was happiest, and lightest, when she felt appreciated. Usually Paisley knew just when to give her mother a compliment: your hair looks nice, the pies smell wonderful, I love it when you tell me that story, can you tell me again? That's when Eudie's best side would shine. She'd let you into this wonderful world of possibility.

She'd feel seen and so you'd feel seen, too. She had a pretty great imagination, because she'd read lots of books about the things she wanted to do. Paisley had found a grocery list pad in the kitchen drawer once, and on a page that started out with *bread, flour, lard, strawberry jam, whatever's on sale*, there was another list at the bottom: *things to do before I die*. That list had on it: *see a Bengal tiger, write a bestseller romance, take French lessons in Paris, become a vet, do some rapids, pose nude, save someone's life*. It made Paisley see a different side to her mother, one she never shared. And it made her wish she could see much more of this Eudie than the regular one.

But this moment with the pies was the other side of Eudie. The darker side. More explosive. Paisley knew to tread carefully now. One false move and—

"Where else would he be but at the farm?" Eudie said. "Where else is he ever?"

No way out but down—or maybe out. Paisley could see Rory Whit walking along the road. She poured all of her cereal back into the box.

"I'm going birding with Rory," she said, and headed for the door. "I'll be back in an hour, plenty of time to help you get the pies to the social."

"What a ridiculous thing to say—can you drive my car? No. I'm asking where your father is. No one ever helps out. That's the truth. It's never going to change. So go!"

Paisley was no fool—she made her exit. She grabbed her notebook and binoculars, slipped into her jelly sandals, and made sure the screen door didn't slam behind her. She'd escaped Eudie's rant. Clever.

NOW

Paisley read the eviction notice. The building owners were now using misspelled but strident language like we will have to remove you forsibly from your domisile, emphasized with capital letters, bold, italics, underline, and several exclamation marks in a row. *Forsibly from your DOMISILE!!* As if she could be removed from someone else's. It would all be laughable if it weren't so tragic and terrifying and paralyzing. Paisley wished she could meet these people right this second to tell them what they could do with their big words and absurd font usage.

The tenants had been getting monthly notices since September; the building, a utilitarian 1960s four-storey brownstone on Toronto's Dale Avenue, just north of Bloor and Sherbourne, was slated for demolition. Everyone had to be out by May 15, eight weeks from now. There was the number eight again, and not in a good way.

This, of course, was having an effect on tenant morale. Many were elderly, like Paisley's friend Mrs. Feldman, from 2B. They were upset about having to leave the place they'd called home for thirty or forty years and didn't know what moving meant for their next stage of life. Would their families dump them in a seniors home? Would they have to move in with their children, no matter how distasteful they found them?

Paisley was only thirty-nine—about half the age of most of the other tenants—but the eviction was unsettling her, too. Want to provoke a mid-life crisis? Lose everything you know on your way to forty. A spectacular benchmark of pathos and nowhereness, basically. She'd lived in her one-bedroom apartment since the age of eighteen. It suited her fine, and she'd become accustomed to its peculiarities. Yes, it was a little decrepit; the balcony was in poor shape, and you wouldn't want to lean on the railings. There'd been many rounds of cockroaches and mice, and recently, a rash, so to speak, of bedbugs. Plumbing problems. The electricity was spotty. In the summers, the building heated up, and management had long ago put a ban on costly window air conditioning units. Worst of all, at least once a winter there were problems with the heating—like tonight. It had failed that morning, and the problem was not yet resolved.

Heating problems or no, Toronto in the winter, especially the late winter, when you'd really had enough, was hard. To get through, you had to focus on the city's merits: how at any time of the day or night you could get dry spicy squid on Spadina Avenue, or the best falafel up on Eglinton West, or curry to die for in Little India, over on Gerrard Street.

At least, these were points in Toronto's favour that Paisley had heard. Fact was, she'd never ventured to Gerrard for curry or to Spadina for squid; she'd only read about it. But she liked that about Toronto, that you could go somewhere if you wanted to, if you had an opening in your schedule. And one day she would. Absolutely.

Paisley wasn't a recluse. She was friendly with the other tenants at Dale Manor. On the first Tuesday of every month, she attended a Toronto Birders meeting in the basement of a church on the Danforth. On Sundays, she went birding with a birders group. Paisley had 267 birds on her Ontario checklist card. She didn't have a car, but often the group would go on day trips or sometimes overnights together, and she'd get a ride, which meant she'd been able to visit Point Pelee, Moose Factory, Long Point, and innumerable conservation parks to add to her sightings. Every third Friday, she attended bird trivia night at a pub on Sherbourne and regularly kicked ass with her encyclopedic bird knowledge and swift hand on the buzzer. An answer was considered complete only if you knew the Latin names; bonus points for interesting facts about said bird. (Q. Can you name the bird that has the longest bill in the world? A. The Australian pelican (*Pelecanus conspicillatus*), found in New Guinea, Fiji, and Australia, has a bill measuring a half-metre. Interesting fact: the Australian pelican is also found in New Zealand as a vagrant. Paisley loved tracking which birds were considered vagrants, and where they'd strayed outside their normal range. Why did birds become vagrants, moving where they might not otherwise move? Severe weather sometimes, malfunctioning inner GPS, genetic mutation, mid-life crisis? Good one. That was the beauty of birds—they did not go in for the proverbial life crisis like overthinking humans. They didn't take that bullshit on.) On Mondays and Wednesdays, Paisley worked at the Canadian Ornithological Archives. Mostly she maintained files, worked in the library, and did data entry. She was very good at keeping things in order. In that way, OCD was an asset. In fact, it earned her praise. Paisley could easily take the lead on a massive project like changing the library's book and photo labelling system or overhauling the archives' membership software. What Paisley liked was that everyone who worked there was just as obsessed with birds as she was. The job would never be more than part-time, and it paid poorly, but she didn't do it for the money; she had enough to live on—just. She did it for the community: she felt comfortable in that environment and could banter with her colleagues while still getting her work done. Mostly, she did it for the birds. All the world's exquisite birds, those that were endangered and those that weren't.

Oh, and she had a Flitter account, for birders people who liked to date other birders. Beyond that, though, she always wrecked any possible long-term romantic relationships early on. The first few dates would go fine. Paisley was good-looking enough, quick-witted enough, smart enough. But weeks into any relationship, no matter how deep the meeting of minds or bodies, she'd sabotage things. Stop answering their phone calls. Or lie about trying again with an old flame who had come back into town. She did not need a relationship. She did not want people in her apartment where she might have to act normal when she wasn't feeling normal, and most of all, she did not want to share her secrets. Seeing herself—and all her rituals and compulsions—through someone else's eyes made her feel terrible. And she'd spent a long time getting things just right, in the right order, so that she didn't have to feel that way.

Paisley put today's eviction notice back into the envelope and thought about Dale Manor. There was no real reason to be so attached to the mediocre building, and yet it was full of familiar people, and personalities, and it was in a good area of town—better than good, really. Rosedale was posh, mostly populated with sprawling, dignified homes. Paisley's third-floor hallway had a rickety fire escape on the south side that gave her quick access to Dale Manor's courtyard, and her apartment's equally rickety balcony was on the building's north side. This allowed her to keep track of apartment dwellers and socialite residents alike on Dale Avenue. She monitored their comings and goings on the street: their daughters' sweet sixteens, their sit-downs for twelve in panelled dining rooms, their ugly fights fuelled by too much Scotch, their migratory patterns between the city and cottage in Muskoka. Even though Paisley didn't go many places herself, she liked knowing others did. And so she watched, perched on her balcony, no matter the weather, sometimes into the late hours of the night.

Maybe she could find a bigger, better apartment, but this was the one she knew. This was where she'd picked herself back up. That was the key: to do what you were capable of, no more, and hopefully no less. She couldn't picture herself moving somewhere else, where everything could shift and slip out of control.

Next February she'd turn forty. Being turfed from the only place you've lived your whole adult life, into the great unknown, felt emblematic of the overall shittiness of stumbling unceremoniously into middle age and not having one goddamn clue about anything. Paisley took the eviction notice, emphatic as it was, the food flyers, and her birding magazine and headed for the lobby. She could ignore the problem for one more day.

THEN

Paisley kicked a pebble out of her jelly sandal as she caught up to Rory. At six foot four, he towered over her, and his much longer legs covered more ground with each step.

"Hey, Rory."

Rory turned and grinned. "Paisley!"

"Going to the social?"

"Sure am!"

"Wanna count grosbeaks first?"

"Sure do!" Rory was always good for counting birds of any kind.

Paisley loved birding. She felt it should be called "birding" as opposed to "birdwatching," because birdwatching implied that you only used your eyes, but birding was so much more. It was listening, too. You could identify many more species if you knew their calls. It was also about being organized: planning your outings, keeping excellent notes about the birds you saw, and knowing a lot about those birds before you saw them, so you'd know what to look for. And you had to behave properly when you were birding: not disturb the birds—just watch, listen, record, count (especially that), and appreciate them. In fact, the American Birding Association had a code of ethics that all birders were supposed to follow. Paisley liked that. A code was her style.

You could draw birds in the special notebook you use for your birding life list (every decent birder had a life list—a list of every bird they'd ever seen) and highlight the parts that make them unique, like the colour of their feathers or eggs. In season, you could record nest sites, egg size and colour. You could help scientists learn stuff about birds—like if you were seeing lots of them or none of them. That was what was so neat about the species. Birds were the signs of what was happening around you. If the weather changed, they might not migrate at the same time as the year before. Or if there was danger afoot, they could sense it and would fly away. They were sensitive. And instinctive. And smart. And symbolic. They brought messages—if you listened and watched hard enough.

Paisley felt lucky because Amherst Island had both a birding community and a place called the Owl Woods, where birds of all sorts, particularly owls, of course, could be counted. The island's birders—even the birders from the mainland—were mostly adults. She was the only teenager. And secretly, that made her feel special.

The women on Paisley's father's side—her grandmother Mabel; Mabel's mother, Alice; and Alice's mother, June, Paisley's great-great-grandmother—had all been birders, too. Paisley had found an old crate of birder things in the shed when she was little: binoculars in an old case with a strap, a 1940s Lennox and Addington County field guide that listed all the local birds with their plumage, behaviours, habitats, and range, a pair of rubber gumboots, a sun hat, a map of Amherst Island so old it had some of the early-twentieth-century land divisions written on it by hand. But June's notebook was Paisley's most prized possession. It was leather-bound, with June's initials in gold embossed lettering on the front cover: J.A.M., for June Andrea MacIntosh. With its weathered, yellowish pages of notes and drawings, it was a cross between a journal, a life list, and field notes. Paisley loved June's observations—about herself, and birds, and the things that were happening in the area back then in the 1860s. Imagine—the 1860s! June dutifully drew every bird she saw on Amherst Island, labelling each part of their bodies and trying to get the colouring of their feathers and beaks and eyes just right. June had been very serious about birding. Ahead of her time. Paisley could only hope to be so serious. She wanted to have an impact. She wasn't too sure how, but that was the dream.

Paisley had started birding at the age of ten, and, so far, her count was 127. But she had big plans. There were around 10,000 bird species in the world, give or take, and it was entirely possible she could see over half of those species in her lifetime, if she really, really tried. She would have to be dedicated. And travel. And be meticulous in keeping notes.

When Paisley grew up, she was going to be a twitcher, a person who travelled really far to glimpse rare birds and tick those birds off their list so the world could breathe a sigh of relief knowing such beautiful creatures still existed. It was a funny word—*twitcher*—but Paisley's other book on birding, which had everything there was to know about the history of birding around the world, said it came from a British birder, Howard Medhurst, who had some kind of nervous habit. Paisley liked knowing that a nervous person could do important things.

Some birders looked down on twitchers, saying they weren't in it for the study of birds, only for the excitement of it, but Paisley felt excitement every time she saw a bird, and what was wrong with that? Twitchers even had their own language. For example, they spoke about a person's spark bird—which was the bird that made them first interested in birding (for Paisley, it had been an awe-inspiring immature female snowy owl—*Bubo scandiacus*—white with dark brown markings, and yellow-and-black eyes that had looked right at Paisley, seeing her, actually seeing her). Finding a bird that was very far away was called a chase, or a twitch, which Paisley thought sounded dramatic and heroic. If a group of twitchers set out to spot a bird and all the twitchers save one saw it, the unlucky one might go so far as to say that they were gripped off. And twitchers were very competitive about their lists, which could lead to suppression: one twitcher not telling others that they had seen a rare bird.

Paisley promised herself she would never suppress. Ever. Just as she would never lie that she'd seen a bird when she hadn't. She liked to colour inside the lines. She liked to stay clean and on the right side of the law, no matter which law it was.

Paisley checked her notebook. So far, she had five hash marks today.

"If we spot one more grosbeak before the social," she said, "that'll mean six in two days."

Grosbeaks on Amherst Island were either evening grosbeaks (*Coccothraustes vespertinu*s) in the winter or rose-breasted grosbeaks (*Pheucticus ludovicianus*) in the summer. The sighting of any grosbeak warranted a tick. A male evening grosbeak, the most likely to be found along the Stella 40 Foot (the forty-foot-wide road that cut the island in half), was yellow with a greenish beak and wings that were yellow, black, and white. A flash of gold over its eyes made it look like a bird superhero. What Paisley really wanted, though, was to see the São Tomé grosbeak (*Crithagra concolor*), a reportedly extinct bird found on São Tomé Island off Africa's Atlantic coast. A large finch with a very large bill, it was known from only three specimens spotted in the nineteenth century. Three! Paisley loved grosbeaks so much, she was certain that if she went to São Tomé, she would find one. Only, she didn't speak Portuguese...and she had no hope of travelling as far as Africa. Still, wouldn't that be something? She'd be a star.

Paisley also felt strongly that a good birder recorded not just the beautiful birds but the ugly ones as well. Amherst Island, for example, had a cormorant problem. For some time, their population had been declining across the Great Lakes, but since the 1970s they'd had a wild resurgence. People also called them shags, because of their crest, although the ones on and around Amherst island were double-crested cormorants (*Nannopterum auritum*), or crow ducks. Paisley loved how the word *cormorant* was a contraction of the Latin *Corvus marinus*, meaning sea raven, as in big black crow of the sea. If she squinted hard enough, she could pretend the lake was the ocean. A far-off ocean of sea ravens.

The birds had taken over corners of Amherst and entire little islands in the lake. They stripped leaves off trees and broke branches with their weight and the weight of their nests. They'd catch fish—that angered the fishermen—to feed their young. Their excrement and leftover regurgitated meals killed ground vegetation, and soon enough their nest tree, so they'd move on to the next tree, and the next. Eventually, the little island they'd taken over would be a ghostly version of its former self, not a green thing in sight. If all the trees on a little island died, the island was vulnerable to erosion. Enough erosion, thought Paisley, and an island could just tip sideways, one end pointing to the sky, the other to the lake floor, and then disappear. Basically, she'd heard, the islands turned into blighted landscapes, and it was all the cormorants' fault.

But to Paisley, cormorants held their own sort of beauty. They weren't pretty like cardinals or finches, but if you looked at them for what they were, you'd see elegant, black, streamlined pieces of God's universe. And despite their destructiveness and poor ability to get along with others, they were successful. They fed themselves, they reproduced, they survived, and when they needed to, they moved on. This Paisley appreciated. So even though islanders hated cormorants, she recorded them on her list, because that was what any decent birder would do.

Paisley knew from her birding-history book that twitching was very big in England and Ireland, and even in places like the Netherlands, Sweden, Finland, and Denmark. Because those countries were small—at least, compared to a place like Canada—twitchers could travel quickly to a new spot to find a bird. Paisley figured she would move to England when she grew up. She'd find a trench coat and some kind of dashing hat to set off her dark hair and pale skin. She'd ditch the jelly sandals and use her grandmother's rubber boots so she could really get in the brush and do some proper birding. She heard it rained quite a bit in England—misty, foggy rains over rolling lands called heaths. So dreamy.

After establishing herself as a professional birder, Paisley would become an ornithologist. Garnet Mulligan, the biggest arsehole in school, had told her that ornithologist was just a fancy name for loser, but Paisley knew otherwise. Ornithologist meant twitcher and birder all wrapped into one, only better: a birder who used scientific methods to identify birds and who did research projects that helped discover new and fascinating things about those birds. An ornithologist was a winner, no doubt about it.

Rory had no ambition to be an ornithologist—it was a word he couldn't even pronounce—but he liked Paisley and was always willing to lend a hand. No one else on the island would hang out with Rory. He was a full-grown man, in his forties at least, but also still sort of a boy.

Like Paisley, Rory had lived all his life on the island. At the age of eleven, while working his family's farm, he'd gotten knocked off a bale wagon and hit his head. Hubert, Paisley's dad, told Paisley that Rory had lost all his smarts in that moment, as if they'd just dropped out of his head and into the field, sown there beside the corn. Since then, Rory had been simple. He'd quit school to help his father, Rory Senior, on the farm. He loved those cows. He'd dole out heavy bales of hay and spread it down the barn's feed alley. He'd sing them "Waltzing Matilda," "Bicycle Built for Two," and the old Brylcreem ad his dad used to sing to him, in that order, a hundred times a day. Rory liked repetitive things. In that respect he and Paisley were similar.

Rory also liked playing hide-and-seek in the cemetery or helping Paisley bird. And when he wasn't doing one of those things, he walked the roads between his farm and the ferry dock, back and forth, back and forth, watching over the island's business. With one hand, he waved to every car that passed. In the other hand, he carried a red-and-white pinwheel made from a drinking straw and construction paper; it fluttered all the time, what with the island's generous supply of wind. Rory had recovered one once from the trash after an Amherst Island Canada Day parade, and when that pinwheel broke, Rory Senior made his son another. This business—of waving to each car that passed and spinning the pinwheel while walking the roads—kept Rory busy every day. Then he'd head home for milk tea and biscuits, and to help his mother peel potatoes or wash lettuce or whatever needed doing for dinner.

The other farmers just waved back or doffed their Massey Ferguson caps and thanked God in heaven above for their children's good fortunes. Most of the island kids, Garnet and his brother Shawn in particular, were brutal to Rory, playing pranks on him and treating him like the town fool, but the adults—and Paisley—knew that Rory cared about others, and that it didn't matter what the island kids thought.

"See you at the social," said Paisley, as they parted at the top of her driveway.

They hadn't found another grosbeak to make the count six, despite going all the way to the bend in the road and back.

"See you at the social," Rory repeated.

NOW

Paisley stepped from the Dale Manor mailroom out to the lobby and spotted Mrs. Feldman through the front door, getting out of a taxi, probably on her way home from bridge. Paisley ran out to help; the front walk was an ice rink, which made it especially easy to slip. Mrs. Feldman was in her late eighties and not happy about the building's concierge, who was slow to tend to the slippery sidewalks.

"He's a jerk," she said.

"Yes," replied Paisley, "but he's our jerk. How was bridge?"

"My friends are in Forest Hill. I should be in Forest Hill," said Mrs. Feldman. They inched toward the front door like novice skaters, Paisley taking care to step over the sidewalk cracks, not on them—today, it just felt better. "It's all my son's fault."

"Have you spoken to him about the eviction? Maybe he can help find you a place," said Paisley. This was not a new conversation between them. Paisley played her part well.

"You mean, has he spoken to me, and the answer is no. That boy. Almost as thick as our super."

"Really?" said Paisley, trying hard not to careen toward a snowdrift and drag the old lady with her. "I thought your son was doing well."

"In money, yes," said Mrs. Feldman. "In brains, no. And his heart..." She tapped her chest with her arthritic fingers. "He holds in his love for his mother. He wants to make me suffer." Paisley had heard enough about Mrs. F's son to know it was likeliest the other way around. There were a lot of retorts to Mrs. F's statements Paisley was dying to let loose, but she knew her place in this relationship. With Mrs. Feldman, listening was king.

A brilliant crimson red male northern cardinal (*Cardinalis cardinalis*) alighted on a nearby branch. You could see them year-round in Toronto—they didn't migrate, they were happy right where they were. Paisley was the same. This cardinal's feathers were fluffed against the cold, and it alternated tucking one foot and then the other under its body to keep warm. The bird was close enough that Paisley could see the black mask and crest, feather for feather. It observed her back. Amazing thing about cardinals: they were known to sometimes cover themselves with crushed or live ants. It was called anting, and scientists thought the birds used the formic acid ants secreted to get rid of lice and other pests. Come on. How clever was that? She would have stayed out in the cold to watch the cardinal in all its glory, but for Mrs. Feldman.

They were almost at the door. Mrs. Feldman clutched Paisley's arm. Paisley reached for the handle and managed to grasp it even as Mrs. Feldman threatened to take her down.

"I should just move to Florida for the winters like my friends. I'd be far away from my son. We get along much better long-distance. You could visit me in Florida. You'd like it there."

"That's a nice offer, Mrs. Feldman." Paisley wondered if she could go to Florida, become a snowbird like Mrs. F. She'd like to. But where would she get the money? It sounded expensive, to keep two places. Her part-time job could never pay for it. And could she just pick up and leave like that? That felt like a lot of change. And change, Paisley wasn't too good at.

"Or you could buy in Florida, next to me. Then we could sit on the beach together and watch the waves roll in. Would you ever buy in Florida?"

"It's not a bad idea," said Paisley. The conversation had reignited the looming question of where she was going to live. Of where they were all going to live.

"Thanks for the hand," said Mrs. F, stepping through the door. "Ooh, it's frigid in here! That damn man—he told me the heat failed last night, the bloody boiler again, but where are the boilermakers? More jerks. We're surrounded by them. We're outnumbered. See what I mean? That super cares for no one but himself. Himself and his television."

Paisley saw her to the elevator.

"Do you have a space heater?" asked Mrs. F. "I've got three. I can lend you one. It's old, but it works. It smells a bit like burning metal, but at least you'll be warm."

Paisley shuddered. "No thanks, Mrs. Feldman. I'm fine."

THEN

She came back in, hoping for good Eudie rather than you-don't-know-what-you're-going-to-get Eudie. Even though it was not a nice thought, she wished her mother might be more like Rory's, who was a little boring but very predictable, always smiling, always saying things like "Bad weather looks worse through a window" and "When you reach the end of your rope, tie a knot in it and hang on."

Eudie snapped her apron and a cloud of flour fell to the floor.

"Let me tell you something," she said, picking up their conversation as if Paisley hadn't been gone for an hour, stirring a pot on the stove that smelled of fresh lemons and sugar. "This is not what I signed up for. Do I look like I'm going to earn my university degree by baking pies? No. Am I going to travel to Europe baking pies? I don't think so."

Eudie had dreams of going to Europe, too, like Paisley, only not for birding. For living.

Paisley put down her binoculars. She told herself not to forget her allowance for the social. Soon they'd be there, and she would staff the post office game (her first time running it solo—a big responsibility), and her mother would be behind the pie table with her best friend Delilah and be happy again. Maybe.

"I did not sign up for this," said Eudie. There was that tone. This wasn't going to go well.

"Tell me about meeting Dad for the first time," said Paisley, aiming for a distraction. "You were smitten."

"Yes, I was smitten, it's true," said Eudie, running the hot water for dishes. "I was looking for something, and like God's zap of the finger, suddenly there he was."

"At city hall, right?" If Paisley could get Eudie off track, it might break the spell.

Eudie nodded as she rolled out the pastry on the counter. "That's right. I was taking the minutes at a conference my boss was attending in Kingston. We'd taken the train from Toronto—my boss, me, colleagues, one other secretary, Donna. Donna with the giant earlobes. It was a big deal. I was travelling for work. It was a promotion, and I was going places. I mean, I was a single girl in Toronto, living in a bachelor apartment with my cat, a cat named—"

"France."

"France, that's right. I'd found her mum run over in the road by a driver, flat as a pancake, eyes all bulged out. And France was mewing, by the side of the road, and needed saving. So we lived together in Toronto. I was taking French lessons at the Alliance Française. I practised my pronunciation with France. I'd recite all my good French to her, and she'd listen, swear to God: "Oui, monsieur, un café au lait sans sucre, s'il vous plait." And then, when I had enough money to move to Paris, I'd take France with me. We were good, France and I. We had plans."

Eudie loved cats as much as Paisley loved birds. Cats ate birds.

"So you ran into Dad in the corridor?"

"Not exactly," said Eudie. "I was outside in the corridor, killing time, bored to death by the meeting. I'd been falling asleep, and I thought my boss was going to catch me, so I asked Donna to take the minutes and I went to the bathroom. And then I stopped to look at the paintings in the hallway, because I didn't want to go back into the meeting. And that's when I saw your father. He was stiff in his plaid shirt, top button done up, and his work pants were clean with a crease up the middle, just like dress pants. I had on a wool skirt, stockings, penny loafers, cardigan, with a sequined butterfly right here. I was so clearly from the big city—not Kingston. He could tell."

Eudie used the flat icing knife to unstick her pastry from the counter. "So I'm standing there, and I look fine, if I do say so myself, and he opens his mouth but nothing comes out other than a frog. Like he was fifteen. It was…sweet. And so I helped him out—told him I liked this certain painting. And it turned out he knew the name of it. *Evening, Lake Scugog.* His voice came out better the second time. 'It's a Tom Thomson,' he said. 'Beautiful, don't you think?' I didn't know what I thought. I wasn't much for art, really, but he got all doe-eyed when he looked at that painting, and I fell for him right there."

She patted the pastry into a pie tin and threw in the little smooth white stones that prevented it puffing up during baking. Then she put the crust into the oven, set the timer, pressed the last bits of raw pastry from the kitchen table into a ball, wrapped it in waxed paper, and tossed it into the freezer.

"Help wash up, Paisley. You know how I hate to wash up."

Paisley did as she was told.

Eudie dumped dishes into the already overflowing sink.

"He smelled like dirt and soap," she said as she stirred the pot. "I tried very hard to focus on the painting. I told him I'd never been to Northern Ontario. He said it wasn't really northern in the painting, but it was Canadian Shield, all right.

"He was there for some kind of regional Ontario Federation of Agriculture meeting. But he stayed there right beside me, and he was big and strong, especially his arms, so I asked him out on a date, just like that. He said 'Now?' I said, 'Now.' He said, 'I don't even know your name,' and I said, 'Are you in or are you out?' and he said 'In.' And I could tell he thought I was wild and beautiful, like the painting."

It's strange, thought Paisley, listening to your mother be young and poetic when she's standing in front of you in her old nightgown. And it's not at all the mother who's been waking you up every morning since you can remember and bothering you about chores and homework and sitting up straight and yelling at your father because he hasn't done any of the things she says a normal husband would do. It's not the same person, but it is, because you're not dreaming, which means you don't know the mother you think you do. Which makes you give her another chance, because any moment now she might change and be better.

"So I took him out to dinner in Kingston."

"Right then? What about the other secretary taking your place?"

"Oh, Paisley, I don't know. I guess I finished the meeting and then I met your father later. I can't remember the details. Point is, I ate out a lot in Toronto, and he never ate out at all, and so we made quite a pair in the restaurant. And he used the teaspoon, not the big spoon, to eat his soup and made terrible conversation."

The oven timer dinged, and Eudie pulled out the pastry, just barely golden and piping hot.

"I talked to him about living in Toronto. He didn't really care. Of course, I never knew how much he didn't care about Toronto until I married him, but at the time I found it charming.

"But here's the thing," said Eudie, slowly pouring the warm lemon mixture into beaten egg yolks. "I told him I didn't really care about living in Toronto either. What I cared about was living in Paris. In my mind, I lived by the Seine—that's the river that flows through Paris—and every day I drank gorgeous coffee and walked somewhere new in Paris, the Eiffel Tower, I suppose, with a baguette in my shopping bag and a hunk of excellent cheese. I made that perfectly clear—I mean crystal. I talked about that dream all night at dinner. And he said yes. *Yes.* Which meant he understood."

She stirred the egg yolk mixture back into the pot, and turned up the heat.

"He told me he lived on an island about twenty minutes from Kingston. He said, 'It's not Paris, but it has its pluses.' I said, 'Like what?' He said his parents were born there, and so were their parents, and he knew pretty much everyone who lived there. And he went on about it, sipping his soup with his stupid teaspoon. I kept thinking about the giant from 'Jack and the Beanstalk.' This huge man in a plaid shirt, buttons done up to the top, sipping his soup with a spoon so small it disappeared in his hand. I would have laughed if I hadn't been so smitten. So I asked him if that was a good thing, to know everyone who lives somewhere. He said he thought so. His dad ran the quarry, for example. In his teens, Hu helped out, hanging out with his father after school and on weekends. The quarry had layers and layers of earth and rock: it revealed the island's insides. And when islanders used the quarry's gravel, he felt like he and his father had given them little pieces of the earth's insides to build the foundations of their barns and houses. And in those houses, babies were born, families were made.

"He talked about helping build several barns on the island. Sure, there were construction crews that came from the mainland, but islanders pitched in. When he was a boy, he carried the nails; when he got older, they'd let him bang in a few nails himself. He once watched a barn burn to the ground in seven minutes flat, and when the crew came to rebuild, he and his father were right there to help out. He kissed a few girls in those barns, too. Carved his initials in square barn beams. It was like that, his story. Romantic. He made it seem more romantic than Paris."

Even if her stories were sort of sad and sour around the edges, Paisley thought her mother had a way with words. That could be a thing to aim for, she supposed, so that people could say, "That Paisley, isn't she just like her mother?" But in truth Paisley didn't think they were similar at all. The lemon mixture was thick and big bubbles were bursting at the surface. Eudie removed it from the heat, whisked in some butter, and spread it into the warm pie crust. Paisley watched Eudie work and wished that she could wrap herself in her mother's arms—that that was even something she wanted, but it wasn't. Was that bad?

"And I fell for it," said Eudie, getting started on the meringue. "I flushed my dream of the Seine down the toilet for a tiny island in Eastern Ontario—an island shaped like an octopus, for God's sake—an island whose ferry dock is two minutes from a huge cement factory that belches God knows what into the air and two minutes from a penitentiary for kidnappers and axe murderers."

The island is shaped like a squid, thought Paisley. Not an octopus. A squid.

Eudie turned the mixer to high and a scream filled the kitchen.

"As soon as the last pie's done, we'll head to the social. Maybe your father'll be back, maybe not. Who knows. Who cares. Just shake a leg, that's all."

NOW

After delivering her neighbour home, Paisley retreated to her frigid apartment, shoved her hair under a wool hat that she pulled right down to her almost-black eyebrows, changed into long johns, two pairs of socks, her nightie and a hoodie over top, and stuffed her thick, farmer's daughter fingers into gloves.

Becoming a snowbird would be appropriate, given her interest in birding, though ironic. She would be part of an annual human migration; she, like the birds she'd studied for so long, would leave home for warmer climes and return when spring had sprung. Migration was fascinating. Birds knew an amazing amount about what they needed and when. Year after year, they followed strict migration routines that varied only by a day or two. They knew the change of seasons from the amount of daylight and from the angle of the sun. They could sense when migration was near. Their hormone levels changed, allowing them to bulk up for the long flight ahead. One bird—the ruby-throated hummingbird (*Archilochus colubris*)—could almost double its body fat a mere one or two weeks before migrating. It migrated as far as Central and South America, travelling more than five hundred miles over the Gulf of Mexico. Without stopping. Paisley found this extraordinary.

Birds migrate as a critical part of their life cycle—to find food, to produce a healthy brood, to survive harsh winters. Species like hawks, swallows, swifts, and many waterfowl migrate during daylight hours, while many songbirds do so at night. This is partly because the cooler nighttime air makes flying more efficient—although species that migrate during the day do so in order to soar using solar-heated thermal currents. Nighttime migrators prefer to avoid predators like raptors. All of these facts captivated Paisley.

One of the world's abiding mysteries is how birds know where to go—how to find a particular location on their journey, and the next, and the next, and the next. Ornithologists spend their lives observing migration patterns and postulating how they are followed. Some feel that Earth's magnetic pull has something to do with it—that compounds in the birds' brains allow them to use magnetic fields as a guide. Some feel the birds' extraordinary eyesight allows them to recognize familiar landmarks. Some feel that birds' parents teach them the proper route, passed down from generation to generation. Others think that daylight migrators use the sun as a guidepost and nighttime migrators use the stars.

Paisley gazed out the window. Dale Avenue glistened with snow under the street lamps. Across the way, there was a party happening at the Smalleys'. Paisley enjoyed spying on them. A guilty pleasure.

The Smalleys' enormous front room was all lit up, and they had at least fifty guests. Everyone was dressed very F. Scott Fitzgerald, the women in fringed flapper dresses and little sequined hats with feathers sticking out the back, cigarettes in holders, and velvet gloves up to their elbows, the men in black tuxedos and ivory smoking jackets, everyone drinking champagne.

Paisley ate her favourite meal, New Orleans fried chicken, while watching her favourite show, *The Private Life of Birds*. As she brought her plate back to the kitchen, she heard the elevator down the hall. She raced for the door to see who it was.

She spied on Dale Manor, too—she wasn't fussy. Between the elevator and her door, she'd learned as much as one could possibly glean about her neighbours on her floor: what kind of groceries they bought; what they wore to work, on a date, to the symphony. She overheard snippets of conversation—the most private kind—from neighbours who had no idea they had an audience.

Paisley pressed her body to her door, one hand on the chain to make sure it didn't rattle, the other hand pressed against the wall for support. Her feet always found the same spot, spread as wide as possible on the dingy hall carpet so they wouldn't cast a shadow through the wide, sloping crack between door and uneven floor.

A plumbing problem in Mr. Burnside's apartment, directly above hers, had caused water to trickle down behind the drywall and underneath the hardwood floor inside her door, lifting it into an undulating topography. Paisley had watched as the hills and valleys grew more pronounced by the day, until it was just about impossible to open her door more than a foot. She'd had to call the super several times—an effort she didn't appreciate. She had a deep sense of privacy for someone whose favourite pastime was spying.

Finally, the super had agreed to send someone. The man had called in advance to arrange a time—which seemed gentlemanly after the super's curt responses—and she found herself excited to meet him. Not that she was desperate; there was always Flitter. But Paisley let this one play out like a fantasy. He might surprise her: maybe he was a professor, well-travelled and sophisticated, who'd one day decided he'd had enough of academia and sought the simple life of working with his hands. She wrestled with choosing an outfit and landed on Lycra leggings, a little athletic top, and bare feet. As if he'd just caught her doing yoga. She hoped to look unintentionally hot.

But then he'd squeezed through the offending entrance, his pants sagging and body odour pungent, never even glancing at her. He looked at the floor in all its moist, mountainous glory before throwing open his rusty tool kit. He pulled out a saw, eyeballed a line across the bottom of the door, and hacked off a good three inches so it could open freely. Then he left.

Paisley had eyed the door's new jagged bottom edge. How could she possibly watch the hallway now? But to complain about the shitty job would mean another call, this time perhaps even a confrontational one. She'd have to make do. And so she'd taken to pressing her feet to the walls at either side of the doorway, forcing them as wide apart as possible so they didn't betray her presence.

Paisley waited to see who stepped off the elevator.

It was Mrs. Feldman, strange and distorted, with ostrich-sized eyeballs.

"Open the door, honey. It's me, Mrs. Feldman."

She opened the door. Mrs. Feldman stood in the hall with the lobby pushcart. Inside it was an old 1970s radiant space heater, the kind with elements behind a grille.

"Now, I know you said no to the space heater, dear," she said as she hauled it out of the cart and into the apartment, "but I brought it anyway, because, first, I'm old so I can do what I want and, second, you're like a daughter to me."

"Mrs. Feldman, really, I'm okay," said Paisley. "I've got plenty of sweaters. The furnace people should be coming soon; the heat'll be back on any moment."

Mrs. Feldman pointed her arthritic finger. "Now, you listen up."

Here we go, thought Paisley.

"This building is cold," said Mrs. Feldman, "cold as six feet under. I'm not going to wake up tomorrow to find you expired in the night just because a neighbour didn't bring you her extra space heater. That's not going to hang over my head. It's a mitzvah to care about your neighbour, to treat her like your own. So here, you plug this thing in."

But Paisley couldn't. She couldn't plug it in. Because that would upset the balance of everything: electricity and plugs and outlets and fires.

"Nah," she said to Mrs. F. "I like being cold. Keeps me on my toes."

"What are you, the Ice Queen from Narnia?"

"Wow," said Paisley, "a random C. S. Lewis reference. On a Thursday evening. And it's Jadis the White Witch, not the Ice Queen."

"Don't correct an old lady, it's not polite. You are not the Ice Queen is what I'm saying. Nor are you the big snowman from the Christmas Rudolph special."

"I'll have you know that was Bumble, the Abominable Snowmonster. And a deft move from literary series mistaken for kids' books to Christmas family movies of yore."

"Anything to make you do as I say."

"Does it work with your son?"

"That's a low blow," she said, pointing at the space heater. "Plug it in."

"No thanks."

"You look like a sausage roll in that getup. Don't be ridiculous."

"Ridiculous is my middle name. Or is it sausage?"

Mrs. Feldman's eyes narrowed. "You're such a sweet girl, and quick with the retorts, but—and now I'm going out on a limb—I've had this suspicion for a while that you have problems with your nerves. Is that true? A nerve problem, like my sister Naomi. Yes, I'm old, but I'm smart. Give me some credit. Am I right?"

Paisley stared at her.

"I'm right. Ha. Now lookit, just plug this in and turn it on. Once you've done it, you can do it a thousand times. That's what Naomi did with spiders; it was a little traumatic at first but it all worked out fine. If you want to throw up like her, so be it. I've cleaned up lots of sick in my time. Do it—just do it. Just once. You'll see."

Paisley didn't move.

"You know how I know? Because they had us march out of Czechoslovakia with our frying pans and our jewellery boxes and our children on our backs, and that was hundreds of miles, but the first step was the hardest. Once you get the hang of it, it's just one more step, and before you know it, you're where you want to go. See what I mean? Now, turn this thing on and then we can sit down for tea. I have a couple of stories about my son I want to share, just to bore you. Go on."

So Paisley did it. She plugged in the heater and turned the dial from Off to On. Directly under it was a warning: "Danger of ignition at high temperature. Keep all combustible items away from unit." Good lord. Her breath came short and fast, but she did it.

Mrs. Feldman barged farther into the apartment, which was no good. Having someone in Paisley's space invited in uncertainty—about which outlets were used, which light switches were touched, any small move that might create a chance for fire—and ultimately meant more counting later. Mrs. Feldman started to make tea, going on about how little Paisley had in her fridge and how she needed taking care of. And then she sat herself down. Paisley didn't want Mrs. F to sit down and make herself comfortable. She wanted her to leave. As they chatted, Mrs. F going on about her son and how no one, not even Paisley, ever listened to her, Paisley kept one eye on the heater, its elements orange with heat. The whole thing was such a bad idea. Space heaters were fire hazards. Paisley's brain tipped into the abyss. She'd turn her head away for just one tiny moment, whereupon the space heater would burst into flames and the apartment would be engulfed, the smoke would be thick, thick and black—

THEN

With only a half-hour until the summer social began, St. Andrew's was abuzz with volunteers. There was still not a cloud in the sky—a good sign. The church's metal roof glimmered in the late July sun; the tops of the trees swayed with the island's ever-present wind. The lawn between the church and the cemetery had been freshly mowed. The flowers were watered. Balloons flapped and jostled, Rory was putting out chairs for the live auction under Mac's supervision, and the Men's Association had already fired up the barbecue.

There were so many good things to peruse, delicious things to eat, ways to spend your coins. The used-books station, the white elephant table, the timeless treasures booth. Paisley eyed Eudie and another church lady, Prudence Bellechamps, setting up the pies. She could help out, try to further mollify her mother, compliment her baking and dress and all the work she was doing for the church, but Paisley was finely attuned to the Eudie days that just could not be won. This felt like one of them, especially since her father was still nowhere in sight. Paisley wanted to please her mother. Satisfy her edict to be the best Paisley could be. Think independently. Go after her dreams. Find joy, somewhere, anywhere. But she didn't see much of that in her mother's life, was the thing. So she went into the church fellowship hall to check out the offerings in the tea room instead.

Two ladies from the mainland hovered near the prepared plates of squares, tarts, and little egg salad sandwiches cut in four, each covered in cellophane. They were angling for what looked best and most plentiful.

"I say we do this thing quickly, then hightail it over to Owl Forest," said one to the other, who looked far more interested in the assortment of goodies than in going on any excursion.

The Owl *Woods*, thought Paisley.

"If we spot it first, then I can give Harv what for. He always thinks he knows better. 'I can spot a rare bird,' I told him. 'What, you don't think I have eyes? Oh, I have eyes all right. And mostly what they do is look at your rapidly expanding behind, on account of how much you sit on it."

The other lady chuckled and snuck a lime square from under some plastic wrap. Some people just couldn't stick to the rules. Paisley adored rules. More importantly, though, her ears were on fire. A rare bird *here*, on Amherst Island?

"Stop ogling the desserts, Eden," said the first lady. "I want to hit the white elephant table first, before the social opens. If you're nice, they'll let you take a gander at what's for sale. Last year, they had this very sweet man working the table. Ben, I think his name was. Single, too. Made eyes at me, I swear to God."

"Made eyes. Olive, really?" Eden said, her mouth still full. "What'd you do?"

"I gave him a piece of my mind, that's what," shot back Olive.

"So, what do you want with him now, then?"

"Oh, for God's sake, Eden. What's with the third degree? I'm going to the white elephant table, and you can keep up if you want."

The women headed outside. Paisley followed. She was supposed to be setting up her children's game, the post office, but she needed to know what bird they'd been talking about. Paisley had helped run the post office for three years in a row. She could set it up in a minute if she needed to.

NOW

"Did I tell you about my brother, Avrum?"

The space heater's elements glowed orange and shot out warmth, but such incredible danger, too. Paisley could focus just enough to shake her head.

"He died last month."

"Oh, Mrs. F, I'm so sorry."

"Don't be. He lived a big life and he outsmarted that piece of crap Hitler and he had seven kids and an okay wife. I never liked her myself, but he seemed to think she was God's gift. His death is what it is. He died over there in Prague. I didn't go to the funeral, because Lord knows I'm too old to travel. I've had my tears—now I'm over it."

"Yes." Paisley kept her eye on the space heater. It had not exploded yet, but there was time. There was always time.

1 2 3 4 5 6 7 8

"Anyway," said Mrs. Feldman, slurping her tea, "Avrum's wife, Anna, she called from Prague to say that they're dividing up my brother's things and what did I want? So I said, 'Nothing. You have seven children who will want his things to remember him by at some point.' Not that he was rich, mind you, but he did all right. Avrum knew how to invest, always did. But on and on Anna goes about 'What can I send back to Canada for you? He would've wanted you to have something.'"

"Did you think of anything?" said Paisley.

"Well, sure I did. I thought to myself, what could I have that would remind me of my brother deep down, who he really was? And then I thought of his diary. And you know what? She sent it over. It's in my apartment. Would you like to see it?"

"I'd love to," said Paisley. Please, God, make this woman leave so I can turn off that firebomb in the middle of my living room.

Mrs. Feldman stood up. "Well, good. I'd show it to you now, but I'm due for cribbage with Mr. Burnside. He's sweet on me, but I'm not that easy. Leave the heater on all night on high. It'll keep you warm."

Paisley thanked Mrs. Feldman, shut the door behind her, unplugged the space heater, and waited for the sound of the elevator. When she was sure Mrs. F had gone, she put the heater all the way on the other side of the hallway outside her apartment, closed her door, locked it, then opened the door again to check that the thing was still unplugged and safe in the hall. It was. Paisley knew it would be: she'd put it there herself. There wasn't even an outlet in the hall where she might have unwittingly plugged it in. And yet she had to check, because of the safety of the other residents. Residents like Mrs. Feldman and Mr. Burnside—poor, unsuspecting, vulnerable residents—depended on her. It sat squarely on her shoulders.

There was the heater in the hall, on the musty carpet, still unplugged. Paisley had closed her door again when it occurred to her that, even though the heater wasn't plugged in, the elements were still hot—maybe hot enough for a spark to fly to the carpet and start a fire. She stared at the heater through the peephole, and while she could see no fire, she felt compelled to open the door again and touch the heater to confirm that the cord was indeed unplugged and there would be no fire.

This happened eight times.

And then eight times again.

That number, her old childhood number, was mortared in her psyche like a brick. It usually reappeared because of something bad. The space heater was bad, sure, but it didn't feel quite bad enough to get her mind going. Paisley went over the events of her day. Ah, yes, the eviction notice reminder. Something bad indeed. Identifying the cause should have helped, but it didn't. Paisley started in on her ritual, inside this time, checking plugs, light switches, and outlets, eight times and then eight times again. She spent all night at it. Round and round she went, unplugging lamps and plugging them back in, in series of eights. Every time she hoped she was done, a new thought arrived, and it would lead to what a bad person she was, and bad people were guilty, and guilty people caused others to get hurt by their badness, by their casual disregard for rules, and, if that were the case, she had probably not checked the outlets properly, which would mean that a fire might start when she least expected it, and, expect it or not, it would be her fault. Her brain was engulfed by fire, flames ravaging the building and killing everyone, and the bad feelings—the massive doubt, the overwhelming fear—would press the restart button and the checking would start again.

By the time the light rose outside, Paisley could barely keep her eyes open—but she'd prevented the building from catching fire. She felt finally that things were safe and under control, and so she crawled into bed under every blanket she owned. She drifted off, dreaming of migration patterns and how it was possible that birds knew when it was time to leave, and how they found the courage to do so.

That, to Paisley, seemed like an impossible feat.

THEN

The women moved to the white elephant table. But Ben wasn't running it this year, James Mulligan was, and he, a stern, take-no-guff sort, didn't take kindly to people jumping the queue. Olive and Eden loitered on the sidelines, watching James unload boxes and unwrap little treasures. Paisley loitered, too. These women knew something about a rare bird here. Paisley couldn't help but follow them.

A couple of tables over, Eudie and Pruc were placing a patchwork of tea cloths over the baked goods to protect them from flies. Del rolled up.

Delilah Cope, Eudie's best friend, was from Bath, a small town a little ways from the mainland ferry dock. She and her husband, Noble, lived above their supermarket. If it weren't for bridge, Paisley didn't think Del was the kind of person Eudie would've fallen in with; she wore tighter clothes than any island woman, higher heels, too, and swore just enough to be scandalous. She was slim and lean, with long legs and arms. Even her nails were long and always painted. A du Maurier dangled from Del's lower lip. Paisley always wondered how she held it there.

Eudie took one glance at Del's outfit and said, "Lord love a duck."

Del was wearing a tight lacy dress in flamingo-pink that stretched across her flat belly and emphasized her big, perfectly round breasts. Breasts that defied gravity. Little ruffled sleeves showed off her toned upper arms. Paisley would have to lose a few pounds if she were ever to fit in a dress like that. Del's hair was piled high on her head— a bird might think it the perfect nest—but somehow the mess of curls was sexy on her. She carried a black patent clutch purse with a jewelled butterfly clasp, a bold choice, too fancy for a church summer social. That was the key, wasn't it? Being bold.

Del stole a folding chair from the live auction, much to Mac's consternation, and waited for Eudie and Prue to finish setting up their station. She crossed one shapely leg over the other and pulled out *People* magazine while Prue talked to Eudie about pie making. Prue had a secret to her pastry crust that she liked to hint at but never reveal. As far as Paisley was concerned, her mother's pastry was just fine, and she wished Prue would shut up so she could hear what Eden and Olive were saying.

Del flipped through the magazine. There was a spread on Princess Diana and Prince Charles. "A match made in heaven," said Del to herself. In the photo, they were shaking hands with people in a crowd at some event alongside the Queen and Prince Philip. "Wouldn't it just fill you with shame to have to walk half a step behind your wife? That's what Prince Philip has to do," Del commented to no one in particular. "Mind you, maybe that doesn't sound like such a bad thing. A man to carry your purse, just out of your peripheral vision, right where you want him."

Prue rolled her eyes and marched off.

"What's her problem?" snorted Del.

"Prue would rather talk pastry," Eudie whispered. "Specifically, how hers is better than mine."

"Is it?" asked Del.

Eudie shook her head. "Greasy, if you ask me."

Then Eudie launched into how Prue had chosen the colour of this year's tablecloth for the pie table, had gone into Kingston to purchase the yardage and stayed up till midnight hemming and pressing the seams, and hadn't let Eudie forget it since. In fact, she'd made Eudie pay half the cost of the fabric. "Let's not charge the church, shall we?" Prue had said. "Let's let the church do God's work with God's money." Which Eudie did, even as she had a hunch that the tablecloth would make its way into Prue's sideboard after the social, where it would do Prue's work with Eudie's money.

"Want me to give her a piece of my mind?" said Del.

"Don't you dare!" said Eudie, though Paisley knew that secretly her mother did want that. Paisley wanted it, too.

"You know the other thing I'm looking for?" said Olive, over at the white elephant table. "Collector spoons. I love those little things."

Prue returned, Ruth's lemon meringue in one hand, her own raisin pie in the other. She put them down on the table and licked her finger. "Ruth's meringue isn't bad, but I know for a fact that her crust—"

"Be nice," said Del, reading her magazine. "Church function and all that."

Prue's mouth opened. Then shut. "I think I know how to behave at a church function," she said. "I'm going to get more pies."

Paisley buried her head in her chest so no one would see her smile.

Eudie couldn't contain her smile either. "Del, you're gonna cause trouble."

"You love it."

"No I don't."

"Yes you do. You can't stand Prue. And yet you're stationed with her."

Eudie shrugged, looking at her short fingernails. "I didn't really have a choice."

"We all have a choice, Eudie. Just depends how clear you are about it."

"Of course I haven't been clear," snapped Eudie. "When I was a secretary in Toronto, I wasn't clear with my boss that I could do more than take minutes and pour coffee. But did I say anything? No. Was I clear with Hubert about not wanting to live on an island? No. Was I clear about starting a family? No. And look at me now. No job, on a piece of floating dirt with other farmers, and a child who—"

"Yeah, yeah, you're all talk, you blowhard," said Del.

41

Del was nice, protecting Paisley like that. Paisley counted photos on the magazine's double-page spread. One, two, three, four, five, six, seven.

"Hubert at the farm?" Del changed the subject.

"I'm not even going to answer that, because of course he is," said Eudie. "The milking pump's broken. He went early this morning, before sun-up. He promised to be here when we open, but is he here yet? No."

Eudie was ready to launch into listing Hu's other faults when Prue returned with another pie in each hand. "Bumbleberry delight," she said, lifting one, "and a very runny marmalade torte. Not mine, of course."

Del lit another cigarette, inhaled, and puffed out a series of bull's-eye rings that expanded, broke apart, and fell languidly in the vicinity of the baked goods. This time, Prue couldn't even look at her, she was in such a rage. She stalked back to the church kitchen.

"I thank God for you, Delilah Cope," said Eudie. "You save my sanity."

"Don't thank God, Eudie. He's got nothing to do with how I turned out. That's all my doing."

"Don't we need to get going to Owl Forest?" Paisley heard Eden say. "I mean, the bird..."

Paisley tried to filter out Eudie and Del.

"Yes, yes," said Olive, "just take a look for spoons first, would you?"

"Now, tell me," Del said to Eudie. "Where's his very Reverend Cuteness?"

The way Del referred to Reverend Willis, you'd think she were after him. Embarrassing.

"He's the best thing at the summer social," Del continued. "You called him a dreamboat yourself at bridge, and since I paid my admission, lemme at him."

"I did not say that," said Eudie, glancing at Paisley, who kept her eyes glued on the white elephant table. She'd heard more than one woman on the island claim the reverend was a dreamboat—always with a smile and ready to chat with anyone who had time. And here was Del, making it clear she had time, all right.

Reverend Arden Willis. They talked about him at Women's Association meetings. The island's women were still aflutter a year after his arrival. He was young—this was his first congregation out of theological college—and he was full of big ideas. Skin so smooth, he couldn't grow a beard if he tried, the slim body of a city boy. Once, he'd offered to help a few farmers during hay season. He got up there into the hot and stuffy haymow and huffed and puffed his way through stacking the entire load of forty-pound bales, so proud of himself. And then he got a look at the next load. And the next. And the next. They'd all laughed entirely at his expense.

Word was that the reverend had a girl from Kingston he took out on Friday nights; Saturdays he reserved for preparing the sermon. At church cleanup days, Paisley listened to the ladies of the Women's Association speculate on how serious the reverend and his girl must be. They discussed whether he'd saved himself for marriage. Paisley wondered if saving yourself included first base and all that. Eudie had clucked disapproval so the women knew she didn't think much of their chatter. In a community as small as theirs, she said, nonsense like that would get them all in trouble. Still, even Eudie acted differently around Reverend Willis.

"His theology's a little newfangled for most on the island," said Eudie. "And he insists on playing his guitar at least one hymn each service."

"Who cares?" said Del. "He's a sight for sore eyes. You've had no one new for years—in fact, it's been an exodus, with all the kids aiming for a one-way ferry out of town. If that reverend brings a whiff of fresh air, then I say let him strum."

Paisley agreed. She liked to watch the reverend's slim fingers on the frets. Soft. She had no idea how to play guitar, but that fretting business had math that Paisley appreciated. She'd also seen Reverend Willis in the small field behind the church cemetery practising his sermons, preaching to the voles and rabbits. She'd seen him walking the Stella 40 Foot, visiting the shut-ins. Walking! No one walked around here except Rory. Even old Mrs. Pettle, ninety-plus years old, still drove the island roads, negotiating bad grading, potholes, and the deer at dusk. Reverend Willis was new blood, all right.

"Who cares if the rev's got a girl in Kingston," Del said. "We all deserve what we want—whether it's the tablecloth at the pie table or a cute man."

Olive and Eden were still hovering near the white elephant table, but James wouldn't budge.

"I'm not giving it much longer, Eden," said Olive. "This church thing doesn't want us. Besides, the Henslow's sparrow is waiting."

The Henslow's sparrow? Oh God, thought Paisley. Oh Lord in heaven.

The Henslow's sparrow (*Ammodramus henslowii*) hadn't been seen in these parts for years and years. Years and years and years.

The Henslow's sparrow.

Imagine.

NOW

Paisley awoke and felt good for a moment, until she remembered the space heater outside the apartment. She couldn't bear to look at, lest it cause another episode. That meant staying home...not such a bad thing. She called in sick to the archives, and emailed Bradley in Catalogues and told him coffee was off. She resolved to start thinning her belongings. She'd work up slowly to packing and finding a new apartment; aiming too high would make for failure.

Paisley started to divide her life into piles of items to keep and items to give away. She could let go of her university textbooks on ornithology...or maybe not. They might be useful. She loved her framed antique bird prints, and all the meticulous drawings she had made of birds during night art courses—the pages of her ringed sketchbook torn out and push-pinned into the living room wall in the shape of a songbird in flight. She needed all the back issues of her birding magazines. She needed two sizes of all her clothes, given her weight fluctuated, so she kept most of them. There were many other things she might need one day: three shades of lipstick, used on sporadic dates with men with whom relationships never worked out; seven colours of nail polish she was always planning to use; maps of Europe from a garage sale, never used at all. She found every bank statement from the last twenty-two years, realized she had almost nothing to her name, and put them aside to take to work for shredding. In the end, she put two pairs of pants with broken zippers into a bag for the thrift store and set aside a couple stacks of newspapers for recycling. They'd been tucked under her bed. Definitely a fire hazard.

Hungry, but still unable to venture out, Paisley foraged her kitchen until she found two packages of frozen wieners. She hacked off a couple, put them in a bowl of water, and microwaved them hot. The water in the bowl seemed fragrant and a little oily, like broth, so Paisley kept it. She imagined this was how people got by during the war. For lunch, she ate hot dogs, stale Melba toast, and the dregs of a jar of marmalade.

She should face the heater. She should walk out of the apartment, return the heater to Mrs. Feldman without any counting or checking at all, and get to the archives, fake sick or not.

But the thought of touching the space heater made her start back in on eights. Every light fixture and plug in the apartment had to be checked. Night eventually fell. Exhausted, she made dinner, using the same water to boil the next two hotdogs. The oil-slick broth thickened and deepened in colour. She was debating throwing it out when she heard the elevator open down the hall. She raced to the door.

It was Lily, from 3F, with a boy. Lily was an uncommonly confident latch-key fifteen-year-old, and Paisley had taken a special interest in her, though Lily didn't know that. Paisley craved Lily's year-round, permanent vibe of je ne sais quoi. It was inspiring to witness her ability to both not give two shits about anything, and also, when she really wanted something, to just go for it. Paisley, on the other hand, felt like she lurched from living a halfway decent life (a job she liked, a pastime she loved) to drowning in eight kinds of torment. The counting. The checking. The guilt that you'd done something terrible, even things you didn't know about yet. The need for rules. The fear of fire. The repetitive negative thought. The capitulation to being at the mercy of OCD—not always, but sometimes. OCD was the fucked-up hydra gift that kept on giving—and on a capricious schedule.

Lily's gangly escort was having difficulty negotiating the goodbye.

"Yeah, so…" he said awkwardly, staring at the carpet.

"Yeah," said Lily, looking right at him.

"Tonight was cool," said the boy. "Did you like the movie?"

"Sure."

Their bodies were close. He hid behind his long bangs, unable to look at her.

"So..." said Lily.

It was a cue, even Paisley could see that. The boy, not so much.

"So..." he said.

"Guess I better go," said Lily.

Shit or get off the pot was Lily's style. No doubt at all—just what Paisley craved. Still, the boy kept his hands shoved in his pockets, shifting his weight left and right.

Kiss her, Paisley thought. It's so easy. Live a little! No one will see. And then, for a heartbeat, she realized that *she* would see. But she pushed the thought away. No one cared that she was there, a fly on the wall. And she was the best secret-keeper in the world.

Paisley had kept similar knowledge to herself before now. Back in high school, Fidelity Parker had been a racy one; anything she said made good gossip. Fidelity's father was a pastor at the Baptist church in Amherstview, one of the towns on the mainland near the Amherst Island ferry dock. Fidelity's mother volunteered at the Kingston Young Christian Parents' Hotline, where she busied herself on the phone saving teenage girls' souls by dissuading them from premarital sex, slutty apparel, and abortion. Fidelity's parents would have had a fit if they'd known what their daughter was up to on weekends, and how free she was with the tales of her escapades on Monday mornings.

One time, Fidelity had gathered her girlfriends in the washroom. Paisley was trapped in one of the stalls, trying and trying to poop before the first bell. She'd had no luck, not even after an entire week of high-fibre cereal. When the girls piled in, she'd tucked her feet up onto the toilet seat, trying to remain still so they wouldn't know she was there.

"So I told him, 'Get in the car,'" Fidelity said. "He has a great car, by the way."

"We know, we know," said another girl, whose voice Paisley didn't recognize, "a two-door LeMans, midnight blue. Get to the good part."

"I told him, 'Drive, just drive. I'll tell you when to stop.' Boys like it when a girl takes charge."

"Yeah, right," Cherie said. She was Fidelity's best friend. "If I said that to my brother, he'd punch me on the side of my head."

"While we were driving," Fidelity continued, "I put my hand in between his thighs and gave him a boner. He nearly swerved right off the road."

"Wow," the first girl said. "Nearly getting killed for a boner. Good times."

Paisley leaned over to see if she could catch a glimpse of the girl through the crack between the door of her stall and the wall. She liked the way she talked, so confident and sarcastic. But all she could see was clothing—skirts and shirts—and bare arms. She leaned further for a better view, steadying herself with an arm against the wall and her other hand holding on to the toilet-paper dispenser. It was a new girl; she'd transferred from a Montreal high school earlier that month. Her father was teaching for a year at Queen's. The boys panted at her. She was smart and laid-back and she dyed her hair jet black.

"It *was* good times!" Fidelity protested. "And if you don't want to hear the rest, I'll just stop."

Fidelity may have been trashy, but she knew when she had the floor. Paisley thought she'd turn out to be an actor. Or maybe...a stripper.

"No, go on," the new girl said. "Don't stop now."

"So, yeah, he has this huge boner, and I'm just playing with him, toying with him, and saying, 'Keep your eyes on the road. I'll tell you when to turn off.'"

"And so?"

"And so as soon as I saw the lane to the Morrow property, I waited till the last possible moment, and then I screamed, 'Turn now!' And he did, and his tires squealed, and I looked back and we left these cool marks on the highway."

"And then what happened?" Cherie again. She hadn't lost her virginity yet, but she had plans and needed ideas.

"We drove into the bush, and I finally told him to stop the car, and then I told him to fold down the seats, which go way back, almost like you could sleep in the car, and then I did it to him."

Cherie squealed. "Did what, did what?"

"Tortured him. Made him pay for being a guy. Never even let him pull it out of his jeans, just blew on his crotch and told him all the things I would do next time, until he moaned and groaned. He wanted to unzip and pull it out, but I said, 'No, no way, you stay just how you are or I'll stop,' and then his face got all tight and he did it all by himself. You know, in his pants. I tell you, it's totally worth it. They only want more, and you don't have to get yourself all messy, nothing in your hair or anything."

Cherie exploded into giggles.

"Plus," Fidelity said, bringing the whole story home, "I think my mum would approve, because there's no chance of getting pregnant, so, like, I'd never have to call in and disguise my voice and ask my own mother for advice she's too stupid to give."

This made Cherie dare Felicity to call in to the hotline. Cherie even offered a month's allowance.

"Big fat hairy deal." That was the new girl.

"What do you mean?" Fidelity said.

"I mean, if you were really in control, you'd have gotten the guy to take care of *you*. Now he wants more, but he figures it's all about him. He thinks you serve him. It's got to be the other way around." Paisley heard the bathroom door open. "Then you've really got him by the balls."

The new girl was gone, the bathroom door creaking closed behind her.

"She's totally a bitch," Fidelity said.

"Totally," Cherie said. "I'll even write it on the wall. Gimme a pen."

Paisley had told no one about that exchange—even when Fidelity had to leave three weeks before the end of Grade 12 because they found her running what amounted to a blow-job brothel for the school's male population out of the girls' washroom—ten dollars a pop. That's how good a secret-keeper Paisley was.

"Guess I should go," Lily said to the boy for the second time. He was missing his chance: going, going, gone.

She pulled her keys from her knapsack. "See ya."

The finality of those two little words catapulted him into action. He yanked his hands from his pockets and wrapped them around Lily's waist. He bent at the knees and pulled her close, but the physics weren't in his favour. He couldn't hold on to her like that and he straightened up. The moment was fumbled—all was almost lost. Paisley let a tiny sound escape, a breath of desire for them both that she instantly regretted. She hoped it hadn't betrayed her. But it was Lily who took the leap. She stepped her scruffy black army boots forward and onto the boy's size-fourteen running shoes. Their eyes met. They tilted their faces in the same direction and crushed noses, then readjusted. Mission accomplished.

Paisley couldn't have been more than four feet from that first kiss. Her legs went weak and she stepped away from the door, letting go of the chain carefully so it wouldn't make a noise, turning back to her lukewarm hot dogs. Her excitement couldn't be denied: she wanted to take chances in life the way Lily did. Leaping without any regard for whether it might be right or wrong, whether it made you a bad person or whether you might somehow inadvertently start a fire because of the tiniest decision. But Paisley couldn't bring herself to be as cavalier about the unknown as Lily. Plus, a relationship was too much trouble. Yes, generally, because of the eights, but also now because she had to find somewhere to live. Just a little too much on her plate, in other words.

THEN

Olive and Eden decided they wouldn't leave the social until they could buy a few precious somethings from the white elephant table, and James wouldn't let them touch a thing until it officially opened at eleven, so this was Paisley's moment to set up the post office. She now had only one thing on her mind: beat these women from the mainland, these women who were not worthy of the Henslow's sparrow, and find the rare bird before they did. After all, she knew all the spots on the island where a bird like that might hide. They didn't. She could go back home and collect her bicycle so she could get around fast. She would beat them, hands down: find the sparrow, add it to her list, and make it known as soon as possible that she had found it. She could tell the president of the Kingston Field Naturalists. She'd be famous—at least among local birders. She'd be important. She'd be able to honour her great-great-grandmother June and her early birding work.

Paisley raced over to her spot, which was nestled among a clutch of oak trees. The table was already there, covered in brown parcels of all sizes. A banner strung up above the table read *Post Orifice*.

Paisley looked around. People in aprons and coveralls bustled about the church grounds. Two ladies argued over how to put up the canopies for the book nook and the clothing corner. No one was watching her.

Paisley looked back at the banner. *Post Orifice*. Only one person was capable of such a thing: Garnet Mulligan.

Running the post office wasn't a bad assignment. In the tea room, one false move could leave you washing a thousand cups and saucers. At the white elephant table, you ran the gauntlet of ladies with sharp elbows like Olive and Eden. Paisley had taken on more responsibility at church since last year, when she'd moved from Junior Sunday School to the CCC Room, otherwise known as Christ's Cool Cats.

Reverend Willis had come up with the CCC Room as a way to get young people more involved. He'd organized a day when the elders, parents, and kids painted the old church storeroom in electric blue (vats of which were left over from Mildred Mickie painting her barn) and decorated it with bright red beanbag chairs, an avocado-green couch donated from someone's family room, and a battered drum kit for the kids to make joyful noise.

Now that Paisley was a CCC, she was invited to church meetings. Just last month, she'd attended the planning session for the summer social. Prudence Bellechamps had also been in attendance. While waiting for things to start, Prue held court with the other women, going on and on about what was growing and not growing in her garden while dominating the cheese-and-biscuit plate at the back of the fellowship hall. Paisley had wished she'd stop talking and free up access to the food table. Then the meeting could get under way, and Paisley could get elected for her job and go back to birding with her pockets full of cheese cubes.

But church people liked to talk. They smiled and chatted even though Paisley never knew what to say in response. The weather was what it was—why talk about it? Of course, school was just fine, and if it wasn't, would she really say so to them? Word got around like lightning on the island, so it was best to share the least and think the most, said Hu. Paisley agreed. There was more certainty in doing tasks as opposed to talking about them, counting problems so you knew where things stood, and putting every object you owned into its rightful place so you didn't have to worry about it afterward. The more of the world you controlled, the better; that was just the truth, island or not. Many things Paisley didn't know, but this she knew for sure.

So Paisley had volunteered to run the post office all by herself this year—a safe bet, a not-too-onerous responsibility.

"Do you need help?" asked Reverend Willis.

Paisley preferred not to work with others. They might smell bad. Or they might want to chat about friends, school, boys, life, and she did not like to chat about those things. White-tailed lapwings (*Vanellus leucurus*), sure, and how the ones found in Russia migrated in the winter to the Indian subcontinent or the Middle East or North Africa and were very occasionally found in Western Europe. She'd talk about things like that for sure. But teenage things? No, thank you.

No hands shot up to help Paisley with the post office booth. Everyone was already on two or three committees: set-up, tear-down, white elephant, pie table, entertainment, tea room, dry goods raffle, or live auction. People wanted another job like a hole in the head. And while for a moment Paisley felt bad that no one wanted to work with her, she was mostly glad.

Mrs. Mulligan lifted her hand. "What about Garnet?"

Garnet? Oh God, and God's only son, Jesus Christ. Not Garnet.

Ever since they'd moved to the island from Ireland three years ago, Mrs. Maeve Mulligan had been volunteering her sons for committees and haying and barn raising and tree cutting and just about anything else, trying to set them straight, to no avail. Garnet was only thirteen, true, but he'd already been hauled into the police station on the mainland twice, once for stealing mail from the Stella Country Store (he'd stolen lots from there, everything from a single stick of licorice to a hacksaw, but mail was a federal thing, more serious), and another time for letting all the cows loose from Old Man Sperry's back pasture. Garnet had also been suspended more times than anyone could remember for picking on kids and pulling pranks. He'd made it pretty clear in class, in the schoolyard, any time anyone asked: he hated it here. He wanted to be home, back in Ireland, with his mates, as he called them. Where his life was. Only problem was, Garnet's father, James, said life was here now, and Garnet should get used to it. James Mulligan was the one who'd made the decision to move his family to Amherst Island to take over his great-uncle's farm—a farm dating back to the island's Irish settlers, who came after the English, who came after the French, who came after the Indigenous people, of course. Mr. Mulligan said they had ties here—just look at the headstones in St. Andrew's Cemetery—Murphy. Brennan. Walsh. Gallagher. Byrne. Mulligan. Good Irish names. Look at the island's dry stone walls—built by so many Irish. None of it was good enough for Garnet. Ever since they'd arrived, Garnet had undertaken a major protest campaign to punish his parents. He was determined to make the whole island miserable so he'd get sent home.

Mr. Mulligan had taken a more proactive route than his wife to setting his son straight, getting him to plant his feet and grow roots here. He'd grounded him, confiscated anything that mattered to him, and beaten him on several occasions. A few times Garnet had appeared at school with a black eye or a few bruises. But that just made him mad like his dad, madder even, which made him cause more trouble, which made his father more furious—which was fine with Garnet, because rebelliousness and insolence were the only real revenge he could dream up.

More than once, Paisley had used her eavesdropping skills to listen to him in the schoolyard. When the Mulligans had left Ireland, he'd left his friends, and his football career, as he called it; they used the word *football* for soccer over there. And Garnet wanted to be a footballer more than anything. He was very, very good, from what Paisley could see. She'd watch him practise keep-up in the schoolyard. He could juggle the ball for hours. He was never beaten in the recess soccer game, or during gym. Ever. He did an "around the world" trick—kick the ball up and then go around it with his foot and catch it again with the top of the same foot and keep juggling—absent-mindedly with his right foot, but the fact that he could do it with his left foot, too, impressed the boys. The fact that he could toss the ball between his foot, his head, his neck, and his chest, his muscles glistening with sweat, impressed the girls.

Every August, Garnet and his brother Shawn went back to Ireland to live with relatives and attend football camp. Amherst Island breathed a sigh of relief while they were gone, because there was a respite from the shenanigans. Until the boys returned in September and Garnet's resentment was right back to where it had started. Worse, even.

Everyone assembled in the St. Andrew's fellowship hall to divide up summer social tasks looked to Garnet, who was slouched in his seat, his feet on the back of the chair before him. He wore a short-sleeved T-shirt and had a farmer's tan on his big biceps. Well, not big exactly...defined. The kind that looked like he had tennis balls underneath his sinewy arm skin. Lean and strong at the same time. Paisley eyed him while pretending not to eye him and thought that, even though he was so evil, he was also sort of hot. Okay, totally hot.

No one dared tell him to put his feet on the floor, not even Reverend Willis.

"Sure," said Garnet, "I'll work the post office with Paisley." He only had a bit of his Irish accent left. "That'll be fun now, won't it?"

Reverend Willis shot Paisley a look as if to apologize, and her heart sank. Yes, Reverend Willis was young and full of verve. He was also, in Paisley's view, sort of a dork who made dubious decisions.

NOW

Paisley made hot dogs twice a day for the next few days, using the same water each time, until both packages were gone. She felt badly about lying to the archives, saying she was sick, but technically, she was, wasn't she? Sick in the head? Having a bout of OCD was just like being down with the flu, wasn't it? No. Not really. OCD was the sort of nonsense you should be able to put an immediate stop to. Get your pants on and get out the door. Get your mental act together. But try explaining that to anyone normal. Paisley might run through the list of imperatives, the rules, the bad feelings, the endless doubt that made you double back and count and check everything eight times, and then eight again. Even if you used a cool, calm, and collected voice to explain that although you knew the OCD rituals were mostly irrational, they were the only thing to make you feel okay—in fact, helped you lead what was mostly an ordinary life like everyone else. But when you looked into their eyes, you knew they didn't believe you. So, the sick-not-sick debate—the moral dilemma of lying to your employers, but not, really, but yes, really—was the very oxygen that fed OCD to become bigger and stronger. Trying to stifle that line of thinking was cutting off one head of the hydra and having two grow back.

In the past week, Paisley hadn't managed to weed out more possessions, had packed very little, hadn't done any searching for a new apartment, and had nothing left in her kitchen except uncooked rice—and given she couldn't use the stove for fear of causing a fire, what good was rice to her? The situation was both absurd and visceral—two terrible words that described much of her life, at least at the moment.

So she stared at the fridge, which was empty save for the bowl of wiener broth. She pulled the bowl out and examined the contents. The water from the wieners had become almost gelatinous, with a thick film of something—nitrates, maybe—on top. She microwaved it and ate it for dinner. Wiener soup. A new low.

On Friday, the heat came back on. There was a knock at the door. It was Mrs. Feldman. "Haven't seen you for a week," she said. "Can you open the door?"

"I'm just out of the shower," lied Paisley. "I'll be down to get my mail later. Can we catch up then?"

"Sure."

Paisley watched her through the peephole. Mrs. F was staring at the space heater.

"I'll just take this old thing, then," said Mrs. F. "Hope you got some use out of it."

"Oh, I did. Thank you very much."

Paisley should just open the door. Do it. Do it now. But she couldn't. She was sick with herself and sick with the world. She could not face another human being.

"I suppose you know the furnace men finally came," said Mrs. Feldman. "It took two anonymous phone calls from yours truly, though. I threatened to sue the owners, and they were scared, I tell you. I said to them over the phone, 'What's that going to look like on page one, you numb-skulls? A little old lady, survivor of World War II, who froze to death in her Toronto apartment because her landlord refused to fix the boiler?' They hopped to, lickety-split."

"You're great, Mrs. Feldman," said Paisley.

"That I am," said Mrs. F. "It'll take a couple of days for the boiler to get up to speed, but eventually it'll be warm again."

Paisley watched her pick up the space heater. Happy to see it go.

"See you downstairs, then," said Mrs. Feldman. "I'll be there after cribbage with Mr. Burnside. Did I tell you he was sweet on me?"

"I think you did."

"Well, don't hold your breath for wedding bells. I'm not on the market."

"Shame for him."

"I should say so."

Mrs. Feldman started to walk down the corridor, then turned and came back. Paisley could see her hot-roller-perfect curls through the peephole.

"I *will* see you downstairs, yes?"

"Yes."

"Because, honey," she said through the door, "life is only as interesting as the number of times you say yes."

But to get out of the apartment later took a full hour of counting and checking. Paisley finally made it into the elevator and managed to let the doors close, resisting the urge to dash out and check her apartment again.

The Dale Manor lobby was empty. Mrs. F was probably still at cribbage. Or getting laid by Mr. Burnside. Paisley eyed the cold sunshine and decided to keep going.

THEN

As Paisley approached the post office table, she saw him. Lounging just beyond the nearest oak tree, muscled arms folded under his head, chewing on a blade of grass, waiting for her reaction. He looked like a centrefold but with clothes on. (Paisley had seen a *Playboy* magazine once in Mildred Mickie's barn. It belonged to Stanley, the farmhand. She knew because when she found it, his metal coffee cup with the joke on the side—"What do you call a cow with no legs? Ground beef!"—was sitting on the open magazine spread. The coffee cup rings had made the pages wrinkly so that the naked woman's globular breasts were wrinkly, too.)

"Come on over," Garnet said.

"No, I—" Paisley spun on the spot, trying to think quickly. She caught Del's eye from over at the pie table. Del. Yes. "Del said she'd help us—Del?" Paisley's voice was soft. Caught in her throat.

"Don't mind her, she's busy," said Garnet. "You haven't said anything about my sign. Like it?"

Paisley turned back to Garnet with reluctance. He stood up, spat out the blade of grass, yanked down the Dublin track pants he wore pretty much all the time, and mooned her. "See?" he said, looking at Paisley between his legs. "Post orifice. Wanna come over here and see if mine's big enough for any of those parcels?"

Paisley was horrified. Not only because Garnet had phrased that as a question, which required a response, but also because his teenage bottom was hairy in the crack, and his testicles were purple and shrivelled.

"Love to." Another voice answered Garnet's question.

Garnet looked beyond Paisley and stood up, yanking up his pants in the same swift movement.

"No, no," said Del, approaching with a sway of her hips, smooth, confident, pausing only to take a drag on her cigarette. "If you want a parcel shoved up your orifice, I can oblige. Just let me pick the right one."

"I was joking," Garnet said. "Can't you tell when it's a joke?"

"I'm not joking," said Del. "Can't you tell when it's not?"

Garnet didn't reply.

"So...Shitballs Mulligan. If you're still here in two seconds," said Del, blowing a smoke ring, "I'll choose a parcel for just what you suggested, and I'll make sure it's big and square. With sharp corners."

Garnet walked off.

"Learn how to defend yourself, Paisley," said Del. "At least keep your eyes open and your head in the world. Get a personality. Stand out. Stick up for yourself. Kids don't bully kids with personality. If all you want to do is blend in, fine. But you're liable to get crushed in the process."

It would be hard to get a personality now, thought Paisley. She was thirteen. Surely the die was cast. "I'll try."

"Atta girl, Paise. And by the way, boys don't pull their pants down for a girl if they don't like them."

That was a new idea, even if it also made no sense.

"I'm off to stop your mother from poking Prue's eyes out. Think you'd best hide that sign somewhere. Everyone knows this is the post office, the same way we all know Garnet's a jerk. Right?"

"Right."

Del headed back to Eudie, who was wiping tables as Mac unstacked them from the shed. There was Reverend Willis, teetering on the top rung of a ladder, pinning up the last of the banners.

And there was Garnet, leaning against the old outhouse, with a glare and a set jaw.

NOW

It was still frigid in the apartment when she got back. That damn boiler was taking its sweet time. Paisley had collected eight boxes at the liquor store and a few groceries, and as long as she kept moving, she felt warm. The contents of her hall closet had been packed, except for her coat, boots, scarf, and mittens. Her birding magazines were packed and she was back into the filing cabinet, feeling proud of her progress, but still wobbly. Where would she live? How would she afford rent at current prices? Surely not around here, on the perimeter of Rosedale—the poor side of the street, yes, but it was still an upscale neighbourhood. She'd been in this apartment since she was eighteen—the rent, despite annual increases, was far below market. In this fictional next apartment, what would her new neighbours be like? She couldn't afford to live in a new building, the kind with a doorman or amenities, so where would she go? And wherever she landed, would there be safety issues? Oh God, the safety issues. The heating system. The boiler. The wiring.

She pulled out another bunch of files. One was marked *Warblers*. The next was *Women of Note*, clippings of interesting women whom Paisley at one time thought she might emulate. Ha! The next was labelled *Wills—Eudora and Hubert Ratchford*. She stared at the legal-size papers.

Paisley's mind flashed to her childhood home on Amherst Island: classic Ontario house, about a hundred years old, not big—two floors, three bedrooms—shed, big lawn stretching to Front Road on the south and the Bay of Quinte on the north. What had happened to it? It must still be there. Why wouldn't it be?

Could she live there?

Suddenly, a possibility.

She got off the floor and stood in the mess. She could write a letter to her mother's law firm in Kingston, the one who'd handled the estate, just to see.

Would it cost money to ask questions? Lawyers liked to make money any way they could. She worried about the embarrassment; it wouldn't be a proud moment to let other people in on the fact that she had no idea about her own affairs. She was flooded with anxiety just remembering the whole thing, sitting there in that office in Kingston, facing the lawyer... What was his name? Bertram. John Bertram.

But if she was ever going to find out what had happened to the house, now was the time.

> *Dear Mr. Bertram,*
>
> *You probably don't remember me, but my name is Paisley Ratchford, and a very long time ago my family was a client of yours.*
> *I was wondering if—*
> *Would it be possible—*
> *I am inquiring about my family's estate on Amherst Island. Specifically, I am interested in finding out what happened with my mother's house on the north shore.*
> *I trust wish hope you are well.*
>
> *Sincerely,*
> *Paisley Ratchford*

She read it over several times. It didn't sound needy or pathetic, but Paisley was always concerned about offending people. Hopefully this was short and sweet enough to get the information she needed without revealing too much. She wrote out a good copy of the letter and made a plan to post it that evening. Then she microwaved the New Orleans fried chicken she'd collected on her last outing and ate it for dinner, tucked under two blankets.

THEN

It was eleven o'clock on the nose. The pies were on display, the auction chairs set up, the games ready to go, the second-hand books laid out. Cyrus, who worked on the ferry, was directing people where to park on the church lawn. He lined up cars and trucks more loosely here than on the boat, so people could leave when they wanted, but everything was still nice and organized.

"Welcome to Amherst Island's thirty-second annual summer social," announced Reverend Willis from atop the large stone set at the church entrance a century earlier to help ladies out of horse-drawn carriages. Behind him, over the double doors, a sign read, *The Worship Is Over, the Service Begins.*

"We're glad to have you here! As many of you know, this is my first year on Amherst Island, and I have been warmly received by so many..."

From her vantage point, standing tippytoe on a tree root, Paisley noted several women who no doubt longed to receive the reverend even more warmly. She also kept an eye on Olive at the used-book table and Eden at the pie table, eating furtively and chatting with Prue.

"So I want to extend a big thank-you to one and all," said Reverend Willis. "You know, back in theological college..."

Del also scanned the crowd. "Is Hubert coming or not?"

"Who knows," said Eudie.

"You two hardly spend any time together," whispered Del. "That man's more married to the farm than to you."

"Del, please."

"It's true," said Del, lowering her voice. "You're dying on this island, Eudie. You married a man who treats Mildred's cows better than he treats you."

Eudie shushed Del but kept her eyes on the minister. She

didn't like how Del had a way of hitting the nail exactly on the head—but it was also the thing Eudie most liked about her.

"I haven't seen Hubert in ages," Del went on. "Is he having a fling with Mildred? That'd be convenient. Tends to her barn in the morning, tends to her in the afternoon..."

Eudie shot Del a look. Paisley wanted her to stop talking, too, wanted her mother to say, no, no, she loved Hu just as she had that day she first met him, loved his pressed work pants and his strong arms and how formal yet down-to-earth he was all at once. She wanted Eudie to say that the cat called France, left behind in Toronto, couldn't hold a candle to the man she'd said yes to on Amherst Island. She wanted her mother to put Del in her place for even suggesting Hu was fooling around with Mildred—a repulsive notion. Mildred, the woman who owned the farm where her father worked, had one black tooth from a slip down the stairs, and was fattish, made all the more evident by her determination to tuck her blouses into elastic-waist pants.

Paisley waited for her mother's reply, but whatever her response, it was drowned out by applause. The reverend had wrapped up and his audience was dispersing. The summer social was officially under way.

Reverend Willis stepped off his perch and began to circulate, charming the little old ladies and chumming around with the men. He meant well, but for Paisley he held no spiritual authority. He was too young. Too inexperienced. Too much of a pushover maybe, like Paisley herself. She longed for someone to offer her certainty, to take the pressure out of her head, calm her, tell her it would be all right. She would love it if God were truly in control. But she couldn't trust Reverend Willis as her rock of salvation. He was too soft for that.

Garnet appeared at her elbow. "C'mere," he said in a low voice, reaching for her arm.

Paisley pulled away and dashed for the post office table, already crowded with children. She threw on the postmaster hat and turned the sign from *Closed* to *Open*.

She doled out parcels, a dime each, keeping one eye on Garnet and the other on the birding ladies.

Garnet and Paisley had both just finished Grade 8 at the island school. It had so few students that each class was a multi-grade split—so really, there was nowhere to hide if a boy like Garnet set his sights on you. Paisley had managed to keep herself invisible enough up until now—sure, she was weird; sure, she had bad days when she couldn't help but count in front of the other kids—but he'd had no reason to pay attention to her. Paisley was pretty inoffensive, and he preferred to focus on the boys, where competition easily escalated into fistfights Garnet invariably won. But now that Del had embarrassed him, and Paisley was responsible, there was a score to be settled.

Garnet approached. Olive and Eden over at the barbecue tent looked like they might soon leave. What to do? Paisley threw off her hat, yelled, "Post office holdup! Take what you want!" and darted away from the table, leaving mayhem in her wake.

She headed for the timeless treasures display: little brooches and costume jewellery from old ladies' estates sold at higher prices to fund the church's new roof. Garnet changed direction and pursued her. He grabbed a long switch from an oak tree and whipped it through the air.

Paisley changed direction again and found herself facing the birding women at the barbecue tent's condiments table. Her only way out. "I hope you don't mind, but I happen to have overheard you're looking for a rare bird," Paisley told Olive. "I'm a birder, too. I can show you around."

Olive squinted at Paisley. "That's nice of you, but I thought birders were competitive about that sort of thing. Spotting a rare bird."

"Only the bad ones."

"Isn't that nice of you," said Eden, taking a large bite of

her hamburger. "We could go after the entertainment."

Paisley looked over their shoulders at Garnet, who was still whipping the switch. She could hear the sound of it cutting through the air from here.

"Except there are some competitive birders here," said Paisley, "and they know all the same spots I do. So if you want to be the first to see it, I'd say we should leave now."

"I think she's right," said Olive. "I'll get my burger and we can go."

Waiting for Olive's burger gave them a chance to see the first performers of the summer social entertainment, the Kingston Tappers. With all eyes on them, Paisley was protected for a few minutes.

Twin sisters Mary and Margaret had porcelain skin, smooth, hairless arms, fire-engine-red lipstick, matching dyed chestnut beehives, and long legs cased in thick hose. It was difficult to determine their age. Fifty? Seventy? They wore homemade fifties outfits—wide purple circle skirts with crinoline petticoats, and tight blouses and cardigans on top with matching purple embossed poodles near their hearts. Their cardigan buttons strained against their ample bosoms, and their shiny white patent tap shoes bore big purple bows to match their skirts. They travelled with their own recorded music and amps.

They had laid down four-by-eight plywood boards for stomping. Margaret blew into the microphone and twisted the dial on their amp to shush the feedback. "Ladies and gentlemen," she said, "we're gonna perform the piece that won us a red ribbon at the Napanee Fair two years running. Feel free to get on up and dance a little yourselves!"

Margaret extended her foot in a preparatory pose, one arm up and one arm down, and froze her lips in a toothy smile. Mary started the music, then dashed back to the plywood to match her sister's stance. The music blared. The plywood bowed and popped with every stomp, but their beehives never moved and their smiles remained steadfast. Mary and Margaret tapped with vigour and pep, cheeks jiggling, breasts jiggling more. They finished to great applause and then removed their plywood to make way for Melvin Duney ("Get tuney with Duney") and his Yamaha electric keyboard.

NOW

A week had passed since Paisley mailed her letter to the Kingston law office. She'd done a bit of packing, enough to require another trip to the liquor store for boxes.

"More boxes. Good for you. Have you found a place to live yet?" asked Mrs. Feldman, as Paisley collected her mail.

"No, I'm just packing up what I don't need now, and then I'll look."

"That's backwards, but you didn't ask me," said Mrs. Feldman. "You'll have all your bags packed and you'll be out on your tuchus in six weeks with nowhere to live."

"But what a tuchus," said Paisley. Mrs. F had often commented that Paisley had a lovely shape, and that the sagging that arrived in your eighties was less than desirable.

"True," said Mrs. F, "but should it be out on the street, sitting on a damp piece of cardboard, rain or shine? I don't think so. Who am I to say? Suit yourself."

Paisley got into the elevator and looked through the mail. There was a card from a holistic health centre on Bloor Street, offering services in homeopathic remedy, oxygen tank therapy, Rolfing, and aura readings. The tag line read "Change Yourself Now!" That was laughable. A Chinese food flyer. A brochure for Drive-A-Booze, a service that delivered beer, wine, and liquor to your door. And there was a letter from the law firm in Kingston, Bertram & Associates.

Days of packing had left the apartment looking empty and sad. Sadder than usual anyway. Paisley sat on a box of magazines and opened the letter. Written by a clerk, according to the signature, it said that the head of the firm, John Bertram, with whom Paisley's family had originally dealt, had developed Alzheimer's and had retired. Paisley's file had been assigned to one of the junior partners, who would be in touch after familiarizing himself with the details. That lawyer was Garnet Mulligan.

THEN

Paisley took Olive and Eden on a wild goose chase around the island. Sure, she showed them the Owl Woods, the one island birding spot they knew by name, but a Henslow's sparrow would never nest in the woods. Only, the women didn't know that. Paisley didn't like lying to them—that would probably prompt some penitent eights later on—but she did love birding and being in nature, and she didn't mind showing the women around even if they were terrible birders: talking too loud, rustling grasses when they shouldn't, and without a clue as to what they were looking for.

The Henslow's sparrow was the bird they were looking for. It was a passerine bird. Over half of all bird species were passerine, like songbirds and perching birds. You could tell a passerine from the arrangement of its toes: three in the front, one in the back—what it needed to perch.

The Henslow's sparrow's breeding range was basically the northeastern and east central United States and southern Ontario. As a ground nester, it preferred dense, tall grasses, like those in unused agricultural lands, thatch, wet meadows, grassy swales, hay fields, or decaying plant material. It moved to new locations as plant succession changed and the habitat became shrubby. It overwintered in states bordering the Gulf of Mexico and in southeastern states on the Atlantic coast. If disturbed, the Henslow's sparrow took flight with great reluctance, preferring to flee by running through the grass. Paisley wondered why it wouldn't fly in the face of danger. It was both odd to her and understandable. Paisley often felt she deferred to paralysis instead of action. A thing would happen, and she wouldn't know the right response. Like Garnet and his hairy ass. What was the right thing to do there?

The Henslow's sparrow's nest was an open bowl of loosely woven dry grasses built just off the ground. Its clutch size was generally two to five glossy white eggs with speckles and blotches. It ate insects, mostly grasshoppers and beetles. Its song was a simple, thin, two-syllable *tsi-lik*. Insect-like. It sang most actively at dawn and dusk, but sometimes it sang all night long, which was how it was usually detected. Otherwise, the small, shy bird was secretive and had a "nothing song," as one expert said. Paisley loved that. A shy bird. A secretive bird. A nothing song.

Of course, she told none of this to Olive and Eden. Paisley missed most of the summer social—all of the performances save the twin tappers, the live auction, the food—but her escape from Garnet had been worth it. She returned to the church after the two women headed for the three o'clock ferry lineup. Garnet was nowhere to be seen. A few men were putting tables back into the drive shed, taking down tents, tarping over the books so the barn swallows (*Hirundo rustica*) wouldn't poop on them. The books would be out for a few days yet so people could get a good look and take what struck their fancy. The church elders were moving into the sanctuary to count the money collected from each station. Del was also on her way out to catch the ferry so she wouldn't have to lift a finger. Mavis and Trixic, spinsters from an apiary on the north shore, washed the mountain of teacups in Javex and water, while Eudie and Prue took care of the remains of the pie table.

Christ's Cool Cats were on litter duty, so Paisley grabbed a garbage bag and walked the grounds, filling it with trash. Then she decided to search for Rory. She hadn't seen him since that morning and figured he might have ventured into the cemetery. It was the perfect place for hide-and-seek, another of his favourite pastimes. In the cemetery, even big Rory could find places to hide behind monuments. He'd worked out a version of the game he could play by himself—hiding, jumping out to reveal his location to no one in particular, and hiding again. If she could track him down, they could start actually looking for the sparrow. Plus, Rory could protect her from Garnet if he reappeared.

Paisley wound her way through the maze of monuments. The entire Dutchie family, each dead from encounters with pieces of farm machinery. The Crummey boys, four sons taken by drowning in the days before the ferry, when people boated themselves to and from the mainland, whether or not their vessel was seaworthy, whether or not they could swim. The Reverend Bertrand Hascall, 1914–1959: "Promoted."

Paisley went to look for Rory behind the drive shed, where the remnants of every Sunday's fellowship hour were tossed: the crusts of minced beef sandwiches, fruit peelings, shavings from huge blocks of local Wilton cheese. The deer knew to visit later, after the commotion had died down, for a good meal. They munched on everything: young tomatoes grown by Reverend Willis at the manse, beds of petunias planted by church ladies outside the church door. Eudie might get a scare if she came out from the kitchen and Rory was hiding there. Paisley veered off through the tall grass, past the old outhouse, into the cool, quiet shade behind the drive shed.

She heard a rustle in the grass; shadows moved. She peeked around the corner.

It was Reverend Willis and someone else. Paisley craned her neck to see. Eudie, dumping leftovers from the pie table.

"What's that you have there?" Eudie asked the reverend. Her voice was light. Singsong.

"Scraps from the tea room," he said.

"Sweet you'd pitch in like that," said Eudie. "Mavis talk you into it?"

"No, no, I'm here of my own accord," said Reverend Willis. "Ate one too many of Mavis's brownies—six, I think—then came back for one more. That dealt the lethal blow."

"Oh, stop it," said Eudie, balancing a stack of pie plates.

"If I'd been five minutes earlier," said Reverend Willis, "I could've helped with counting the donation plate. But I arrived just as it was all cleanup." He flashed her a smile and tossed coffee grounds into the weeds. They looked at each other. Smiled again.

"Where's Hubert?" asked Reverend Willis.

"Not here."

"Sorry about that, Eudie." He used his gentle after-service minister voice, the one for congregants with problems, not the voice for sermons. "Is it something you'd like to talk about?"

Eudie paused a half second. "No." She held out a plate with some pie still on it. "Did you try my rhubarb pie?"

"No, that I missed, unfortunately."

He stepped toward the plate. She stepped toward him. She picked up the piece of pie and fed it to him with her hand. He laughed a little and stumbled forward. Two adult bodies collided awkwardly, in slow motion. Eudie leaned in to Reverend Willis. The pie plate tumbled into the tall grass. Eudie and Arden Willis's lips met, like they were suspended in time and space. Under the cool shade of the trees, a big sense of nothingness ballooned in Paisley's head. Eudie's lips were moving on Reverend Willis's mouth. Her hands travelled up his slim arms to his shirt and his neck with that funny bump. His white collar popped off and fell into a patch of burdock, like a long, thin boomerang-shaped asteroid spinning into space.

"Eudora…"

Reverend Willis talked as if through a fog. No one ever used Eudie's full name.

And only then did Paisley register it: her mother was kissing the minister.

"No, Eudora. No."

His voice, firmer now, was like a shot of adrenalin in Paisley's body. A bad thing was happening. The reverend was fighting off Paisley's mother, but not very well. He was too polite. He was too weak.

"Not here..." he said, which implied that elsewhere might be okay, sometime later. Paisley could see he had the same realization, heard the implication as he made it. He'd wanted to be strict and clear. Eudie was still on him, her weight given to his weight, no air at all between their bodies.

"Please," whispered Eudie.

Paisley's mother never begged for anything. She had one hand on her skirt, hiking it up, the other under his shirt, hiking it up, too, and Paisley saw the smooth furrow leading down from the reverend's hip bone, the slim curve and silky skin, all lean and—

"Paisley!"

Arden Willis was looking straight at her. He shoved Eudie away with a strength he hadn't shown before, straightening her up onto her own feet, like a tourist pretending to right the Tower of Pisa.

"Paisley— I— There's nothing—" He turned away and bent down. It seemed very important for him to find his collar.

Paisley felt a gurgle in her gut.

"For God's sake, Paisley, go!" screamed Eudie.

Paisley leapt over the crabgrass and milkweed. She ran faster than she'd ever run in her life. "Olly olly oxen free! Olly olly oxen free!" she yelled.

Rory jumped down out of a tree. "I tricked you. You didn't see me. I been watching you a long time now!" He clapped at the excellence of his hiding. "Want to go again? Count, Paisley, count!"

Paisley wanted to count all right, just not with Rory. "I'm not playing."

"But you like to play with me."

"I need to go home. Right now." She ran toward the road, counting her steps to make sure they came out even. The parking lot was empty except for Cyrus, who was having a smoke.

Twenty-seven steps.

"I'll walk you home, Paisley," Rory called after her.

She couldn't respond or she'd lose count.

Past the stone gates, the sign announcing the hours of service. *Rev. Arden Willis welcomes you. The sermon this Sunday: Sanctity in Everyday Life.*

Thirty-four.

Down the road, dead centre of the road.

Forty-four.

Forty-eight.

Fifty-seven. Uneven numbers were terrible, they were good for nothing—

The worship is over, the service begins. The worship is over, the service begins.

Run fast, Garnet might be anywhere, waiting to ambush, waiting to—

Sixty-eight.

Seventy-two.

Counting.

The only sure thing.

NOW

The confluence of needing to find a new place to live and the re-emergence of Garnet set Paisley back. Her counting and checking hadn't been this bad in years, and as a result, she abandoned any notion of recovering the house on Amherst Island—she couldn't fathom what had possessed her to indulge that fantasy in the first place. It had cracked open memories of a time and place that were too much to handle on top of her current state of affairs.

She had to focus on getting a new apartment. It couldn't be hard; people did it all the time. She could find a newer building where dependable heating was a certainty, or where concern about electrical safety wouldn't be an issue. She would get her counting and checking under control again.

The following week, Paisley worked a few shifts at the archives, and on her breaks sifted through online rental ads. She'd write a few options down to call later. Then she'd pass by the liquor store to collect more boxes. She'd go home, pack a box or two, and then she'd get close to calling the numbers for the apartments—she'd dial, then hang up right away. A round of counting and checking would ensue. She would feel certain she'd left the stove on. She hadn't used it in years, but she could have bumped into it in passing—that was within the realm of possibility. And the plugs needed checking. Several rounds of eights would solve this anxiety, would get it under control again. Her swan song at Dale Manor couldn't be burning the place to the ground.

And so she'd swap calling new apartments for counting and checking. One round of eight led to seven more to make the eights complete. The hours ticked by. Midnight would pass. Exhausted, Paisley waited to feel the click in her head, the panic abating so she could collapse into bed. Eyes closed, tucked under the heavy blankets, she knew her struggle was taking on bigger proportions. There she was, trying to nudge herself toward the precipice of change; behind her, the counting and checking, a fanged monster, its eight arms pulling her back to this old, tired, terrible place. She had to face the truth: Everyone was due a relapse at some point.

Garnet Mulligan had called more than once from Kingston to follow up on the law firm's letter. Paisley had no idea what to say to him, so she pretended Garnet's messages weren't there and that the message light on the phone base wasn't blinking.

Something had to give, so she decided to change her approach. She'd turn this into a positive experience. She'd make it like a birthday, a new beginning. After all, she'd just turned thirty-nine in February—why not celebrate now? She hadn't back then. She'd let it drift by unnoticed, "the birthday before the birthday that shall not be named." She'd get fresh rental leads. She'd buy herself a bottle of wine. She'd buy some ingredients and she'd bake herself a cake. Steeled with alcohol and sugar, she'd call her entire list of landlords and line up some viewings in one fell swoop. She'd get this shit done.

Paisley pulled on her coat, grabbed her bag, and headed for the door. But first—she needed just one tiny check to feel okay. One round. That was all she'd do.

She examined each outlet to make sure it wouldn't burst into flames. Today, just looking wasn't enough, so she took off her mittens and did one more round, unplugging and replugging every electrical appliance eight times—including lamps, the toaster, and two clock radios, the most bothersome to reset. There was no telling how many rounds of eights she'd have to make, plugging and unplugging a lamp, or turning a light on and off, on and off, on and off, to feel just right.

The stove was last. With the stove, Paisley was always confronted with her own sheer stupidity, because she didn't cook—she never cooked. And yet today she was determined to bake herself a cake, so anxiety was starting off higher than usual. Regular people used their stoves all the time, and, goddammit, so would she. Even though, if the stove were left on, it might burn down the building and the tenants with it, all because of her carelessness.

Exhausted by the rut she was in, she forced herself out into the hall. She locked her door, made it halfway down the corridor to the elevator, and then stopped.

What if, after checking the stove, she had bumped it by mistake? The knobs were on the front; the galley kitchen was small. She had used the fridge before leaving; she'd opened the door. The fridge was past the stove, so she could have knocked one of the knobs. It was possible. An element could be on right now. A fire could happen. She pictured the terror: she'd return to Dale Manor and find it engulfed in flames. Mrs. Feldman would be on her balcony, unable to escape. Lily, with all her potential to change the world, would be lost. The pumper trucks would arrive, the firefighters would do their best, but the building would go up like a tinderbox. Finally, on the brink of exhaustion, the soot-covered firefighters would sit on the curb in shock to watch the blaze, wondering who'd started it.

1 2 3 4 5 6 7 8

So Paisley found herself turning around, opening her door, checking the stove, which was, of course, off. And now, back in the apartment, she had to start her whole routine again, because it wasn't just the stove; she might have missed something else, too.

Filled with self-loathing, she revisited every outlet, every stove knob, every lamp switch eight times, and just as she felt herself propelled to do one last round of eight, the phone rang. She could tell it was Garnet again, and so she bolted from the apartment, pausing only to lock the door, and ran down the hall to the elevator.

THEN

Drenched in sweat, Paisley ran-walked as fast as her thighs could take her onto Front Road, which followed the island's north shore. She needed to be home; she needed to be surrounded by familiar things.

Grass rustled on her left, from the MacNicoll farm.

Normally, she would have veered into the field to track down the sound like a detective. Vole or raccoon? Bluebird or finch? But not today. Today, she kept on, right down the middle of the road.

Five hundred and four. Five hundred and eight. Five hundred and twelve.

Paisley checked over her shoulder to see if Eudie was trying to catch up, trying to give her what for—change what Paisley had seen, dole out a consequence—when Paisley knew, *knew*, it was her mother who'd done something wrong. Eudie must have gone crazy. But her father. What would he think? Did he know? How long had things been like this?

Sixteen things to think about that are not this awful thing at hand, sixteen being two times eight:

1. Chlorine from pools gives you shiny hair but dry hair, a lot like straw.

2. Plantar warts are ugly to think about and very difficult to get rid of. You have a choice of wearing your flip-flops at the public pool or having a skin doctor burn the thing off your foot—like smell-your-own-flesh burn. Gross.

3. If you try to catch a garter snake, your hands will smell like the stalest pee ever. Worse than pee. Like something rotten pulled out from under a rock that's been there for a hundred years. That was peed on.

4. Hairy moles are possibly the most vomit-inducing thing seen on a person's body. Scratch that: bums like Garnet's are worse. Bums with hair in the crack.

5. Trainer bras are ridiculous and get you unwanted attention at school, plus they don't really do anything because usually there's nothing to bra, unless you are unlucky, of course, with plenty to bra. Two shirts one on top of the other works better but gives you bad BO. Then you have to try to fit in two showers a day, which isn't allowed because it drains the well water.

6. When people's big toe and second toe are half-connected with skin, they look like whatever a platypus looks like. Probably no one's ever seen a real platypus, they're just in books. The platypus sounds like a lie, something someone invented for a history of nature textbook. Or wait—am I thinking of the dodo? The dodo is a bird. I should know everything about it.

7. The problem with snowshoes is that they aren't ladylike. In fact, everything about snowshoes is dumb. They are the lesser version of cross-country skis. If your family can't afford skis, you get snowshoes instead, hand-me-downs from a dead relative, a pair your parents found in the shed. Now, it's true that in winter, snowshoes let you cut across the fields instead of sticking to the roads, which can trim a good twenty minutes off a trek. But they can also get you called "fat penguin," which is what Garnet Mulligan yells if he sees you in them. He'll imitate the way you waddle in them and make sounds more like a dolphin than a penguin, but don't be foolish enough to correct him.

8. When Sonya at school—and Wanda, too—say the only cool way to wear eyeliner isn't underneath your eyelashes but in that bottom part of your eyelid itself, so that the pencil leaks onto your eyeball every time you blink, you wonder if you'll end up going blind just for the sake of beauty. Imagine, thirteen-year-olds going blind from eyeliner, all over the world. That's something that would end up in history textbooks as a dumbest-ever moment in humankind.

9. I wonder what it feels like to be kissed like that.

10. When vomit comes up, it burns your throat.

11. Think of anything that doesn't keep coming back to kissing someone you're not supposed to kiss. In the 1840s, the population of Amherst Island was either one thousand or two thousand, depending on whose account you believed, and that was basically its peak population. This was because of a wave of Irish immigration, but the rest of the story is kind of hard to remember.

12. People sometimes said that Amherst Island was shaped like a giant squid (not an octopus like Eudie said, a squid, a squid), swimming away from Prince Edward County, but did that mean islanders were standing on a giant squid? What would that be like, to ride a giant squid? Giant squid could reach over thirty feet long with eyes the size of dinner plates. (This made Paisley think of Jonah and the whale—even though people got the Bible story wrong; it wasn't a whale, it was a giant fish that swallowed Jonah. Paisley knew that from Sunday school. Jonah didn't do what God wanted him to, so God sent along a big fish to swallow Jonah, and he survived in the fish for three days and three nights.)

13. Three is a pretty big number for God and in the Bible. Jesus rose three days after his crucifixion. The Magi presented three gifts to Jesus on his birthday. And there was the whole trinity business—Father, Son, and Holy Ghost.

14. If Paisley didn't do what God wanted her to do in this very moment, could the Giant Squid she was riding swallow her whole for her sins, and would it spit her back out in three days or eight days—hopefully eight, because it was her number?

15. What did God want her to do with what she had just seen?

16. Even numbers are the best things in the world because they are fair, right, nice, and clean. Multiples of even numbers, like eight, are even better.

NOW

Paisley turned onto Bloor Street and walked toward Yonge. Surrounded by buildings that blocked out the sun, she found it bitter. She zipped up her coat and tried to avoid the sidewalk cracks. Step on a crack, break your mother's back. She stood beside a rock pigeon (*Columba livia*) at an intersection, waiting for the light. People think pigeons are dirty, but they're actually quite clean. And smart: they're one of only a handful of species that can pass the mirror test—recognizing themselves in the mirror. And excellent navigators, known to use landmarks as guideposts and roads as routes—there's a reason they were used as homing pigeons. They know how to find home better than I do, thought Paisley.

She'd go to the library and find new apartment rentals in the papers. Then she'd buy herself a bottle of wine and a cookbook—nothing too challenging. A late birthday gift for herself. She'd collect the ingredients at the grocery store. Then she'd go home and drink and bake and call landlords. She'd do these things because *she* was in charge, not the counting and checking. She'd do these things because she could get a grip, and that was that.

Paisley marched toward the library, avoiding the cracks. She sidestepped a man flicking a lighter that refused to work. What if it didn't work and didn't work, and then the buildup of butane produced a flame that caught the wind and ignited the cuff of his suit? Paisley hurried to put more distance between them.

1 2 3 4 5 6 7 8

THEN

Paisley was still on Front Road, still in a fog. She just wanted to be home. In bed. Alone. And then Garnet stepped out from behind a bush, cigarette dangling from his mouth. He took one look around to make sure no one was watching, grabbed Paisley's elbow, and yanked her back off the road and down toward Stella Bay, stopping just far enough from the road that no one looking in that spot would see them. He pulled so hard that she tripped but managed to recover.

"Made a fool of me at the social. Proud of yourself?"

"No, I—"

"What?"

Paisley didn't know what to say. Didn't know where to go. He was bigger than her. Stronger. Faster. Running was pointless. But surely someone would pass by. To go for a jump off the dock, maybe? To fish?

"You need that lady from Bath to fight your fights?"

"No."

"But you called her over."

"I didn't mean to."

What did he want her to do? Rewrite history? You can't change what's happened. Or who you are. Or where you are. Or even where you're going.

"So fight them yourself."

"I don't want to fight you."

"Too bad. 'Cause I wanna fight you. Del told my Mam and Da about that business at the social. They told me if I'm not careful, I won't be going home in August."

"To Ireland?"

"My club is doing trials."

Paisley looked at him blankly. She didn't know what that meant.

"Tryouts. Soccer. My football club has players trying out for the academy in Dublin. And I'm going to be there for the trials, not here. I fucking hate it here."

In this moment, she hated it here, too—this business with her mother, her father not being there when she needed him, her need to count, not being able to go anywhere to get some breathing space. In this moment, she felt they were wading in the same intense emotion—all Garnet ever spoke about was getting out, wanting to be elsewhere, and now that's all she wanted, too. He suddenly didn't seem so imposing—just sort of in pain. But then he tossed his cigarette into the uncut grass with the same energy he'd swung the twitch at the social. Short. Fast. Mean.

Paisley's eyes followed the cigarette's descent. Panic. She had to pick it up and put it out.

He smiled. "That flip you out?"

She counted under her breath. 1 2 3 4

"Make you want to count?"

"No."

5 6 7 8

"Really. 'Cause I know you've got a thing for counting, right? But maybe fire's in there, too."

The cigarette would be fine as long as she could find it.

"I think it is," he said.

"Can I go?"

"No."

He pulled out a box of matches. Shook it. *Shook-a-shook-a*. They rattled around inside the little box. He slid it open. "That's not right in the head, what you do."

"I'm sorry about Del. At the social. I'm sorry."

He struck a match. Its flame leapt up and settled in.

"Too bad."

He threw the match down. Paisley's eyes followed it as it disappeared into the tall grass. Had it gone out?

"Please don't."

He struck another match and threw it more in her direction this time. The flame extinguished mid-air as it fell at her feet. At least, she thought it did. She stepped back.

"Just give me one little count and I'll stop. I want to see what it looks like."

Paisley's brain hurt. No one had ever asked her to count for them before. She could do it and hope it made him stop. But was Garnet the kind to ever stop?

"I don't—"

He struck another match, then stepped forward and held it right up to her face.

"I don't want to be here. I want to be home. If you stand in the way of that, I'll murder you."

The flame burned down the wooden match, reaching his fingertip and thumb and extinguishing against his skin. It must have hurt. He didn't flinch. The charred end of the match, shrivelled to almost nothing, barely held on.

Garnet flicked the extinguished match at Paisley. Then he walked away.

Paisley waited until he hit the road and disappeared past a clutch of lilac bushes, and then dropped to her knees and scrambled about the unkempt grass to recover all three spent matches. There had been three, right? Three? Plus the cigarette.

NOW

Paisley went into the liquor store, where she bought a bottle recommended by a woman offering little plastic glasses of Australian red wine alongside appetizers. The wine was expensive, but what the hell. I am celebrating this moment, thought Paisley. I'm starting fresh. If that isn't worth seventeen dollars, I don't know what is.

Then she headed to Between the Lines for a cookbook. The bookstore was a fixture at Yonge and Bloor, housed in a turn-of-the-century building with a white-and-black-tiled floor and dark wood bookshelves. It was staffed by people who knew everything there was to know about books. Not that Paisley had ever asked for help, but on occasion she'd browse, wandering up and down the aisles, spying on the salespeople and other customers.

A clerk was putting finishing touches on a new window display. He crawled backward toward her. Paisley glanced at his suede runners. His button-down shirt. His skinny rear end.

"Need help?" he asked. He had long, curly locks and wore horn-rimmed glasses that made him look like some New York art critic.

"Who, me? No, no thanks, I'm fine, I'm..." She wanted to hide in the alcove reserved for leather-bound classics. Of course *me*, she thought. Who else? Hemingway? Maupassant?

"Feel free to browse," he said. "Or holler for me at any time. I'm at your disposal."

Paisley took care not to let the wine bottle in its paper bag sleeve slip from her armpit. She wandered down an aisle. What should she do? Had she sensed a smidge of interest? Was that possible, especially now, when she was in such a bad way? Possible, she guessed. Remotely possible. He had no idea what a big bag of crazy she was.

Maybe I should ask for help, she thought. But she couldn't think of a single title or author. She felt sick. It might have been the appetizers from the liquor store. They had tasted wonderful and exotic, but her frozen-dinner stomach wasn't used to anything new. Any moment now, she might be in need of a bathroom. She headed for the door.

"Find what you were looking for?" There he was again. She'd almost made it to the exit.

"I— No— It's just—" She was flustered. "I was looking for a cookbook, an ordinary cookbook. Any cookbook'll do."

"Sounds like a line from a Broadway musical. 'A cookbook, an ordinary cookbook, any cookbook'll do.'" He smiled and led her to the cooking section. There was no getting out of it now.

He suggested *The Joy of Cooking*, which he said was the standard, not using the word as in "lesser than" but as in "benchmark." Perfect. As he hiked up his low riders, Paisley pictured him hiking her up. A fling with a bookseller to escape it all, to shut off her brain for just one second.

She bought the book and escaped to the grocery store, hiding behind a display of dried pasta and tomato sauce to leaf through the recipes. There was one for devil's food chocolate cake, but it looked complicated. She settled on a hurry-up cocoa cake, hustled to aisle four, and collected the ingredients.

THEN

Paisley had three dead matches in her pocket and a cigarette butt. She'd run down to the public dock to dunk them in the lake. But then, when she turned to head home, she worried a fire might have started back in the grass after all, so she scooped some water from the bay to douse the grass where Garnet had thrown them down. But by the time she reached the spot, most of the water had leaked out of her cupped hands. So she did it again. And again. And then it seemed she needed to do eight. Thirty-two trips later (eight times four—eight for obvious reasons, four for the number of matches and one cigarette Garnet had lit), she wrenched herself away and continued home in a state.

Her house loomed up ahead and it suddenly occurred to her that home was exactly where Eudie would go, too. Paisley would be cornered. She turned around, but didn't know where else to go. So she darted into the field by the MacNicolls's barn and paused there, unsure. She could be seen from the road. What if Garnet came back? She ducked inside.

Built with thick, hand-chiselled square beams, the barn was dark, cooler inside than out. Paisley found a straw bale and sat down. She couldn't imagine what might happen next. If she went home and her mother tried to talk about what had happened, the world would fall apart; if Eudie didn't talk about it, the world would still fall apart, eventually.

Paisley climbed the ladder into the haymow and sunk into an old red velvet chair; springs stuck into her hips. Stuff was piled up on the loft's wide planks: trunks and chests and boxes of books, a few dusty antique tables and chairs, old farm tools. Barn swallows banked around the barn, their fork tails darting in the glimmers of light between boards. They nested inside buildings, while cliff swallows (*Petrochelidon pyrrhonota*), with not much of a fork in their tail, made mud nests outside under eaves and bridges. Paisley knew of two cliff swallow nests on her birding route: one in the doorway of the public school and one on the outside of Mildred Mickie's barn. Other interesting facts about swallows: their streamlined bodies allow them to swoop around at speeds of up to twenty-five miles an hour, which lets them efficiently hunt insects on the wing. They are insectivorous—an excellent word. Father swallows are some of the most caring parents among passerine birds. And barn swallows mate for a nesting season, which makes them basically socially monogamous. Unlike some mothers Paisley knew.

And there she was, back to Eudie and the minister. His Adam's apple. Their bodies. His pelvis, his shirt, her skirt—

A black barn cat crept across the haymow, body low, inching forward, eyeing the swallows. Paisley wondered if her mother's cat, France, had been black and if it had hunted birds. Not, she supposed, if it was an indoor cat. Although to hear Eudie talk, that cat was capable of anything. It had personality, Eudie said. It had wisdom and emotion. This Eudie knew because, the evening before she left Toronto to marry Hu and live on Amherst Island, the cat had sensed it was being left behind. Eudie took it to her best friend Lisbeth's place, and it had meowed into the night. France would have a good home with Lisbeth, but Eudie felt—despite her hopes for a fresh new life, with fresh new adventures—that she had abandoned the poor feline, and she had never forgiven herself.

The barn cat darted into a pile of hay, forgetting the swallows in favour of a mouse. Wildlife coexisted here in this barn. Paisley thought there might be enough room for her to live up here, too. A person could easily sleep and get dressed and get off to school before anyone saw her, then later get back in unnoticed. That person would need a light for nighttime, but maybe a flashlight would do. It could get very dark in a barn at night.

Paisley built a bedroom in her mind. She chose her furniture from the things piled around her. She decided how she'd arrange it. An old spindle bed. A box spring but no mattress; she'd have to find one somewhere. A little side table, dark wood, with three fancy curved legs and birds carved into the stand. The African sacred ibis, actually. *Threskiornis aethiopicus.* A wading bird with a curved bill, native to Africa and the Middle East. Some of Eudie's lemon oil would bring those carvings right up. The African sacred ibis was thought to be the living incarnation of Thoth, the Ancient Egyptian god of wisdom. Paisley could use some wisdom right now.

She planned her room and sang "How Great Thou Art" under her breath, relishing the lowness of her favourite hymn, the sombre sound's echo through the big dark barn.

> *O Lord my God, when I in awesome wonder*
> *Consider all the works Thy hands have*
>   *made.*
> *I see the stars, I hear the rolling thunder,*
> *Thy power through the universe displayed.*
> *Then sings my soul, my Saviour God, to*
>   *thee:*
> *How great Thou art, how great Thou art.*
> *Then sings my soul, my Saviour God, to*
>   *thee:*
> *How great Thou art, how great Thou art.*

She felt calmer. Her bra pinched. When the "transformation" had started, as Eudie called it, she had full-on announced at the kitchen table that Paisley was growing breasts (had Eudie thought she hadn't noticed?) and needed to be "discreet." Paisley had no idea how anyone was supposed to hide knockers like hers. They took up space. They had volume. They jiggled and bounced when she ran. Mortifying.

She had gone to the Country Store, where a bookmobile came to the island every second Thursday. She waited until the librarian wasn't paying attention and looked up *breasts* in the pocket dictionary on the trolley. The entry read, *Soft round organs on each side of the chest in women and men. In women, the organs are more prominent and produce milk after childbirth.* Milk? Gross. Paisley started wearing her father's old undershirts, which her mother took up in the straps. But Paisley quickly outgrew those. Next, she was poured into brassieres that Eudie went into Bath to order from the Sears window in the back of Del's supermarket. Paisley skipped a training bra and went straight to the real thing: stiff, pointy, $16.99. It was a scant year before she was a full-on 38C. How could she be discreet? Answer was, she couldn't. Before you knew it, boys like Garnet and his brothers are calling you Bazongas and there's nowhere to hide.

Except here, in the MacNicoll barn. In the distance, cows mooed idly. A heavy vehicle disturbed gravel as it sped along the road. Farther off, a tractor. Then quiet.

Paisley jolted awake. Where was she? She had dreamt something, something embarrassing.

> *Then sings my soul, my Saviour God, to*
> *thee:*
> *How great Thou art, how great Thou art...*

An Adam's apple, a shirt, a collar, a dress, a breath, a lip, a kiss. How could she possibly go home?

If her Saviour God was indeed so great, why would He let something as terrible as this happen? What kind of a God did that?

NOW

Paisley gathered her mail and made it past the superintendent without having to face questions about when she might
move out. She caught the elevator and stepped in carefully
over the crack. Inside her apartment, she avoided looking
at her phone, set the table for one, cracked open the bottle
of wine, and poured herself a glass. Then she stepped into
the kitchenette, laid out the ingredients she'd bought, and
read the instructions for the cake.

Preheat the oven to 350 degrees, it read.

She had to do this. No oven, no cake. No cake, no celebration. No celebration, no calling numbers for apartments.
Paisley took a big gulp of wine, turned on the oven, and
stepped back. The metal ticked and clanked; it wasn't accustomed to being used. She took another step back. She was
not going to be lorded over by a stupid oven. The kitchen
would not catch fire. The building would not explode.

There was one therapist, Nolan—she'd seen him two
years ago during a rough patch, but she hadn't stayed with
him long. He wasn't a psychiatrist, and so the government
didn't cover the cost, and it was too much money. He had
talked her through her worries—explaining how ovens
and light fixtures and outlets worked, how electricity was
conducted through a building, how there were preven-
tive measures built right into the walls to ensure that fires
rarely—if ever—occurred. Objections and exceptions were
rooted deep in Paisley's mind, but Nolan stood by his story,
and time had supported his case. There had never been a
fire in Paisley's world, not from a frayed wire or a faulty
oven or anything else. She had never known where to look
at the end of Nolan's long talks. She was ashamed of her
problem, understood its lack of logic, and yet this was what
she believed. She would tell Nolan with conviction and self-
effacing wit that although he was convinced it was good

workmanship and design that prevented fires, she knew better. It was her worrying that prevented the world from falling apart, and history had borne her out. If she worried with great feeling and ritual, nothing would happen. That was how the world worked.

The oven ticked and clanked again, loud and resentful. She gulped down a second mouthful of wine for courage. It warmed the space between her lungs. It had been a while since she'd had a drink. On occasion, the staff from the archives socialized, and there were the monthly trivia nights at the pub. She might have a glass of wine or two at these sorts of things, but she was always cautious about her budget so never drank to excess. And because she didn't, she never got rowdy, never (okay, rarely) flirted with her co-workers, and didn't bring them home. Sometimes she wondered if she should. She drank again and stared at the oven. Just as Nolan had promised, nothing terrible was happening. The little orange light above the dial said the oven was preheating.

She peered at the *The Joy of Cooking*'s next instruction. It said to grease the pan, and so, giving the oven a wide berth, she unscrewed the cap on the vegetable oil and looked for something with which to apply it. Would a spatula do? The back of a piece of cardboard? The recipe advised wax paper. Paisley hadn't thought to buy any. A tissue, she thought; after all, this cake was just for her. She grabbed a tissue and dabbed it in the oil. *Grease the bottom of the pan*, the recipe read, so she turned the pan upside down and rubbed it with her oily tissue. There. Excellent.

Paisley combined the ingredients in a bowl and whisked them with a fork. *Do not overmix.* She didn't own a beater. The batter looked a little lumpy; baking would probably fix that. She leaned against the counter, apron on, cookbook open, and took another swig of wine. She could see why people did this on a regular basis, this cooking business. It was satisfying. You followed the instructions and got results.

The oven light flickered off. The kitchen was warm; the whole apartment was heating up. It felt comfortable for the first time this winter.

Emboldened by wine, Paisley poured the batter into the pan, carefully slid it into the oven, closed the door, and set the timer magnet on her fridge.

She stepped into her dining nook, satisfied. Look at what she had done!

Wait. Was that burning she smelled?

It was. It smelled like a burning hairdryer. It smelled like Mrs. Feldman's space heater.

Sometimes, Nolan had said, if you haven't used an element in a long time, it might smell. It was not a fire. It was nothing. The smell would dissipate.

Paisley tapped and counted a bit and didn't feel any better. She considered going for a walk to get some distance from the oven, but that was absurd: you couldn't leave an oven on unsupervised. She tapped out an eight just to punish herself for the thought. That lack of vigilance on her part was unnerving. A bad omen.

Find something to distract yourself with, Nolan had said. Read a book, do a crossword, a word search. Power through the fear, and you'll see that nothing happens.

I'll drink instead, thought Paisley. She refilled her glass of wine and settled in the living room. She flipped through her latest bird magazine. It was taking everything she had to stick with this program.

The burning smell was worsening. She was sure of it. She wasn't having a stroke and she wasn't being obsessive; she was really and truly smelling burnt air, burnt pan, burnt everything. An old oven. An underused oven. No. She was in control of her thinking; it was not in control of her. She would drink the rest of her glass of wine and then check on her cake. That's what she'd do.

She should have eaten something first. Her insides felt

odd. She was now downright hot and floppy. But still: she did smell burning. She did. She put down her glass and got up. The apartment reeled a little. She walked to the kitchenette and found the oven smoking.

In a flash, she knew she'd done the wrong thing. Eudie had never let her near the kitchen, but of course the grease went on the inside of the pan, the hell's bells inside of the pan! She turned off the oven and grabbed a pot holder and pulled the smoking pan out of the oven, the cake batter still jiggly and raw.

She heard the elevator doors open down the hall. She had missed it clanking into action.

Even as her head spun, Paisley sprinted toward the door, still holding the smoking cake pan. She glued her feet to the edges of the floor, so her shadow wouldn't be seen through the generous gap at the bottom of the door, then grabbed the lock chain with her free hand and pressed one eye to the peephole. For a second, she saw herself—the absurdity, the desperation with which she'd raced to catch a glimpse of someone else's life.

Whoever had come out of the elevator hadn't made a move. It wasn't Lily. Or Mr. Li, or Mrs. Berkowitz, or Adam the dog walker, or the Schultzes.

So who?

Someone confirming an apartment number, pausing before deciding which way to go. A pizza delivery driver or a window washer or a canvasser who had sweet-talked a resident into letting him in the front door. The stranger approached. Paisley tried to muffle her breath.

The stranger reached her door and stopped. It was a man. He looked familiar. He was someone she knew... He was...

Garnet Mulligan.

Oh Christ.

He leaned forward and looked right into Paisley's eyepiece, straightening his collar.

Paisley jerked her head to the left, out of any possible line of sight. Could he see her through the peephole? Was it possible to see anything from that side? She'd never tried.

He grasped the knocker and rapped. Now what was she going to do, stuck here, pressed up against the door? If I open it, she thought, if I even make a noise, he'll know I'm right here. If I delay, he might go away, which as an option was equal parts misery and relief. Not opening the door didn't seem to be an option at all.

He knocked again. Paisley took one giant, quiet step back to make sure her feet wouldn't be seen under the door, but she stepped onto the rug in the hall—an old, unanchored rag thing from the thrift store—and it was her downfall. Her back foot slid; she was headed for the splits, but there was no way that was happening so she fell instead. The cake pan clattered to the floor, flinging batter everywhere.

Garnet called out from the other side of the door. "Paisley? Holy crap, are you okay?"

Now he knew she was in there. She'd claim she was sick. That she'd taken a fall in some kind of delirium.

Crimson-faced and discombobulated, she got up and opened the door. He was really there. Garnet. Older. Fit. Different but the same.

"Did you fall? Are you hurt?"

"Yes, I— I—" Her mind was a drunk blank.

"Can I come in?"

She couldn't think what to say. She couldn't think of anything. She found herself moving to the side—and all of a sudden Paisley Ratchford had her first visitor, other than Mrs. Feldman, in years.

THEN

Paisley didn't know how long she'd been in the haymow, but it was late—dinnertime late. She had to head home.

"Halt!" It was Little Jack, in the deep grass outside the barn. He was in Grade 2 but hadn't grown since kindergarten—some kind of hormone deficiency. He wore oversized rubber boots, dark blue Adidas shorts, a tie-dyed T-shirt, and a Viking helmet with horns. "What doeth you in my barn?"

"I thought I saw one of your dad's rabbits running loose," Paisley lied.

"Did not." He picked a wide blade of grass, placed it between the pads of his thumbs, and whistled. It was loud.

"Did, too," Paisley said, walking toward the road. "But it ran away. Check the cage."

"Don't want to." Little Jack grabbed a plastic shield and sword from the grass and ran after her.

"Don't follow me. I'm going home now."

"You're on my property; I can be on yours." Little Jack was only seven, but he had four older brothers who had trained him to be bothersome.

Paisley walked along Front Road. Little Jack followed a couple of feet behind, stabbing the air with his sword.

"I'm a Viking, you know. Take that. And that!"

Paisley picked up the pace.

"Vikings were masters of the fight," he said. "They could hack and slay anyone to pieces. They could sneak up to a village, quiet as anything, then pounce on people while they slept. It was a gory mess, blood and guts everywhere!"

"You're not very quiet now."

"But I could be."

"So prove it."

"Fine." Little Jack shut his trap all the way to Paisley's driveway.

"Get outta here, Jack."

"You get out."

"No, you."

"You."

Paisley could hear her parents' raised voices inside. She stood on the porch, frozen.

From behind her came a loud, long whistle: Little Jack, blowing the blade of grass between his thumbs.

Paisley watched Eudie catch sight of her and Little Jack through the window.

"Idiot!" whispered Paisley.

"I can blow on grass if I want," said Jack. "It's a free country. I don't have to be a quiet Viking. I'm the loudest Viking alive!"

The door swung open. "Get inside, Paisley," said Eudie, standing there barefoot. "Go home, Little Jack."

"But—"

"You're not welcome here."

Little Jack stared at her, slack-jawed. He dropped his blade of grass, grabbed his sword and shield, and stomped off, horned helmet bouncing as he went.

NOW

"Did you slip?"

Garnet eyed the pan and cake batter mess on the floor.

"You mind?" he said, stepping into the kitchen, returning with a roll of paper towel. She could still hear the Irish accent. Faded from when he was a kid, but there.

Paisley sat down at the table in her dining nook, in shock more than anything. It was a little hard to believe. Garnet was in her apartment. In a good suit and a wool coat—a proper coat. His shoes were polished. His face was older, more angular. Paisley knew she looked older, too.

"I should explain why I'm here," he said, mopping up the batter with paper towel. "I called a few times to see if you'd gotten my firm's letter, and you didn't call back. Which makes sense, given I was a complete prick back in the day." He shot her a look. "I had to be in Toronto for meetings, so I thought I'd take a chance and drop by. There was a delivery guy downstairs and he let me in and, I don't know, I just ended up at your door. Did you...get my calls? No—wait—it's okay. Don't answer that. I'm going to deal with this. Hold on."

He took the cake pan and the sopping paper towels into the kitchen.

There was a pause. Paisley knew what he was looking at. The leftover cake ingredients. *The Joy of Cooking*, open to page 635. The oven, smelling like a grease fire. The silence was as loud as a pneumatic drill.

"Hey," he said from the kitchen, "maybe we could go out to dinner, talk about your paperwork. Or even a cup of coffee and a piece of, um, cake?"

But Paisley's head was spinning. She didn't feel well.

"Or maybe we could postpone until tomorrow," he said. "It's late, and you had a fall."

"Yes," she managed to say. Her left side hurt; there would be bruising. And she was pretty drunk, that much was clear.

"Okay then. Tomorrow. What time would be good?"

Where should Paisley even go with this?

"Would you...be coming home from work?"

"Yes." She didn't need to explain that she'd been home for a week counting eights.

"So would six work then?"

"Yes." There was an absurd inevitability to all of this.

"Six it is. I can come by here to get you. That good?"

"Yes." God. How many times could she say the exact same word?

"Great." They eyed each other for a moment. And he smiled—not making fun of her, just a gentle "isn't life funny" sort of smile. "I'll let myself out." He headed for the door. "You sure you're okay?"

She nodded. "I'm just going to sit here for a minute, and then maybe clean up a bit more." How could she even begin to explain? "I hope I don't have the flu." Maybe he'd buy it. "I should head to bed."

"I hope you don't have it, too. The flu." Nice of him to go along with it. He turned to go. Then he turned back. "It's good to see you. You seem well."

Lie of the century.

"You, too."

Not as big a lie. Because he did look well, with his well-paid job, taking care of people's estates, making something of himself. Not like her, pathetic OCD-riddled Paisley Ratchford from Amherst Island. What a colossal fuck-up she was.

THEN

The air in the living room was still. Hu sat in his recliner. Paisley stood near him, wanting the comfort of his presence even if he did still smell like Mildred's farm.

"Paisley," said Eudie from the kitchen, washing the pie dishes she'd used at the social, "you're thirteen, so I think it's high time you knew a few things."

Paisley wasn't a big fan of knowing things. Whenever Eudie told people things they should know, Eudie felt better and everyone else felt like crap. Paisley leaned on the worn armrest of her father's recliner.

"When I got close to giving birth to you," said Eudie, "I took the ferry and stayed with Del for a couple of days in Bath, just to be safe. Finally I went into labour, and Del gave me a lift to Kingston General. Dropped me at the front door and let me check into the hospital myself. Your father was still on the island. He planned to come, but the lake froze over that night, and the ferry stopped running. No way to get across, not until the lake was frozen good and solid."

"First off, Eud," said Hu, "that was thirteen years ago, and it was the way it was done. Plus, I had the farm to tend."

"I'm getting to that," said Eudie, slamming down a dish and opening the kitchen liquor cupboard. She mixed herself a gin and tonic, her favourite drink, and dropped in three maraschino cherries.

They're getting a divorce, thought Paisley. Eudie's already told Hu about kissing the reverend. Or has she? She searched her father's face. He was staring at his folded hands, weathering the storm.

"The lake was just barely frozen," said Eudie, "so no one could've expected your father to make it over. Fine. But you weren't an easy birth, Paisley. I managed the whole thing without drugs, got you out into the world, all purple and not breathing right. I called you Paisley, and there you were, six pounds even, a scrawny thing, but ten fingers, ten toes. Cried blue murder. Then that day and the next and the next after that, you refused to latch on. I was exhausted and finally gave up. So did the nurse. She gave me bottles of formula and wished me luck."

Paisley thought about the Henslow's sparrow. To make this go away.

"Del and Noble came to give me a lift. I stepped out of the hospital, and the February cold took my breath away. There'd been a storm, and everything was covered in a thin sheet of ice. Icicles everywhere. The sidewalk was a skating rink. I had you, this tiny baby, in my arms, all frail from that poor feeding business, and I remember thinking, what if I break this little thing not ten steps from the hospital? It all seemed so dangerous."

"And I was at the dock waiting, wasn't I?" said Hu.

Paisley thought about her great-great-grandmother June, the first birder in the family.

"Your father took you, swaddled up in blankets, and helped me down to the ice and into the old Ford islanders used to cross the frozen lake. They'd taken a saw to it and removed its doors and roof, to make the car lighter and less likely to go through the ice, and to make for an easy escape if it did. There you were, ripe old age of five days, making the first Ford crossing in the winter of 1968. I'll never forget that trip. The wind blew clear across the Bay of Quinte. Brought back the shakes I'd had right after you came out."

If one of Eudie's stories started with a big windup, it usually came right back at you, as if from a slingshot. Paisley and Hu tried to follow along, but Paisley was thinking about June's birder notebook in the shed and was pretty sure she'd first learned about the Henslow's sparrow from that note-book. Now all she wanted was to escape this and go check. She could even check eight times. Which would be a relief.

"That first night on the island, you cried and cried, so I

fed you a bottle of formula and you finally fell asleep. Your dad snuggled in with us, and I felt like it was going to be all right. Remember that, Hu?"

He ruffled Paisley's hair with his big hand, calluses on the palm, dirt under the fingernails.

"But then, in the middle of the night, there was a phone call," said Eudie. "It woke you up, and you started to cry. It was Mildred. Her cow was giving birth to twin calves. The first one had died right off the bat. The second one was coming out backwards, and she wanted Hu to come. He said he'd be a short time. I pleaded with him to stay, but he went anyway. You cried for most of the time he was gone, and I had to use two more bottles of formula just to keep you settled. He was still gone when the sun came up."

"I called," said Hu.

The notebook, thought Paisley. The Henslow's sparrow and June's sketch in the notebook.

"Yes," said Eudie, "in the morning. By then I'd had about two hours' sleep. I was desperate. I asked if you were on your way home. You said that you'd gotten the second calf turned around and out okay, but that the cow had a prolapsed uterus, and the vet wasn't available, and you were taking care of it yourself. I said, 'I need you to take care of me.' And you said, 'I will, Eud, I will—just as soon as I get this damn uterus back into the cow. It's like getting a wet balloon back into a tiny hole and it just won't go—you get one part of it in, the other pops out. And then I have to sew her up. Mildred's got out the turkey needle from the kitchen drawer and she's boiling it right now.'" Eudie shook her head. "I didn't know what to say. I had this baby who'd cried all night, too, I had stitches in my arse, too, but you were there and I was alone. And even you got the irony. You, who never really pick up on that sort of thing, you said, 'I had two births happening at once, and my own flesh and blood's more important than this one, of course, but here

I am anyway—the cow's not going to get her own uterus back in, is she.' And you laughed."

"I wasn't trying to make light, Eud," said Hu. "I was just caught is all."

"So I asked if you were coming home then," said Eudie, "and you said you'd be along as soon as Mildred got you the needle and you could sew up the cow's arse. And that's what you did. And of course it worked—and the vet, by the time he finally got there, thought you'd done a good job, as good as he could've done. You'd put the dead calf outside the barn, and you'd given the mother some space with her other calf, and it'd finally found the teats and was feeding. I knew you'd left me because that farm would someday be yours, that Mildred needed you because you're responsible and dependable, but in my mind, crazy from not knowing what to do with a new baby, in my mind, you'd picked a cow and calf over your own wife and baby."

"I picked you both," said Hu. "I picked you first, then I picked the farm for you. Farmers can't say no to these things."

"You're no farmer," said Eudie. "You're Mildred's farm-hand, just like your father before you. Family here for generations, but no one with enough mettle to make anything of themselves. Your aunts married and moved away, your uncle ran his farm into the ground, your father was good for nothing. Any one of them could have done something to help you get your footing, but did they? No. You have to own land to be a real farmer, Hu. You can't just run a quarry and manage someone else's farm and pray one day you're going to get it for yourself. Your father knew that, when he was sober, and he left this island with his tail between his legs. But you, you just keep working and hoping. You're a fool. And I was a fool to not understand these things when I got talked into all this."

"Aw, Eudie, enough. I'm going to the shed. When you're ready to talk sense, I'll be back."

The only places with any privacy were the shed and the backyard, where Hu had planted a sprawling vegetable garden—as close as he could get to having his own farm. He collected old farming implements and rusty, broken-down machinery in the shed. He worked on that machinery, tinkering away when he had the time, so that when, eventually, he had Mildred Mickie's farm for himself and could call it his own, he'd be set.

I want to go to the shed, too, thought Paisley. My crate's in there. Paisley angled for the door.

"Stay," said Eudie. The moment Hu was gone, she came right to Paisley and said, "See how long your father's been choosing the farm over me?"

Paisley thought of her father at the Mickie farm, working in the barn, tending the cows, building what would one day be theirs. He couldn't be blamed for it.

"So help me, God, Paisley, if you mention what you saw today..."

Paisley stared at Eudie's bare feet. The bunion that caused her so much trouble.

"What you saw with the reverend was nothing. It was not your business."

"No," Paisley said.

Eudie's bunion pushed the big toe toward the other four toes at a terrible angle. It looked like it hurt. It looked like someone should go into the foot and saw off that big bump with one of Hu's tools from the shed so the toe could just relax again and point in the right direction.

"Dinner will be ready in fifteen," said Eudie.

"I'll tell Dad."

Eudie grabbed her drink and went back to the sink. Paisley headed for the door, her mind filled with June's notebook, the Henslow's sparrow, her mother kissing Reverend Willis: her hand on his body; his cleanly shaved cheeks; her light cotton print dress; how her hair, always worn piled on top of her head, held together with one clip, had come undone and tumbled down her shoulders, loose.

Paisley would erase it all from her memory. She would force it from her brain every time it flooded in. It was nothing, just as Eudie had said.

1 2 3 4 5 6 7 8

1 2 3 4 5 6 7 8

Two sets of eight. Not quite enough to make things right. "Go," said Eudie.

Paisley did as she was told, counting six more sets of eight by tapping her thumb and index finger, thumb and middle finger, thumb and ring finger, thumb and pinkie—four on one hand, 1 2 3 4, and four on the other hand, 5, 6, 7, 8.

NOW

Paisley awoke the next day on the couch, still in the same clothes. She wasn't sure if it was morning or afternoon. She tried to get her bearings.

The clock said it was noon. Garnet would be here in six hours for coffee or dinner or whatever, and they'd discuss her pitiful affairs.

She had agreed to it. What had possessed her? Knowing him, he could be a con man now, a sexual predator, a bank robber. Or was he just who he said he was: Garnet Mulligan, remade as a lawyer? His letter had come on Bertram & Associates letterhead.

Maybe that was fake.

Don't be ridiculous.

Paisley got up from the couch. Her body hurt everywhere. Her head pounded. What should she wear? What would she say? What to do first?

She saw herself in the mirror. She looked like hell. Her face was puffy, she guessed from the wine. And she had a zit. How was that even possible at thirty-nine? From stress maybe? She could squeeze it and it would go away. She squeezed. Nothing happened. She squeezed harder. Now it looked mad. She squeezed again and made things worse. Stop touching it. Have some breakfast. Lunch. Nothing greasy. Think up topics of conversation. Get dressed in something...but what?

She needed to clean up. If Garnet had to go to the bathroom before they went out, he'd need to use hers. Men lifted the seat, which meant cleaning the toilet, but she'd run out of toilet cleanser. She grabbed her wallet but was stricken by the urge to check. It took a full set of eight checks to get out of the apartment. Downstairs, she ran into Mrs. Feldman.

"What's the rush?" said Mrs. Feldman, who was dead-heading the lobby's flower arrangements.

Paisley didn't want to talk. She wanted to clean. "I just read somewhere that if you run places instead of walking, you can burn an extra three hundred calories a day."

"You don't need slimming," said Mrs. Feldman. "You're beautiful the way you are."

Paisley headed for the door.

"You know," said Mrs. Feldman, "my cousin Erma grew up a little zaftig, too, which is how I think men like it, but she was convinced otherwise. 'Oh, Erma,' I used to say to her, 'if you put as much energy into your art'—she was a painter, you know—'if you put as much energy into your art as you put into wishing your thighs were smaller, you'd be in the Louvre.' But did she ever listen to me? No. I used to say to her, over and over, I said..."

Mrs. Feldman went on and Paisley remained planted politely on the spot.

"Oh, Erma, Erma," said Mrs. Feldman. "May she rest in peace."

"It's been nice talking," said Paisley, "but I have an errand."

"Well, don't let me hold you up," said Mrs. F. She passed Paisley a handful of dead flowers. "Throw these out as you go."

Paisley bought toilet cleanser at the corner store and ran back to the apartment and scrubbed the bowl to within an inch of its life. Then she raced about, hiding laundry and stray papers in closets. She did what her father used to call the bachelor vacuum, pulling her running shoes backward against the pile of the carpet, dredging up tangled messes of dust, lint, and hair. This helped to avoid plugging in the vacuum, always treacherous, always involving counting—one never knew for how long. This was much better. It exercised her thighs and reminded her of her father.

Wouldn't Hu be proud of her? Dealing with her personal affairs. Getting things done.

Paisley picked up the last clump of lint and checked her zit. It was definitely worse. She would get a hot face cloth. That would make the swelling go down. But a hot face cloth required hot water. That meant plugging in the kettle or boiling water on the stove.

Boiling water?

No, no, she would not be deterred. She would use the stove again. She hadn't burned down the building baking her cake; she could do this. Or—she could use the microwave. Excellent idea.

She dipped the cloth into the hot water and pressed it to her face. The zit would be nothing by the time Garnet arrived. The face cloth only burned initially, and soon the heat sent her adrift.

THEN

For the next few days, Paisley was very careful. She kept an eye out for her mother and avoided getting cornered by her; she kept an eye out for Garnet and avoided getting cornered by him. She spent time with Rory walking the island and counting birds; she spent time with her dad while he worked on the farm or in the shed behind their house. He'd tinker with some fix-it thing; she'd read her birding books in a fold-up chair, feet propped up on the old tractor.

She'd been right: June's leather-bound birder notebook had a sketch of the Henslow's sparrow, page 79. Imagine: a Henslow's sparrow from 1895. June MacIntosh would have been forty-seven, which made this notebook all the more special. To think that June had started birding and keeping field notes and reflections when she was a teenager, and had kept adding to it. On the corner of the page was scrawled *rare*. And beside it the note: *most often seen in Southwestern Ontario, not where we are!* June had taken great care with its colouring: a pale green head and hind neck, chestnut-brown wings, brown-and-black-streaked back.

Paisley was copying June's sketch of the Henslow's sparrow into her own notebook and trying her hand at zoopraxography. She'd learned the term from her birding books. Paisley didn't have a camera, so she was drawing the Henslow's sparrow in flight across the fold of her notebook. First the wings were up, then they came down slowly, then they reached the bottom of the movement. Maybe she could be a zoopraxographist when she grew up. Zoopraxographer? She'd have to do more research, find out what the proper term was. But just imagine if that was a thing she could do for a living.

She heard Hu's boots in the shed gravel.

But it wasn't Hu. It was Garnet.

Paisley panicked. She looked past him for her father.

"He went inside. Then he had lunch. Then he went off in

the truck."

"My mother's—"

"Not here either." Garnet set a gas can on the tractor seat. Paisley's throat went dry.

"I'm getting ready to go. Shawn and me."

The Mulligan boys could not go across the ocean for an entire month fast enough.

"My Mam's been on me about mooning you. She's all, 'You've ruined my reputation at the church, all the ladies know.' Plus Delilah Cope runs the supermarket in Bath and she's got a big mouth and now the women in Bath know, too."

He was wearing his usual track pants. Paisley noted that one knee was almost threadbare. Soccer was his life. In that moment she felt for him, being stuck on an island of a few hundred farmers with no proper field or team or club. Lost. Abandoned. Ignored. She felt some of these things, too.

"She's been on it for days," he said. "How I do nothing but ruin her life, how reputation is everything."

On that score, Garnet's mum and Eudie had something in common, too.

"She made me shovel the sheep shit for both me and Shawn. He sits there and calls me a loser. Shawn's got an IQ of like four, and I'm the loser? So finally I said I wouldn't anymore, I threw the shovel at Shawn, and my Da came at me and pointed his finger right in my face and told me to pick up the shovel. I said no. And it went on like that until we were screaming. Then he said, 'You pick up that shovel or there's no going to Ireland, this is your second warning.'"

Paisley wanted Garnet to go to Ireland. She was as invested in his departure as he was.

"So why was it you told on me to Del?" he asked. With genuine confusion, like he really had turned over the incident at the summer social in his mind and couldn't figure out how it had gone awry.

"I was scared."

"You seem scared a lot."

This was true. She felt scared of everything, to be honest.

"I figured I'd help you with that." Garnet unscrewed the gas can lid. "Siphoned this from my Da's car. Screw him."

Paisley closed the notebook on the sparrow.

"Thing is, he decided we'd come here. Did he ask me for my opinion? No. He hauled us all the way over here. And now he's pissed 'cause I'm pissed." He picked up the gas can and walked to the shed entrance. "But what I really don't need is you making it worse. So if I have to be taught a lesson, it's only fair you get taught one, too. I was thinking, if there was a little fire right here"—he pointed in a line at his feet across the shed entrance—"what say we watch you jump over it? So you don't have to be scared all the time."

Paisley stood up like a shot. Her birding notebook fell to the floor.

"I figure you could do your counting, and then when I yell 'Go,' you can jump over. That'd probably cure you of the counting and the fire thing both at once. It'd make us even."

Garnet stepped back farther, maybe three feet from the entrance. She'd have to squeeze past him to escape. She could do it. Now was her chance. He poured a trickle of gas across the grass. Paisley watched from where she stood. She could bolt now. She could.

Garnet pulled out the box of matches he'd played with off of Front Road. Shook it. *Shook-a-shook-a*. He slid it open, pulled out a match, and struck its head against the black striker. "All you have to do is jump over."

He dropped the match onto the ground. The fire sprung up at his feet and, with a *whoosh*, ignited the line of gasoline. "Come on, Paisley, jump."

Paisley watched the flames, her feet planted in the gravel.

Garnet jumped over the thin line of flame back into the shed. "See? Easy. Easier than shovelling shit." He jumped back out. "Count and jump."

But she couldn't. The pressure in her chest held her to the ground.

Garnet eyed her. Maybe for a second, he looked at her with something other than contempt, like he could feel her misery. "Pathetic. What are we going to do with you?"

And then the wind shifted. There was so much wind on Amherst Island. It changed on a dime, blowing into the shed and into Paisley's face, fanning the flames. They sprang higher, caught the grass between the shed entrance and the line of gasoline. The fire spread.

Garnet knew they were in trouble the same moment she did. "Paisley, jump!"

But she didn't. She couldn't.

Garnet jumped over the swath of fire and grabbed her by the elbow like he had at the social. He pulled her back toward the entrance and forced her toward the flames. "Jump!"

Every organ in Paisley's body shut down, including her brain. She couldn't breathe. She couldn't see. She must have jumped, though, because she ended up on the other side of the flames. Garnet grabbed the gas can and ran for the water's edge.

Paisley turned and saw that the fire was an inch from the shed's wall. She looked around her for someone to help.

It was Rory's umpteenth walk of the day along Front Road. Whenever he passed Paisley's place, if he saw her, he'd wave and she'd wave back. This time she saw him but didn't wave, only looked back at the shed. So he turned down the ungraded driveway, waving harder.

"Hi, Paisley!" That's when, like Paisley, he saw the fire catch the shed wall. He bolted forward.

"Fire!" Rory yelled.

No one was close enough to hear except Paisley. "Fire, fire!"

NOW

Paisley checked her face in the mirror. Not only was the pimple still there, her face was also red from the heat of the face cloth. She knew she should just leave it alone, but she squeezed it again. Of course, that only made it worse.

She paced. She counted to eight. She dipped the face cloth several times into the hot water and pressed it to the zit, willing it to disappear. Where would Garnet even look, if not at this?

She had a meeting with the boy who'd tormented her when they were young. He was trying to be nice now, to make up for it, and she should let him, but how could she if she was so hideous she couldn't even show her face?

Counting took over. Her head swam with eights. She vowed never to use the stove again, never to challenge the status quo, never to hope for anything. She counted eight eights. It made no difference. She hated everything.

She tore off her clothes and climbed into bed, pulled the covers over her head, and prayed for a nap to stop the counting. A nap to give her some peace.

THEN

Cyrus was putting the ferry hawser onto the bollard when he saw the plumes of smoke from Hu's shed. He got right on the horn to get the phone tree happening. The island's volunteer fire department had its first real blaze to contend with in fourteen years, not a drill.

The four o'clock boat waited to load, in case there were any injuries, so people in the lineup heard about the fire, too. Several folk left their cars, keys still in the ignition, and ran to Hu and Eudie's place to see if they could help. In the meantime, Rory had dealt with the fire, and the front of the shed was only a little charred, no major damage done.

Unlucky for Garnet, though, Cyrus and a number of ferry passengers had spotted him running along the shoreline with his gas can. Garnet had pulled something everyone only ever thought Shawn would be dumb enough to do. So when Paisley was asked about the incident, she left out the part that Garnet had set the fire while she was inside the shed to teach her a lesson. There was no need. Even so, James and Maeve Mulligan yanked Garnet's trip to Ireland.

For Rory's part, when word got around (which it always did on Amherst Island) that there had been a fire at Eudie and Hu's, and that he had saved the day, he was immediately dubbed the Mayor, something that made him feel very proud indeed. He was a fool no longer.

NOW

When Paisley awoke, the clock read 5:40 p.m. She had twenty minutes until Garnet arrived. She raced to the bathroom and flicked on the light. Her pimple was still there, positively topographical and more disgusting than ever.

Life is futile, she thought. She was propelled back to the island school. A moment from Miss Montgomery's English Grade 7/8 split. Garnet was sitting in front of Paisley. She stared at the back of his head for a whole term. His neck was tanned. His hair was greasy and unkempt; like the eddies in an Amherst Island inlet, some went this way, some went that.

Miss Montgomery believed in self-expression. Every day, she assigned class time for journalling. She put on classical music at top volume and asked the students to write about whatever came to them while it played.

On this particular day, she chose Garnet to read his writing aloud. The music they'd listened to had been dark and dramatic, full of big drums and cymbal clashes. Paisley had written about the ferry trying to dock in a bad storm. Garnet stood up in class to read: Paisley looked at the taut rear of his jeans and noted how both back pockets were covered in dirty handprints from the number of times Garnet had wiped his hands on them. Four fingers on each pocket. She wondered what her hands would look like in the same position.

He read his story; it was about his mother's kitchen hutch, a large piece of furniture that had belonged to the Mulligans, who'd run the farm on Amherst Island for generations. The hutch had been brought over from Ireland on a boat decades and decades ago. It was so big, it lived permanently in the kitchen, but when Garnet's family had arrived three years ago, they'd decided to put in insulation, because that back kitchen was frigid in February—like standing in the great outdoors in your altogether. They'd taken everything out of the kitchen to do the work, but the hutch didn't fit through the front door, "the back kitchen door neither," as Garnet said his father had put it. His mother had insisted; that hutch was family, as much family as anyone else. She wanted it.

So after Garnet's mother had cried into her apron, his father had taken a saw to the thing, cleanly slicing it cross-ways into two pieces, a top and a bottom. The bottom came right on out through the kitchen door, and the hutch top had come after. Garnet's father had gone to the mainland to buy extra-long screws to reconnect top to bottom, and then he'd lost the screws somewhere, so the two halves had stood side by side for quite some time, much to the consternation of Garnet's mother.

But one day—this was where the drums and cymbals must have come into the music—it was revealed that Garnet had taken the screws. His father had blamed Garnet for some trouble on the island, even though Garnet had sworn up and down he'd had nothing to do with it, and Garnet had stolen the screws to get back at him. When his father found out, he'd—

Garnet stopped reading. Miss Montgomery, who'd been sitting on the edge of her desk, mouth slightly open, waited for more. Everyone waited for more.

"And?" said Miss Montgomery.

"The music stopped, so I did, too," said Garnet. He sat back down and slouched. The muscles in his back readjusted beneath his shirt.

"Do you feel like telling us the rest of the story?" asked Miss Montgomery.

"Not much more to tell," said Garnet. "My dad beat my rear with a wooden spoon till I couldn't sit for a week. He did it out near the barn, in the wide open, so everyone—my brother and the farmhands, too—could see. So while everyone else was at church, I took his saw to the hutch. I cut it up. I cut up that whole thing until it was kindling, top and bottom. And it wasn't till after that, till I'd finished, I realized it was my mother who'd cry about it, and did she ever. She didn't look me in the eye again for a month."

A hush fell. For all of Miss Montgomery's talk of self-expression, she had nothing to say. She searched for another piece of music—a polka.

Instead of writing, Paisley found herself watching Garnet's strong back just inches in front of her. She was flooded with feeling. Part of her feared his pent-up anger, family trouble or not, tossed in the direction of pretty much anyone who crossed his path. The other part wanted to wrap her arms around him, lean her cheek on his shoulder blade, and whisper into his hot skin that she wouldn't have stopped looking at him. She would have forgiven him. He was in turmoil. So, often, was she. In some ways, she felt he was the only one on the island who understood her, maybe more than Rory.

Paisley was pulled back to the present. Her face in the mirror. Her zit. And a noise. The elevator.

She flew to the door, pressed her feet to the wall on either side, grabbed the lock chain for balance, and pressed her face to the peephole.

Garnet appeared at the door. He was dressed in yesterday's suit with a new shirt and tie. She stepped back quickly. He knocked.

Paisley could stand there and do nothing, not even breathe, and Garnet would leave, and that would be that. Or she could open the door and let him see how monstrous and vile and repulsive she was, and that, too, would be the end of that. Or she could... What else could she do?

"Paisley?"

"I'm here."

"Can you...open the door?"

"No. Because I'm hideous."

"What? No. No, you're not."

"You don't get it. I have a problem. With my face."

"Oh."

"Hard to know what to say, I know. It's so dumb."

She hated everything. She hated what her life had become. Hated every day, since the day she was born, that had led to this torturous moment. She blamed everyone who had ever failed her—especially herself—and she forgave no one anything.

"So I can't meet you today," she said. "But I'm okay with just leaving things as they are. I don't really need any updates on the house. I don't need…anything really."

Silence. She watched him through the peephole. He pulled on his tie a bit, as if to breathe better.

"Jesus, Paisley. I was so terrible to you back then. I'm sorry. I turned up like this on your doorstep because, yes, I'm on your file at the firm, but also because I've owed you an apology for a long time."

Paisley clutched the lock chain for dear life. Sobs welled up in her. The tears trickled down her face to her neck to her clavicle into her bra.

Garnet could hear her. He stepped up to the peephole.

"Don't cry," he said. "I suck. I don't want you to be upset."

"You do suck, it's true."

They laughed from either side of the door. How they could be laughing about anything together, after all this time, just confirmed what a strange, unpredictable world it was. Paisley's mind snapped to bird migration patterns, and how generations of birds flew to a far-off place, mostly twice a year, for climate or breeding reasons, or in search of food and resources. Just like Garnet was trying to help her migrate—migrate back to a place, that is.

"Did you hear me, Paisley?"

"What? No. Sorry."

"Obviously you don't have to open the door with your, um, face, but I want you to know that I did look into your file, and your mother did do a ridiculous thing with her will. You're right, you don't have the house. But I think I can get it for you. So, with your permission, I'd like to try. It'd be pro bono, of course."

"Why?"

"So I can make up for, you know. How I behaved."

"And your firm would be okay with that?"

"They're okay with that."

"I'm not a charity case."

"I know."

Lily came strutting down the hallway and stopped short at the sight of Garnet peering into Paisley's peephole. "Who're you?"

"I'm a friend of Paisley's."

Paisley pressed herself to the door again to see what was going on. Lily wore a short plaid skirt, knee-high socks, twelve-hole Doc Martens, and a safety pin through her lip. That was new.

"And you're looking through her peephole because?" asked Lily.

"Because..." Garnet didn't continue. Interesting. The lawyer Garnet, who must be good at talking himself in and out of things, didn't have anything to say.

"Paise?" ventured Lily.

"Yes?"

It took Lily aback that Paisley's voice was so close to the door. She eyed Garnet. "Do you mind?"

Garnet took a step back. Lily stepped up.

"This guy bugging you, Paise? 'Cause I can call the super. He doesn't like strangers."

Paisley and Lily both knew the super avoided all conflict. If Garnet had been harassing Paisley, the two women would have had to deal with it themselves. But Paisley liked that Lily was creative enough to think up a good ruse.

"It's okay, Lily," she said through the door. "I'm okay."

Lily shrugged. "Fine. G'night then." She moved down the hall.

Garnet waited until she was gone and stepped back to the peephole. "So...you okay with me trying to get the house?"

"I guess so. I mean, sure. Yes."

"How much longer before this building gets demolished?"

"How do you know about that??

"I read the sign in the lobby."

"In five and a half weeks, we're evicted. I left it a little late."

"Do you have a place lined up if things don't work out?"

"I'm working on it." Which she wasn't. Dumb, dumb, dumb.

"We'll see what we can do. I can't make any promises. I'll call you as soon as I know."

"Okay."

She watched him head for the elevator.

THEN

Several days passed without any Garnet sightings. Eudie caught Paisley alone and asked if Garnet's little arson prank had been an attempt to punish her, not Paisley. Had Garnet also seen her behind the church after the social with Reverend Willis? Or had Paisley told him Eudie's secret? Paisley swore she hadn't, but Eudie didn't believe her, and her mood worsened.

Paisley tiptoed around, trying to be invisible. Or she hung out with Hu—stuck to him like glue. That morning before breakfast, she'd heard her mother go at her father for all his past sins, his lack of attention and romance, his settling for less, things she brought to the fore like they were only yesterday. The good thing about the house was that it was small and you could hear everything, no matter what room you were in. Mind you, the bad thing about the house was that it was small and you could hear everything, no matter what room you were in. Eudie stormed into the laundry room to get going on chores. Paisley laid out Wheaties, sliced bananas, and four pieces of toast for her father. She found yesterday's paper and opened it to the crossword. Her goal was to stay as far away as possible from Eudie and let things cool down.

Soon enough, Hu emerged from her parents' bedroom in his overalls. Paisley sat at the table, toes tucked under her nightie, and watched her dad eat. He sank the Wheaties into the milk and held them down until they doubled in size, while he methodically filled in the crossword. He finished his cereal and drank the leftover milk out of the bowl. Then he wandered to the bathroom, where he brushed his teeth, shaved, and ran a comb through his brown curly hair. Paisley followed him as he strolled over to the back door and clicked his overall straps into place.

"Can I come to Mrs. Mickie's today?" she asked.

"Nothing better to do with your Saturday?"

"I'd rather go with you."

"The milker's been acting up. I'll be busy."

"I can help."

"Fine," said Hu. "Get your things."

Paisley dressed and was out to the truck in a jiffy. Hu, his glasses perched on his nose, pencil and crossword still in hand, was humming and hawing about fourteen down, an eleven-letter word for a sudden or violent upheaval. They pulled out of the driveway in near darkness, Paisley watching the sun rise over the water between Amherst Island and the mainland like a blazing ball of fire, orange and pink and promising.

Mildred Mickie's farm had two barns: one for the cows and milking parlour, and one with no doors, for farm machinery. The house, white and red, was old and rickety but grand in its own way. It had shutters, a wraparound porch with gingerbread trim, and lace curtains. Whirligigs outside the kitchen door turned in the wind, a cancan dancer's legs spinning round and round and a gymnast flipping over and over on a high wire that was really the garden fence.

Paisley and Hu pulled on barn boots, and they each chose a mesh cap from the line of nails in the house's cold room. Paisley hoped Mildred wasn't up yet, otherwise she'd get invited into the salon so Mildred could show off her latest auction purchases: cut crystal this and whimsical that. She was planning an antiques business in Kingston for her "next life chapter" and loved talking about every little detail. Just last week, for example, Mildred had shown them a heavy Sir John A. MacDonald commemorative ashtray she'd bought for five dollars and that she'd had appraised for twenty times that, no word of a lie. Mildred vowed to never actually use it for cigarettes lest that lower its value. She could put that ashtray in the window of her future antiques store, and it might create a buzz. A buzz, said Mildred, was what you needed to be successful. And she was always on the hunt for more buzz-worthy items to launch her antique business.

Paisley followed Hu to the cow barn, where Stanley, the farmhand who lived in Mrs. Mickie's spare room, was already filling the feed carts from the silo.

Paisley loved being on the farm with Hu, away from her mother and surrounded by the wet warmth of the barn, the shuffling cows, their swatting tails. Stanley talking to the animals, Hu whistling low.

Hu turned on the milking system and flushed it with water. Mildred and her husband had invested in a state-of-the-art system, circa 1959. It was one reason the farm was a great investment. Once the system was flushed through, Hu herded the cows one by one into the milking parlour and attached the milkers to their udders. Each cow took five or ten minutes to milk and then was sent through the next set of doors into a holding pen. That was how Hu kept them straight—which cows had been milked and which hadn't.

Stanley kept shovelling feed from the silo into the cart. It had a good smell, like a chopped-down field. The calves and their mothers waited for their breakfast, standing close, stomping their back hooves, leaning in to one another.

"They don't stay together for long," said Stanley, as if reading her mind. "Soon as we can, we separate calf from mother and bottle-feed them."

Paisley stared at him.

He shrugged. "Calf gets too big, drinks too much milk, cuts into profit."

Paisley looked at the youngest calves, sucking at their mothers' teats. It was a wonder they didn't suck them right off. The bigger calves were docile in their own stalls.

"See, it's not as bad as all that," said Stan. He grabbed his coffee and walked over, releasing the spigot on the reservoir and helping himself to a shot of fresh milk right out of the machine. "They get on, sort themselves out. Seem happy enough, don't they?"

One calf chomped on its feed. It looked all right—not happy, just all right. Amazing how a cow's mouth moved sideways like that.

"You going to collect some eggs?"

This was Paisley's least favourite job. Chickens smelled bad. Worse than pigs. "I'm sorta busy," she said.

"What, got yerself a boyfriend?" Stan leaned on his shovel and eyed her with a smirk.

"No."

"Sure? You're all developed like a young woman now. The boys paying attention? Not keeping their eyes where they should be?"

"No."

"Any day now, don't you worry," said Stanley.

He fancied himself pretty smooth, pretty much something. He was wiry, not a fleshy part on him. His nails were never really clean. And his lower jaw was all caved in, the product of too many bar fights, which had left him virtually toothless.

"If it ain't a boy you're busy with, then it can wait," said Stanley, passing her a basket. "Collect them eggs."

She took the basket and headed to the coop. On the way, she counted three frogs and a barn cat. Garnet and Shawn Mulligan used to catch frogs and use them as baseballs, batting them across the fields, aiming for a home run. They called that fun. Two summers ago, after the Canada Day celebrations, they stole leftover firecrackers from the organizing committee and blew off the side-view mirror from the family car. Another time, they caught a barn cat and attached a firecracker to its tail with a string. The poor cat's tail was blown right off.

Paisley took a deep breath and stepped into the coop. It was loud in there. The chickens looked at her with mean red eyes. They pecked at her hands when she reached for their eggs. She wondered if they thought she was stealing their babies.

She walked back to the house, careful not to jiggle the eggs, set the basket on top of the cold-room freezer, then slipped out again, quietly latching the screen door.

Rory waved to Paisley from the road in front of Mildred's house, and she waved back.

"Sorry for yelling at you at the summer social," she said. "Wanna hang out?"

"Sure do."

Rory was good like that. Never held a grudge, not like Eudie. Once, Eudie had made Yorkshire puddings for a Sunday roast to impress guests. It'd taken all day, pulsing the blender every time she passed it so the batter would be light and airy. She'd done them in the oven in roast drippings like the recipe said and had made an announcement to anyone listening that they were not to open the oven door. Eudie watched them rise through the oven window and they were just something to behold—light, fluffy, voluminous, and golden-brown muffin-tin cups of goodness—so she'd made a subsequent announcement that these puddings would make it into the church fundraiser cookbook for sure—until Paisley, taken by the size of the things, forgot the rules and opened the oven door to steal a peek. The puddings fell just like that, and when they landed on the dinner plates, they were hard as hockey pucks. Eudie's cooking, the guests quipped, was legendary indeed—not exactly fit for the St. Andrew's cookbook, more like for use over at the Napanee rink. Eudie never let Paisley forget that.

When she came back into the barn with Rory, Hu was shutting down the milker and flushing the pipes with water, and Stanley was hosing down the floor where the cows had done their business. It smelled bad—not as bad as chickens, but bad enough. Paisley and Rory escaped to the back stalls where the barn cats lived.

"Why were you so mad before?" Rory asked.

Two cats approached and brushed up against Paisley's rubber boot. That was how it was with barn cats: one batch would disappear as if into the sky or the forest behind the cemetery, often right after Paisley had managed to get them all straight and categorized by size, colour, and gender; then another batch would appear, usually a few cats at first, and, some weeks later, kittens.

"Why were you so mad before?" Rory asked again, and suddenly Paisley had a desperate need to share her secret. In a way, Rory was the best person. No one talked to him but her.

"I saw my mother kissing Reverend Willis."

"That's nice."

"No, Rory, it's not. My mother's not supposed to be kissing anyone but my dad. Don't you see? She was kissing someone else. And she told me to keep it secret. And I don't know what to do."

"Oh," said Rory. "That's bad. Very bad. Right, Paisley?"

"Right. My mother kissing the reverend is very bad."

Something made Paisley look over her shoulder. There was Hu, pale as straw, bucket in one hand, other hand dangling.

He turned and walked away, rubber boots crunching over the barn floor. She should go after him. But what would she say? What would she do? She thought of his crossword in the truck. Fourteen down.

Catastrophe.

NOW

Paisley's zit was gone.

She sat, legs splayed, in the middle of her apartment, surrounded by garbage bags of clothes, all her toiletries, the contents of her kitchen junk drawer, and a stack of papers dating back to the late 1990s. Some were self-help magazine articles about yoga places in California and India that helped you realign your chakras and other good things; some were interviews with "experts" about how to kick the "habit" of OCD (ha!); some were articles describing twitching tours through the UK, France, and Italy, where staying at agriturismos certainly seemed the way to go.

Paisley had put the clippings into the recycle bin three times, and three times she'd fished them out. While it was true she had only about a hundred dollars to spare each month after expenses, and therefore it was almost a certainty she could never afford a realigned chakra or an agriturismo, she had to believe that somewhere, somehow, these things were a possibility. After all, she'd moved to Toronto on her own at the age of eighteen. She'd had the courage to sign up for ornithology courses at the University of Toronto, one course a semester. She'd found herself an apartment—this apartment—with no one having shown her how to do any such thing. And she had survived by being frugal and trusting herself. She had even managed her OCD, probably better than anyone ever imagined she might. Better than she herself had imagined.

Still, she had to be careful. Take Garnet, for example. Any benevolence she'd attributed to him was probably wishful thinking. It wasn't realistic to think a tiger could change his stripes. Why would Garnet, all these years later, show up on her doorstep in a cool suit, not only to offer his free services but also apologize? I mean. Come on.

Paisley threw an article about boat tours down the Seine into the bin and willed herself not to pull it out again.

THEN

They stayed at Mildred's farm until mid-afternoon. Paisley kept clear of Hu, playing with the barn cats and counting birds with Rory. Mildred fed them western sandwiches and drippy butter tarts, and they each had two. Then, panic rising over the secret she'd failed to keep, Paisley took two more tarts when Mildred wasn't looking and wolfed them down as well. Corn syrup coursed through her body and made her heart race.

Paisley and Rory walked up and down the road. He waved to passing cars, she counted grosbeaks. The middle of the road was where she liked it best, where she could eye telephone wires for birds and keep both halves of the road exact. Two halves, a good even number. Eight strides at a time, carry the eight, start again.

Eventually, Rory went home, and Paisley met Hu in the cold room, where they silently hung their mesh caps on a nail and changed out of their rubber boots. Hu headed for the truck and Paisley followed, eight strides, carry the eight, start again. On the way home, she stared at his crossword, which had fallen on the truck's rubber mat. She wanted to fill in fourteen down but thought better of it.

Hu took his time driving home. Clouds gathered over the fields. The wind whipped the lake into a whirlpool of currents between the island and the mainland. Branches blew across the roads. Hu drove right over it all, not even swerving to miss potholes. The gate into the quarry had come unlatched and was swinging back and forth, banging against the fence. Paisley wondered if anyone was down there. It was a dry quarry—no water for kids to drown in or anything—but no one was supposed to go in except workers; it belonged to the township and was dangerous.

"Tell me about when you worked the quarry," she said.

Hu didn't answer. Paisley didn't ask again.

Eudie's Saturday bridge club was on that afternoon. Paisley loved the bridge club, because she could eavesdrop on the island gossip. Del would be there, presiding over the women with her racy stories, which Eudie pooh-poohed, though Paisley knew it was the racy bits her mother loved best. Del didn't care what anyone thought, whereas Paisley worried about everything: the things she could control and the things she couldn't. And while Eudie admired Del, she also judged her. Paisley didn't judge Del. To Paisley, Del seemed free.

When Paisley and Hu turned into the driveway, they could see that things were in full swing. Hu went to the shed. Paisley, not sure what else to do, went inside.

Eudie was taking extra celery stalks filled with Cheez Whiz out of a Tupperware and arranging them on a plate. She had spiffied up for the party and looked beautiful, not like the "tall drink of water" Del was, but a more practical beautiful. Eudie didn't show off her endowments, but they were there. Muscular legs and arms, covered by the light pink sweater-and-skirt set she often wore for bridge. Long dark hair, usually worn up in a twist to keep it out of her eyes, down for the evening. Strong features: high cheekbones, full lips that looked good with a certain shade of L'Oréal. Del was often on Eudie's case to lighten up. "Eudora Ratchford," she would say, "if you keep your best wares behind the counter, who's going to buy them? Let the customers see the goods!" Eudie would scoff, but you could tell she liked Del's praise. Hu always kept quiet, and though he might have found his wife beautiful, he probably didn't say so often enough.

Eudie passed around the celery sticks to Del, Trixie, and Carol at one card table in the kitchen, and to Ethel, Muriel, Mavis, and Georgia at another table in the living room. Some were drinking tea; some were into gin and tonics, including Eudie and Del, and apparently not their firsts.

Paisley took off her runners and tiptoed toward the food laid out on the sideboard: coconut lemon bars, triple-layer surprises, hermit cookies, cream-cheese-'n'-chive pinwheels, and devilled eggs on her mother's special plate made for just that purpose. Paisley loaded up on food, her back to her mother so Eudie wouldn't see how much she was taking.

Eudie noticed anyway. "Put that back," she said to Paisley. "How will you ever lose your baby fat eating like that?"

"Oh, Eud," said Del, "put a sock in it."

"Life is hard enough without being fat," said Eudie. "We all know what it's like. No man will want you. People will think you have no self-discipline. It's just not worth it for a couple of cookies."

Paisley put half the food back, then wrapped the rest in a paper napkin and slipped it into a pocket. She took her familiar spot on the stairs, three steps from the top. Hopefully people would forget she was there. Prime spot, since you could disappear upstairs if you needed to, or you could survey all the action below. She sat there, wished herself into invisibility, and wolfed down her snacks. It felt good to eat, to tamp down with whatever she could the swamp of guilt and shame in the pit of her stomach.

Paisley listened in on conversations from both sides of the open main floor. Eudie going on about how she had altered the triple-layer surprise recipe. Del talking about improvements they were hoping to make to the store in Bath. She wanted it to feel like a Toronto grocery store, with a deli counter that offered paté and antipasto, a card and floral section, and food demonstrations on the weekends. Carol thought this was nonsense. Where was Del going to get the money to make all that happen? Toronto people could have their Toronto ways; people here had their own ways. Why try to change them?

"Don't be ridiculous," Del said, over the *snap, snap* of cards being laid on the table. "Carol, why'd you cover the queen?" Then, before Carol could answer: "You want to think like an islander? Go ahead. If I want to think bigger, that's my business. I mean, if I want to go to Toronto, I can go on a second's notice—hell, on no notice at all. The Chevy's parked outside the store, and I can jump in and be on the 401 in seconds flat. But you lot, stuck out here?"

This Paisley believed, that Del could be anywhere in seconds flat; she had seen her fly up and down the road between Bath and the highway. The islanders drove the same way from the 401 to the ferry dock, and Lord watch over the little children who lived in the houses dotting that stretch. The ferry left the mainland on the half-hour. A farmer would be coming home from picking up feed or parts and he'd only have four minutes, pedal to the metal, to make the boat. Hu did it, too. Everyone did. Who wanted to sit in their truck twiddling their thumbs for a whole hour until the next ferry? The boat's schedule was unforgiving. The hawser was thrown over the bollard, the ramp was lowered, the cars came off, new cars came on. When the captain gave the nod, off came the hawser, up came the ramp, that was that. It didn't matter if the Queen of England came barrelling down the road, the boat crew would not lower that ramp again.

"We're not stuck out here, Del," said Eudie. "Sorry, Trixie, I didn't have the courage to bid the slam. Carol—another G and T while you're up? Plus two maraschinos and syrup, please." Then she added: "There isn't much I or anyone needs to do on the spur of the moment, Del. Most of life can wait until the top of the hour."

"Not for Art Percy, as I hear it."

A titter passed between the tables. Paisley pricked up her ears. Del knew all the island gossip, even though she lived on the mainland. Paisley had no idea how she kept on top of it.

"Art Percy missed the eleven-thirty boat one night last week," Del continued, "and he chose another pastime, if you get my drift."

"Oh, Del," said Eudie. "That's nonsense."

"I know it from no fewer than two sources, and not one word of it is nonsense," said Del. "Someone, who shall remain unnamed, was at the auction that day. And Art didn't have any luck at all: none of his cows sold at market price. Too skinny—runts, every one of them. The auctioneer told him to his face in front of everyone, including my source, who lives on this island and is maybe someone you all know."

She paused for dramatic effect. It worked. She presided over them all, curls framing her face like a movie star, one shapely leg folded over the other under a satin· skirt the colour of Pop Shoppe grape soda. One hand picked at a cream-cheese pinwheel and the other held a long cigarette, ashes ready to fall onto Eudie's pristine linoleum. The other women, much less glamorous, sat motionless, waiting for the rest of the story. Del had them in the palm of her hand.

"So there he is, Art, at the ferry dock, and he no doubt figures he's there by himself," Del said. "Plus, he's drunk—not too drunk to drive, but drunk enough to take the edge off the humiliation of the auction."

"You can't possibly know he was drunk," said Eudie.

"Betcha."

Del thrust her hand in Eudie's direction, but Eudie wasn't shaking on it. This was the kind of bet she never won with Del. Not that Del's stories were necessarily airtight, but she could win any argument anyway. She'd been president of the debating club in high school. She'd talked her way out of many a tight spot, you could tell.

Nevertheless, Eudie faked disdain for the story. "How could you know Art was drunk," she said, fishing for a maraschino from the bottom of her glass. "Now, come on."

"Because, Eudora, he had a couple beer at the peeler tavern between the end of the auction and the eleven-thirty boat, no doubt to give the other island farmers plenty of time to get gone so he wouldn't have to face them in line for the ferry."

Paisley made a note to figure out exactly what the peeler tavern was, but before the others could ask how Del knew Art had been there, she continued.

"And I know he was at the strip joint"—Paisley's mouth fell open—"because one of the strippers who works there shops at our store. I've made friends with her. And she's not the devil you uptight church ladies think she is; she's just a smart cookie who knows how to make a bigger buck than all the rest of us put together. And, yes, she saw Art there that night, and, yes, he had two beers, and on her break he complained to her about the auctioneer calling his cows runts in front of everyone, and when she got up to dance again, he put a fiver in her outfit in a spot I won't mention."

Silence.

"So, by elevenish, Art knew all the other farmers were long gone, but he probably stuck around for one more beer, and there he was, having missed the eleven-thirty by a couple of minutes, with nothing to do and nowhere to go for a full hour. And he figured he was alone. Only he wasn't alone, was he? No."

"Should we get back to the game?" asked Eudie. But Paisley knew her mother wanted the end of the story as much as the next lady.

"Wasn't it Mac's wife, Ruth?" said Del with satisfaction.

"Ruth Millstone?" squealed one of them.

Del nodded, butting out her cigarette. "Just back from her Bible study meeting at Amherstview Baptist, which went late on account of studying something like 'The many faces of evil in the Bible and in modern society.' Now, if you ask me, that subject can't possibly be wrapped up nice and neat in just one meeting, not by a long shot."

Wow, thought Paisley, Del sure does have guts.

"Ruth was on the Sunday school popcorn drive committee with some of them in her meeting, and they decided to have an impromptu confab about the coming Sunday's launch. And so, having *not* booted it down the road from Amherstview like Art, having more concern about safety than him, she rolled up at eleven-forty, the eleven-thirty ferry almost halfway across."

No one else protested now that their game was waiting. They cradled their cards and drinks, immobile, thanking their lucky stars for being part of Eudora Ratchford's bridge group. Paisley kept absolutely still.

"Ruth saw Art's truck, and she thought maybe his wife was there, too, and they could chat till the next ferry, so she headed over to the truck. She cupped her hands around her eyes just like this and she peered right in the passenger-side window."

Gasps all around.

Del chortled. "And this is what she sees: Art has the visor down, and strapped to it with two elastic bands he has a picture of the Corn Flakes girl, which he's no doubt cut off the back of the cereal box. There she is, all soapy clean and rosy-cheeked, eating her cereal like she'd just milked a buncha cows, which were very probably not runts like his."

Everyone laughed at that, nervous laughter to release tension, but also not so loud as to break the spell and stop Del from finishing her story.

"So Art's praying to his Corn Flake goddess, full-on involved in his *business*, head thrown back there in the dark of the ferry dock, when he sees Ruth, hands cupped around her eyes, glued to his passenger-side window."

The ladies shrieked hysterically. Eudie was loving every minute of it, slightly drunk, hands covering her mouth, laughing and absolutely riveted.

Paisley was desperate now. What was his *business*? Wasn't he a farmer?

"There was Ruth, paralyzed, glued to the window of the truck, and there was Art Percy and his exposed *thing*, longer and harder and wider than anything she'd ever seen. Because between you and me, Mac always came up short in that department. I don't think I'm betraying a confidence, because even Mac knows that. In fact, he's known it since high school."

The women exploded with more laughter.

Trixie wanted to know how Del could possibly know.

"Some secrets I'll never tell," said Del, suddenly coy. And then, without missing a beat, she continued. "But, given Mac's was the only *thing* Ruth had ever seen up until then, she had nothing to compare it to. Well, now she had more than enough to compare it to.

"So Art tried to zip up, but he could hardly get it into his pants. He either burst a vessel by bending it the wrong way or he got it caught in his fly—Ruth doesn't know which—but he screamed, so she screamed, too."

"And?" someone asked.

"And nothing. She got back into her car and he stayed in his car. End of story."

There was a pause. That was Del, brazen as always. Brave enough to stare down Garnet, brave enough to tell a story about someone else's intimates, brave enough to give the bridge ladies something to chew on. There hadn't been a story like that in a good long while. The ladies would be able to dine out on it for months. Who cared about bridge!

What did Eudie think? Paisley looked at her mother's face, and what she saw was a revelation. Envy. Eudie wanted to be like Del as much as Paisley did.

What Art Percy's *business* was, Paisley still couldn't tell exactly, but the image of his giant thing loomed large in her brain. She wished she knew exactly what they were talking about. What would it be like to kiss a boy, soft lips to soft lips, heat to heat?

Hu came in. He threw the screen door open so hard it banged against the siding and whipped back behind him.

"Hi, Hu," said Eudie, trying to assess what was going on.

He took the stairs by twos, past Paisley, without taking

off his boots. The crowd in the living room watched him go. They could sense something was up. Del looked like she was taking mental notes for another story.

He banged around up there. Something was afoot.

"Coffee?" asked Eudie, trying to regain control of the room.

"Not for me," said Georgia.

"Me either," said Trixie.

"Well, I'm into another G and T, Eud," said Del. "In fact, what say we all move on to G and Ts?"

At the upstairs landing, Hu gave a quick whistle to summon Paisley. She stood up and followed him into her room. He had his father's khaki parachute bag open on the bed and her drawers open. He yanked out her nightgown and an armful of folded clothing and shoved it all in the bag.

"Pack your knapsack with whatever else you want. Do it fast and then come on," he said, turning on his heels.

Paisley did as she was told.

The women watched as Hu, followed by Paisley, headed downstairs and for the door. Paisley willed an extra moment so she could grab another devilled egg.

"What's happening?" asked Eudie.

"Milker's still broken at Mildred's," said Hu. "Paisley'll help."

"But—"

Hu was already out the door. Paisley scrambled to put on her shoes.

"Eud," said Del, cool as a cucumber, "you go after Hu to see if he needs a sandwich wrapped for him. Looks like he'll be working through dinner. I'll get us girls a round of G and Ts. Go on now."

Eudie smiled at the room and opened the screen door just enough so she could slip out. Then she bolted after Hu, who was almost to the truck, Paisley in tow.

Hu threw the parachute bag into the truck bed. Paisley, on instinct, darted into the shed, past Garnet's charred wall, to grab her birding things. She shoved them in her knapsack: her own notebook, June's leather notebook, her book on bird identification, the map of Amherst Island—

She could hear her parents outside on the driveway. "If you think you're going somewhere," Eudie was saying. "If you think you're taking Paisley. If you think you're getting the better of me—"

Then Hu: "The better of you? The better of *you*?"

Paisley stood stock-still. "You come here and bewitch me with your difference," Hu said. "I didn't need difference; I needed a wife who would be with me for life. Who would appreciate this place. Where my family's been for generations. Our name's on the original land claims, on the volunteer fire roster, on the church's stained-glass window, on almost every barn. I wanted a woman who wanted that, too. Instead, I got nothing I planned on. I got something different. And I find out just how different not from Paisley telling me but from her telling the island dimwit. The better of you. Ha. Paisley!"

Paisley bolted out from the shed.

"Get in."

She did.

As they pulled out of the driveway, the truck's running lights caught a few of the women in the window, watching what was unfolding from the living room. They caught her mother's eyes, making them glint like a cat's: glassy, mean, and hollow. Paisley had read of that look in books, in fairy tales especially—like when a witch cast a spell on a girl who broke a promise. After that, things went south very fast.

NOW

It was the last week of April, three weeks before the bull-dozers would arrive to demolish Dale Manor. Just in the last few days the pendulum had swung, and it had become unseasonably warm, fooling the gardens and birds into responding. Paisley had sighted a black-capped chickadee (*Poecile atricapillus*) among the crocuses and snowdrops on Beatrice Smalley's lawn across the street. It was a passerine bird that was very common, but so cute and curious, it could almost always distract Paisley from anything distress-ing; she had drawn them many times, and their sketches were pinned to the wall of her living room.

Not this time. Paisley was in a rut. Two and a half weeks had passed since Garnet's visit. Nothing had come in the mail, and he had not made contact—just as she had pre-dicted. She'd been right: he was a dick of monumental pro-portions, doing his best to victimize her all over again.

She had nowhere to go and no one to depend on. She'd given up on packing and looking for a new place. She couldn't admit to anyone at the archives that she'd let it come to this; they'd think she was crazy. She *was* crazy. The enemy had outposts in her head. So did Garnet.

It had become increasingly hard to leave her apartment. Paisley had moved from sick days to using up vacation time. She hadn't gone for groceries in a while, but she knew she had to eat something or she'd pass out. Barely able to see straight, she grabbed her purse and headed for the door. Then she real-ized she'd forgotten to check the stove. She stepped back into the kitchen and checked each of the knobs eight times. Every-thing was off. The toaster was unplugged. She stepped back to the door and was about to leave when she realized she'd left her purse on the counter. That forced a return to the kitchen, which meant checking all the knobs again, eight times. The toaster was still unplugged. Paisley cursed the day she was born, the day she started counting, the absurdity of it all.

She marched through the door, slammed it shut, walked to the elevator, and stopped. Her bout of self-loathing in the kitchen had distracted her from counting. What if she hadn't done it properly? This demon inside her, it had a grip so tight it was choking her to death. She considered going back for a recount, but no. No.

She stepped into the elevator, gasping for air. She wanted to go back so badly, count again, calm herself with numbers...except she was starving.

When the elevator doors opened in the lobby, there was Mrs. Feldman, pinning arm covers back onto armchairs.

"Hello, Paisley. How's it hanging?" said Mrs. Feldman. She chuckled. "That's what my grandson asks me. I say back to him, 'How's what hanging? And what's it doing, hanging?' It's a joke between us. It's not such a clever joke, but he's only up to a penguin's elbow, so it'll do for now."

"It's hanging okay, Mrs. Feldman."

"Honey, pardon my French, but you look like shit. How are you really?"

Paisley was desperate for her to go away. Mrs. Feldman was lovely, like a mother, a good mother, but Paisley could not take interrogation right now. She was barely keeping it together and here was Mrs. F standing between her and the outside.

Paisley saw an escape route. "I need to get my mail."

It was quiet in the mailroom. And warm. The furnace was still blasting, and the spring-like temperatures outside made it hot, Sahara Desert hot. Paisley could hear the hum of the furnace room directly below. The ledge was littered with pizza and takeout flyers. But there was a brown paper package about the size of a shoebox sitting there, too, right by her mailbox. It was from Bertram & Associates.

Paisley peered into her mailbox and saw a letter had come as well. She pulled it out and opened it.

Garnet Mulligan, LLB
Bertram & Associates
Kingston, Ontario

Dear Paisley,

Sorry for my delay in contacting you. I have submitted papers to have your mother's will overturned. It is clear that your mother was not in her right mind when she wrote her last will and testament. I don't know what state the house is in, but the property itself is worth something, and you could always re-build if the house was not suitable for your needs. In the meantime, in going through your mother's estate papers, which I had to retrieve from our archival storage facil-ity, I came upon a box of letters from your mother addressed to you, which—I hope I'm not overstepping—I have sent along. They are, after all, yours. I will contact you when I know more.

Best, Garnet Mulligan

The paper trembled in Paisley's hand. She looked up. Mrs. Feldman was staring at her.

"Everything all right, dear?"

"I don't know."

"What don't you know?"

"Anything."

And then the truth poured out. She told Mrs. Feldman about Garnet Mulligan, her childhood torturer, now assigned as her lawyer. About Garnet looking into the old house on the island so she could maybe live there, or sell it to buy a condo. About the box of letters from her mother, the mother Paisley spent a great deal of every day trying to forget.

"Lookit," said Mrs. Feldman, taking charge, "I want you to listen to me and listen good. We're going to deal with these things one at a time. One: the box of letters. Nothing says you have to read them. Lord knows we had troublesome family members who wielded pens like swords, and for years I subjected myself to that nonsense. If your mother had nothing good to say to your face while she was alive, she has nothing good to say to you on paper after she's dead. Take my word, Paisley. Nothing good will come of reading those letters. You can pass them to me if you like, but whatever you do, don't open them. They hold no power over you unless you let them.

"Next: whatever happens with the house is not your business. It's not your business until it becomes your business. There's nothing you can do about it until you hear what the legal decision is, so leave that be, too. Meanwhile, the only thing you can do is help yourself. We can only ever really count on ourselves. I know it's hard for you, and you want this thing to work out with the house, but it could be uninhabitable, so you still have a problem. I recommend getting your shit together and looking for another apartment here in Toronto fast. Because if you don't, you're up the proverbial creek."

Paisley felt faint. She clutched the ledge for support.

"And one last thing," said Mrs. Feldman. "Write that law firm today—write the head of the firm—and tell him to get Garnet the hell off your case. You can't trust that man as far as you can throw him. He doesn't deserve to represent you. They don't know your relationship with him, and so he should shove off. I'll write it for you. Or I'll call. I can talk to them directly, if you like. I have lots of experience getting what I want."

Paisley said she'd think about it and reached for the box of letters.

"Just leave the box there, dear, until you've had some time. I know you think you have to take it, but you don't."

Paisley left the box in the mailroom and went to the corner store to get two cardboard-like Jamaican meat patties that must have been sitting in the warming display case forever. She ate them on the street, and contemplated everything Mrs. Feldman had said. There was wisdom in her advice.

Paisley would get herself a new apartment.

She would not touch her mother's letters.

She would get herself a new lawyer.

But when she started to think about a new apartment, she worried about the building she'd be moving into: the fire hazards, the light switches, the faulty wiring.

1 2 3 4 5 6 7 8

So instead of going to the library to check for rentals in the paper, Paisley went home to tackle writing the law firm to dump Garnet.

Then she thought of the ways Garnet might make her existence a living hell for humiliating him like that.

When Paisley stepped out of the elevator and turned toward her apartment, there was Eudie's box of letters in front of her door, with a note from the super. It was coming up on recycling day, and he'd been in the mailroom to clean up the flyers and had seen this box. He was leaving it at Paisley's door to be helpful.

THEN

At Mildred's, Hu dropped their bags in the room next to Stanley's.

Paisley had overheard Stanley telling her father several months earlier how the hag he lived with in Napanee, just up from the liquor store, had tossed him on his lily-white ass after she'd found him inspecting the tonsils of the gas station's salesgirl. Now Mildred rented him a room for fifty dollars a month, which she deducted from his pay.

"Well, look at that," Stanley said to Hu. "Room right next to mine. Means you get an extra twenty minutes' sleep. Nothing bad about that."

"Stan," said Hu. "I don't want anyone knowing we're here, understood? It's only for a while, and it's only because Eudie has this ear infection. Even the tiniest sound makes her head pound."

"If that's the problem, why keep it a secret?"

"People talk. You know that," said Hu. "Ear infection or no, there'll be some story come out of it about how this and that means this or that...so best not to say anything."

"Lips are sealed," said Stanley, "sealed shut. What was that again? I already forgot."

Hu went to close the door.

"Maybe Eudie has migraines from the weather," said Stan.

"Nope. Definitely an ear infection." Again Hu tried to close the door.

Mildred had been lurking on the top stair. "Maybe it's an aneurysm," she said. "My aunt Bev had one of those. Didn't know it, of course. Her head hurt so much, she banged it against the wall just to make the pain move somewhere else. Made her forehead go black and blue. Before the doctor got round to seeing her, her aneurysm burst. It was my cousin who found her, dead in the bathtub, big bosom floating up on the cold water. She still had a razor in her hand for her legs and bleach cream on her moustache. Not much dignity in that."

"Eudie has an ear infection," said Hu. "She can't stand any sound, even the littlest one. Paisley and I'll give her a few days to recover. Thank you, Mildred." He shut the door politely but firmly.

"I have dinner on," said Mildred from the hall, "been in the slow cooker all day. It's Daisy's mother. She was some tough, but slow cooking always does the trick. And Paisley can put the lima beans to the side. All right?"

"Very nice of you," said Hu through the door. "We'll be down as soon as we get settled."

Mildred headed down the stairs, *clip-clop, clip-clop*, then stopped. "Stanley! Give 'em some room, for crying out loud, make yourself scarce."

"Yes, ma'am," said Stanley. Then *clip-clop* again, followed by the shuffle of Stanley's slippers.

Hu put clothes into drawers, and Paisley looked at the room—its sloping roof, baby-blue wallpaper over plaster and lathe, twin beds covered in white crocheted throws. Strange to hear her father say a string of untruths.

"No sense discussing what no one else understands," said Hu, as if reading her mind. "I'm going to check on the milk parlour."

Paisley spent Sunday visiting the barn cats. The mother was stretched full length in the hay, and the kittens, which had grown even in such a short time, climbed over one another to reach her teats. Paisley petted them all, smoothing their soft fur and plucking bits of hay from their tails. She counted them, tracked them, and listed them, almost like they were birds in her notebook.

On Monday morning, Hu drove Paisley to the island school, where she was supposed to attend summer camp for all of August. Week one: math Olympics. Camp was populated by island kids too young to help on the farm, or kids whose parents were just plain fed up by the endlessness of summer with too many children underfoot.

When Hu pulled away from the schoolyard, Paisley stood there, self-conscious in a skirt and top that was too tight across her chest. She'd have to collapse her shoulders a bit to make sure the button didn't pop. She decided to walk the perimeter of the schoolyard; she'd been keeping an eye out for the Henslow's sparrow. But when she reached the far end, she was cornered by the Mulligans.

Garnet focused on the soccer ball he was juggling. He was here, on Amherst Island, and not in Ireland trying out for the academy team in Dublin. He was here, attending pathetic island school math camp. He must loathe her with every fibre of his body.

"Your dad doesn't usually drop you off, does he?" he asked.

"Not usually," said Paisley. She prayed for the bell.

"I mean, you live right over there. Wondering why he gave you a lift. Right, Shawn?"

"Yup. Wondering why."

"No reason," said Paisley. Cry out, she thought. Someone will come.

"Really?" said Garnet, settling the ball for a moment and shoving his hands in the pockets of his track pants. "No reason at all? Not like your dad is sleeping out at the Mickie farm, you too. Something going on at home then?"

Paisley felt an urge to throw up—on the blouse pulling at her chest, her shoes, his shoes. In a split second, she measured the problem: vomit would mean being sent home to change. Her real home was a ten-minute walk. But home for the time being, as Garnet and Shawn somehow knew, was at Mildred's, which was quite a ways. No possibility of walking there. And even if she could get there to change her clothes, she'd have to wash the dress herself. In the bathtub. With a bar of Ivory.

"What gives?" said Garnet. "Your parents fighting or what?"

"Her dad's probably been kicked out," said Shawn. "Maybe he's banging another lady." He laughed and made a thrusting motion with his pelvis.

Garnet laughed, too, and that only egged Shawn on, keen for his brother's approval. Shawn made grunting sounds and thrust harder in Paisley's direction, letting his tongue hang out in feigned sexual throes.

Garnet pulled the matchbox from his pocket and shook it. *Shook-a-shook-a.*

Paisley heard that sound and saw floating black spots. Her lunch bag dropped to the gravel and she felt her body tilt sideways, as if she were stepping off a ride at the Napanee Fair.

"What's going on?" It was Mr. Chadwick, math teacher, part-time piano teacher, and camp counsellor. He stared the boys down. "Get going."

They did as they were told.

Paisley could barely focus on the grain of Mr. Chadwick's corduroy pants.

"Anything you'd like to share?"

She could taste bile; opening her mouth was not a good idea. She shook her head.

"Fine. I see you still have your lunch. At least there's that." He checked that the Mulligans were out of earshot. "For God's sake, Paisley. Stay away from the back of the yard, understand? And those boys. Don't give them any opportunity."

The day unfolded with math minutes, calculator Olympics, and popular puzzlers, but Paisley was distracted by how it was that Garnet knew she and her father were sleeping at the farm. She tried to focus. Long division usually made her happy. It had an order to it. Beauty. Math made sense of the world, and when you realized that, you could filter everything within your sight. Math even gave a shape to things that were invisible (germs, chemicals, molecules, atoms, chances, dangers of all kinds) and made them knowable. Math was God's work in action, pure and simple.

When the day was done, Paisley took Mr. Chadwick's advice and sat on the front steps in front of everyone to wait for her ride. It was already a quarter to four, and most kids had either been picked up or wandered home or gone for the ferry. Hu had promised to collect her but was nowhere to be seen.

There were stragglers: the boys competing for marbles; the girls with braids and good shoes tittering over a love note near the swing set; the nerds working on math problems on top of the jungle gym. In another life, Paisley would have been part of this last group; they were a year younger and should have accepted her as the obvious asset she would be to their group. But the truth of it was, they too wanted someone to be mean to, and Paisley was an easy target.

Paisley pulled June's notebook out of her knapsack and looked again at the Henslow's sparrow sketch.

Garnet and Shawn blasted out the front doors and threw down their knapsacks, kicking up dust. Sonya, the leader of the girl group and perfect in every way, shot Garnet a look of disdain. He pretended not to see it. Instead he kicked June's notebook off of Paisley's knee.

Pick it up or no? Pick it up.

She reached for it, but Garnet stepped on it.

"I asked you a question," said Garnet. "We got interrupted before you had a chance to answer."

Paisley had to be strong. She had followed Mr. Chadwick's advice to stay out in the open. There were witnesses all around; nothing would happen. And Mr. Chadwick hadn't even gone home yet. Getting caught twice in one day would mean consequences. Garnet's parents would get a call. He would get a beating. Or they would take something else away. But what more could they take than Ireland?

Mr. Chadwick appeared at the doors. Shawn and Garnet headed off five paces, looking up the road as if waiting for their ride.

She recovered the notebook and shoved it in her knapsack. Where was her father?

The boys waved at Mr. Chadwick, who turned only once as he walked in big strides to the road. He no doubt had registered the scene: Paisley on the front steps, Garnet to one side, Shawn on the other, not exactly close but not far off either, hemming her in. Yes, there were other kids there, but none who would really help in a pinch. Mr. Chadwick knew it, and Paisley knew he knew it. But Paisley knew one more thing about Mr. Chadwick. She had heard Del tell it to Eudie: he caught the four o'clock ferry every Monday and Thursday, not to teach piano but to meet Judith, the married lady who worked the Sears counter in Bath. Apparently more happened behind the Sears counter than taking orders and receiving shipments. Mr. Chadwick wasn't going to hang around.

Garnet grabbed Paisley by the sleeve and yanked her to her feet. Her knapsack slid awkwardly to her elbow and tipped everything out: math booklet, calculator, June's notebook, and *How to Win at Chess* from the school library, which was left open, with no librarian, during the summer months. No escape now.

Garnet stepped back onto June's birding notebook and wiped his feet on its cover. "Helped out in the barn this morning, Paisley. Part of my punishment for setting your shed on fire. Only, I stepped in sheep crap."

"He's clumsy like that," piped in Shawn.

"Shut it, Shawn."

Poor Shawn. He'd need to turn it up just to stay in the game. That didn't bode well for Paisley.

"Want your book back?" asked Garnet. Paisley nodded. "Then tell us why you're living at the farm."

"I'm not." She raised her voice. There you go, Paisley. Atta girl.

"Really?" said Shawn. "You're not living out of a suitcase in the room next to Stan?"

Now it all made sense. Stanley Mills, father of four illegitimate boys: Connor, Spencer, Jim, and Alistair. Connor, twenty-five or so, killed last year after he took to the 401 and drove drunk, way over the limit, in the wrong direction, the father of four illegitimate boys of his own—Morton, Gary, Stewie, Billy with the cleft palate—Billy rejected by Connor's girlfriend the moment Connor was in the grave, taken in by one of Stanley's exes, also not Billy's mother, but the very ex who helped Garnet and Shawn's parents on the sheep farm, in return for board there. So the Mulligans saw Stanley most every Sunday when he came by their place to act as close as he could to a decent grandparent to Billy. Even after Hu had expressly asked Stanley for discretion, he had obviously spilled.

"You can tell us," said Garnet. "We can keep a secret."

What would Del do? She'd make Stanley's life hell, that's what.

"Give me my book."

"Move over, Garnet, I need to take a piss," said Shawn. "Got just the spot to do it."

The other kids had approached to watch. Maybe Shawn would be too ashamed to pull out his thing. Maybe not.

Garnet gave Paisley one last chance to answer, then shrugged and stepped off June's notebook to make way for his brother. Paisley made a grab for it—a brazen, life-threatening move—and Shawn stepped right onto her hand. She yelped but didn't let go.

Garnet reacted strangely. "Move off, Shawn."

Had Paisley heard right?

"You move off!" Shawn said.

Garnet shoved Shawn off Paisley's hand and looked down at her. She pulled June's notebook to her chest.

"It's not about taking a piss, is it, you idiot. It's about her Da. Doing something wrong. What'd he do to get thrown out like that, Paisley? Commit a crime? Sleep around?" Garnet saw Paisley flinch. "There it is. Didn't he sleep with someone."

"Oh, shut up," snapped Sonya.

"What, afraid it's your Ma?" said Garnet.

"Yeah," said Shawn. "Your Ma's not so bad-looking, Sonya. I'd do her." He turned to Paisley. "Your Da's got good taste."

"It's not my father!" spat Paisley. And in that one moment everything changed. All of them—even Shawn—understood the problem wasn't Hu; it was Eudie. It was her mother who had upset the natural order of things. It was a slip Paisley would never be able to take back.

There was a rumble beyond the barricade of legs. It was Hu's truck.

The kids heard it, too. They separated a bit as Paisley collected the rest of her knapsack's contents from the ground. Things had shifted: she was suddenly, weirdly, at the top of the food chain, not below Garnet but somehow alongside him. She had been tortured and had survived; there was dignity in that. Her stock had risen for having an unfaithful mother.

"See you tomorrow, Paisley," said Sonya. She had never really spoken to Paisley before.

Garnet felt the shift, too. "There's some fresh gossip for you, so spread the word," he said to the others. He eyed Paisley. "Your Mam sleeping around this piece-of-shit island. Only a few people it could be. Who is it, Paisley?"

She didn't answer.

He eyed June's notebook. And grabbed it. "Who?"

Paisley stared at June's notebook in Garnet's hand. She would do anything to get it back.

Hu leaned across the truck's wide front seat and threw open the passenger door, trying to assess the schoolyard politics. "Sorry I'm late, Paisley," he called from the truck. "Come on!"

Hu was there. The moment was gone. But Garnet eyed her, conspiratorial, and smiled. He knew he had her—that it was only a matter of time before he'd get the information he wanted. She would participate in her own demise, just as he had participated in his own by setting the fire at her shed and getting caught. He looked down at the notebook, brushed off the dirt he'd left with his own boot, and gave it back.

Signalled by Garnet, the kids parted even further and Paisley walked through to the truck. But as she climbed in, she saw her father's eyes locked on the kids. They were watching him with pity. Shawn, with a look of disdain. Garnet—who knew what he was thinking.

As they pulled out of the school driveway, a new thought occurred to Paisley. Sleeping around meant something different from kissing. Kissing was all she'd seen between her mother and Reverend Willis. So had she, just now, been the one to pour gasoline on the fire?

NOW

Paisley had left the box of letters on the coffee table, untouched. They were sure to be standard, toxic Eudie fare, and yet they were all she had left of her mother.

On the way to her next shift at the archives, Paisley splurged and got herself a supersize latte: rearranging deck chairs on the *Titanic*, but what the hell. As she headed to work, she passed a brownstone just south of Bloor Street, near the fire station. Out front was an *Apartments Available* sign. She listened to the subway rumble. That would be bothersome.

The brownstone was on a tilt, maybe because the subway tunnelled underneath. People might mock her fear of crushing subway passengers, but if the engineering hadn't been done properly during construction, and the building one day just up and caved into the tunnel underneath, killing everyone in a subway car or two, her concerns would bear out. Ample reason not to consider relocating here. As she contemplated the array of possible catastrophes, a portly, unshaven man stepped out to dump a bag of trash into the garbage container.

"Looking for a place?"

"Me? Um...no. Yes. I'm not sure, I'm just—"

"I can show it to you now. It's reasonable, I can tell you that much."

"Oh. Well, I have to go to work. But, okay, I could take a few minutes."

She went to see the apartment.

It was in the basement. A mouldy, damp smell permeated the air. The ceilings were low and peeling. Water damage had yellowed the crumbling plaster. Worst of all, the light switches were old, 1940s-style buttons you had to punch rather than a switch. In her desperation, Paisley might have overlooked everything else, even the mouldy smell, but the light switches caused her stomach to do flips.

The superintendent was called away elsewhere in the building. She could take a few minutes to decide, he said; he'd be right back. While he was gone, Paisley availed herself of the underwhelming facilities without turning on the lights. She sat furtively on the toilet, hoping the man didn't return too soon. Unable to do what she needed to do, all she could think of was how upside down her guts felt, and how upside down her life was.

Paisley left the miserable apartment unrented and returned to Dale Manor. She called in sick, pulled some *Birders International* magazines from a box, and headed for her own bathroom.

THEN

It didn't take long for everyone on the island to find out Paisley's mother was sleeping with someone, and by the second-last day of math camp, Eudie also knew that everyone knew. Shortly thereafter, the letters started. Eudie dropped them off after nightfall in Mildred's mailbox at the end of the driveway.

Dear Paisley,

I want to tell you a few things, and I want you to listen hard. Life is not easy and you're going to find that out soon enough like the rest of us. You will come to regret what you have done. You will come to see that life is not as black and white as you think. Someone else may do something you consider wrong, but it's not up to you to judge and gossip, spread lies in the schoolyard so that young foolish boys can write things on my front door, tell their parents so I'm barred from church meetings, so that no woman except Del will come to my bridge parties. Who do you think you are? I have my reasons for what I did with Arden Willis, but did you ever ask me why?

Let me tell you.

While you and Hu have abandoned me, I haven't stepped out of the house, not once. You've made a public humiliation of me. I'm trapped here. There's nothing left in the fridge, but I have casseroles in the deep freeze and I'm defrosting them one by one. One lasts me two days straight. So there is time to think about how I hate this place, how tired I am, and how I want more. There is nothing to stop my brain turning over and over what happened at the summer social, and how awful I was. My head is pounding with all the questions: Should I stay? Should I go? I can hardly face my friends in Toronto. We got married quietly on the island, and they didn't come, so they never knew what a simple man Hu was. What a simple place this is. Now they're all probably married to doctors, lawyers, businessmen. Can you imagine? I'd be back there with my tail between my legs, single, saying I'd married a farmer who spent half his life shovelling cow shit, and it didn't work out. My cat France, my beautiful cat France who knew me through and through, better than anyone else, isn't even mine anymore. I don't have a penny to my name. My typing skills are stale beyond saving. There's no way out.

Everyone thinks I've had an affair with Arden. A serious affair—tiptoeing around, motels in Kingston, secrets and lies upon lies upon lies. But the only liar is you. You made everyone believe that. You made it so much worse than it was. I wish I had had an affair—at least then someone would have loved me. But no, instead, you've ruined my life and your father's life. He can never recover his good name here. There's no coming back from this. So I made it easy on both of us. I told him it's over. I'm not sure what I'll do next. But this is what you have done.

Paisley spent the entire next day in bed. She could not bring herself to face the last day of math camp, new friend Sonya or not. Hu didn't make her go; he worked in the barn and spoke to no one—not Stan and not Paisley either.

Paisley counted the lilies of the valley on her pillowcase, read the Bible from the bedside table, and flipped through her field guide, looking at sketches of birds, but nothing could distract from the facts: Hu had stopped talking about going back to Eudie. Eudie clearly hated her own daughter. A good portion of the island knew about the situation, and yes, as Eudie said, Paisley was a no-good, terrible liar of a human.

She counted eight sets of eight.

They didn't help.

1 2 3 4 5 6 7 8
1 2 3 4 5 6 7 8

Flies buzzed in the window. A spider crossed the rag rug. The bad thoughts wouldn't quit.

There was a tap at the door, and Mildred came in bearing another letter. Eudie was gathering steam. Mildred, who had spent the last few days at auctions in Prince Edward County, was perhaps the one person on the island still oblivious to the news of Eudie's infidelity.

"I've been to three auctions this week," she told Paisley, "and here's why. I don't want to run a farm for the rest of my life. On the other hand, auctions...now, they hold potential. I once found a gold charm bracelet in the bottom of a musty cardboard box of 1960s *National Geographic*s. I bought the whole box for a nickel, one shiny nickel, and kept my trap shut. Then I took that bracelet in to be evaluated and it was worth $540, I kid you not. I stepped out of the jeweller's and I turned my face up to God and gave my thanks. That's what I live for: the thrill of the hunt. That's what keeps me going. I'd give up the farm in a second to your dad if I just found the right thing. A treasure with my name on it, something I could move to the mainland on.

Something that would make people flock to my antique store because I had this one thing that no one else had. Still looking for my treasure now, aren't I? Wash up, dinner's in ten. You can put the beans to the side."

Paisley closed her field guide and opened her mother's letter. It didn't even have a salutation.

> *You couldn't possibly mind your own business even after all I've done for you—bringing you into this world, giving up everything I ever hoped for, all my own dreams, to let you suck me dry in more ways than one. I laundered your diapers, your endless shit-filled diapers. I might've been out on a Friday night back in Toronto, going with the girls for a good BLT dinner and a drink and a gab where we'd talk about who's dating who and who's gaining weight and the newest styles, but instead I was home on this ridiculous island folding cloth diapers all bloody night. I'm sure I folded thousands. Because that damned women's Welcoming Committee didn't see fit to give me one moment of true companionship. What they did do was take up a collection of the cloth diapers no one needed anymore and wrap them all in a cloth bag and drop it like an unmerciful cow patty on my porch. No one even rang the doorbell, for God's sake—they just damn well left them there and walked away.*
>
> *Where was I? Was I not here? Could I not have used a little company?*
>
> *I had a tin full of orange pekoe like the rest of them! I had cookies in the freezer,*

wouldn't have taken a moment to thaw, so why in God's name did no one ring the doorbell? Couldn't they see I was half crazy with your incessant crying? Colic, they'd say to me at fellowship hour after church, colic, ooh my baby had colic too, cried for three months—ooh, my baby had colic too, cried for six months—like it was some competition. Well it's a good thing that it all came up under God's roof. I was forced to hold my tongue because He was eavesdropping. Mostly I wanted to just holler at the bunch of them, standing around in their fancy hats and mud-caked shoes, Prue's cranloaf in one hand and a cup and saucer in the other. I wanted to say, Paisley cried for a year. A whole year. While Hubert was at your farm, Mildred, milking your cows and harvesting your crops and cleaning your bloody barn, I was home with a baby who never stopped crying, ever. No that's not true—she stopped only to take a breath to cry some more. I thought I was going crazy, I was sure I was losing my mind. A few times I saw angels, and I thought I'd killed myself just to stop the sound, and I was being accepted into heaven anyway for my troubles. God knows. He heard you and He forgave me this one small thing.

You stopped eventually—I have to give you that, like most things in life, the crying stops just before you're ready to slit your wrists. Only then there's always some other fresh hell. All I prayed for was for you to get out of those damn diapers, but no, you held on to crapping in your diapers longer than any other child on the island. Because that's what always happens in my life—whatever normally happens doesn't happen to me, it's always worse. That's my lot. I must've done something bad in a former life, and I am being punished. That's what you were, one big punishment. My hands were permanently cracked and dry and bleeding and smelled like vinegar because of that diaper-soaking solution. And this is why I say don't judge others for what they do to hold on, to stay sane and make believe they have something on this earth that is more than misery. You don't know anything about misery. You don't know anything. And I'll remind you of that as long as I have breath in my body.

Paisley folded up the letter, put it back in its envelope, laid it on the crocheted bedspread, and went out to the back field, where she poked her arm with a stalk of dry grass eight times in a row for ruining her mother's life. Then she lay down and closed her eyes. Maybe a colony of killer ants would swarm her body and eat her from the outside in, leaving only a heap of bones. Eudie might find them later and feel guilty. That would be good.

Paisley hummed, waiting for the ants to come. The grass was cool and prickly. She closed her eyes and let the field take over. The crickets carried on around her, lulling her to sleep. Her body became one with the grass, and before she knew it, her hair was turned to feathers, pale green feathers. She sprouted chestnut-brown wings, and her back was brown-and-black plumage. Her song became insect-like: *tsi-lik, tsi-lik, tsi-lik…*

A mosquito bit deep into the fleshy part of Paisley's ear. She slapped it too late and was left with blood on her hand. She sat straight up. She knew how to solve the problem.

While it was true that her mother was the author of her own downfall, it was also true what Eudie had said in her letter: Paisley had not been able to keep her mouth shut. So solving this situation was her responsibility. And now she knew how to fix it.

NOW

One week left until eviction day.

Mr. Burnside, Lily, Mrs. Feldman—they'd all moved out. Most of Dale Manor's apartments were vacant. The super had placed a call to the building owners about Paisley's reluctance to leave. When the owners—an old Lithuanian couple—came to talk to her, Paisley told them it wasn't reluctance; it was an impossibility. Where would she go? The owners claimed she had been given plenty of warning. Paisley said that while that was true, the length of the warning was not the issue, safety concerns were, and she did not want to elaborate. The wife slipped into Lithuanian and gesticulated enough to make it very clear that swearing was involved. The husband ignored his loud wife and said that in four days they would put a padlock on Paisley's door and confiscate whatever they found inside—all her possessions. Did she want that?

"Of course not," said Paisley. Secretly, she didn't give a rat's ass about her stuff (well, most of it anyway). "It's the electrical sockets and the light switches and the wiring where I go that concern me. I need to know they're safe." Didn't anyone ever listen?

"But soon there will be bulldozers," said the owner, "and the building, it is being condemned. If anywhere will be unsafe, it is Dale Manor, young lady."

"I don't know how to respond to that," said Paisley.

"You will have to be taking that up with the sheriff, then," the man said.

Paisley was momentarily impressed that Toronto had a sheriff.

"She should go to the house for the crazies," mumbled the wife.

"I am not crazy," said Paisley. She resented having to talk about her personal affairs with strangers. "I have obsessive-compulsive disorder. It comes and goes with anxious times. And being forced out of my home qualifies as an anxious time."

"Crazy," said the wife.

"Go fuck yourself," said Paisley.

She waited until after midnight to collect her mail. There was one letter from Garnet. He had indeed managed to overturn Paisley's mother's will. He had put forward a motion that Eudie was mentally unwell when the will was made, and it had been successful. The envelope included documentation to back up his letter.

The house on Amherst Island where Paisley had grown up was now hers. If she wanted to meet with Garnet, they could visit the house, have her sign the papers, and he could pass her the keys.

A trick? A bad joke? Or a lifeline?

Paisley reread the letter. Neither she nor Garnet knew what state the house was in, and yet Dale Manor was also shortly to become uninhabitable—a pile of rubble, in fact.

Amherst Island was her only option. Birds were forced off their migration paths because of many factors, including unusual weather events. This was like a storm blowing Paisley off her own migration path. She shouldn't fight it—fighting would only exhaust her further. She should let the storm blow her somewhere new.

If she didn't want to live there, she could sell the house and get enough for a down payment on a newly built, safe condo.

On impulse, she called the law office, even though it was close to one in the morning. She left a message saying she wanted to discuss the matter further. She still hoped she could deal with someone other than Garnet, though. That might just do her in.

THEN

Paisley's great-great-grandmother June had started her birder notebook in the 1860s and kept it up so carefully, so neatly, for years and years. The gold initials on its leather jacket were J.A.M. Mildred wanted—no, needed—a special thing, a valuable thing, for her antique shop in Kingston before she'd move off the farm and give it to Hu. All Paisley needed to do was tell one tiny white lie: that the birder's notebook had in fact belonged to Sir John Alexander MacDonald, not to June Andrea MacIntosh. They'd lived around the same time. They'd lived near the same place. It was entirely believable that birding could have been one of John A.'s pastimes.

Paisley would hand over June's beloved notebook and share the lie in just the right excited, secretive tones—and Mildred would have her special thing. The notebook was rightfully Paisley's; Hu had given it to her, and she could give it to Mildred if she wanted to. Lying about its author wasn't the honest thing to do, but it was the right thing to do. Mildred had been promising the farm to Hu for years—the deal was that he would work at a reduced income in return for the farm when she moved to the mainland. All she did was complain about farming. She hated the smell. She hated the animals. She hated the relentlessness of it. And yet she held on, always dangling the farm as Hu's eventual prize. This handshake deal had strained her parents' marriage, and it made Hu feel bad. Paisley could see that, and it just wasn't fair. So lying it would be. It was true that Paisley always paid the price for not telling the truth—it brought on days of eights, counting and checking, self-loathing for being a terrible, no-good person—but these were dire times, and it was Paisley's responsibility to set things right, eights or not.

Paisley needed to address one other tiny detail: how she had come to be in possession of June's notebook. She'd have to say it had not come from the back of their shed, but that Paisley, like Mildred, had found it in the bottom of a musty cardboard box at a farmer's auction and had bought it fair and square for next to nothing. In fact, Paisley would say she'd bought that box *on account* of Mildred—because of Mildred's past success in buying boxes of junk just like it. Boxes that—surprise!—turned out to contain the very opposite of junk. Mildred would love that Paisley had followed her advice. And she'd love the notebook: its history, its value. It would be the prize in her new store window. It would give her a reason to move to Kingston. Then Hu would have the farm he deserved. Paisley and Hu would have a place to live. And Eudie might come back.

She and Rory could renew their efforts to find the Henslow's sparrow. If she could spy one, just one, that would make the story she was going to feed Mildred all the sweeter—and slightly more honest. There was the Henslow's sparrow in Sir John A.'s notebook—the rarest bird in the notebook, one that got a double-page spread. And there would be the Henslow's sparrow, sighted for real on Amherst Island, if she and Rory were lucky enough to find it. Those two things together would give the story buzz. Mildred loved nothing more than buzz.

Paisley didn't have trouble getting Rory onside. That Saturday, they looked all over Mildred's property, up and down the Stella 40 Foot, through field after field, and on farm after farm, listening for the telltale song.

They found nothing.

Paisley brought Rory back to Mildred's for iced tea on the side porch, where they could see all the comings and goings on the road, the driveway, and from the barns. Hu was checking the mailbox. He saw Paisley and Rory but headed back up the driveway to the barn, pocketing a letter as he went. It was probably from Eudie. She had taken to delivering letters herself several times a day, walking from their house on Front Road all the way to Mildred's on the

third concession. Hu had been intercepting her letters before Paisley could read them, although if she looked hard
enough, she'd found them and read them anyway.

"Hi, Dad!"

He waved over a shoulder in silence before disappearing
into the barn.

Paisley and Rory sat on the porch swing. She folded her
legs underneath her and let Rory do the swinging.

"We could look on the north shore," said Rory.

"Done that."

"We could look around the fishing village."

"Done that, too."

Swing, swing, swing.

Rory whistled the Brylcreem ad. Paisley kept one eye on
the yard for the Henslow's sparrow.

She wondered about her mother's letter.

1 2 3 4

She didn't want to know what was in it, but she did.

5 6 7 8

What terrible thing had she done now? She wanted to see if
she agreed with Eudie's latest assessment of her. She had come
to believe much of what Eudie said in those letters: That she
was responsible for the demise of her parents' marriage. That
she was a terrible child who brought disaster. No one knew
that it was Reverend Willis, of course, but he did, and so he'd
hightailed it out of town—to do research at the church's head
office in Toronto, apparently. Maybe, if she had the power to
bring calamity to her family, she could unleash it elsewhere,
too. People tripping on rocks, fires being started, buildings
falling down, earthquakes, car crashes, gangrene, leprosy.

1 2 3 4 5 6 7 8

"Whatcha thinking?" asked Rory.

"That there are so many different sparrows," lied Paisley.

Rory pushed the swing. The wind made Mildred's garden
whirligigs fly.

"There's the grasshopper sparrow, for example. *Ammo-dramus savannarum* in Latin. I've found plenty of them around here. They're like the Henslow's sparrow in some ways—they feed and nest on the ground—and they're scared. The book says they're *furtive*."

"Good word," said Rory. "You're smart."

Not according to Eudie, thought Paisley. "But grasshopper sparrows are interesting in their own right."

"Yup," said Rory.

"They find grasshoppers to feed to their nestlings, and they shake the grasshoppers' legs right off."

"Yes, they do."

"But a trained eye can tell that grasshopper sparrows are not Henslow's sparrows. Grasshopper sparrows make a dome of grass over their nest, with a side entrance."

"Mm-hmm," said Rory.

Paisley watched Mildred come out of the house carrying the compost. Hu came out of the barn to get a tool. They crossed paths without acknowledgement. Paisley felt invisible.

1 2 3 4 5 6 7 8

"Let's look in the fishing village again, Rory."

They rode their bicycles to the south shore. All Paisley needed was dedication and good eyes. And faith. She remembered one of Reverend Willis's sermons, where he'd quoted Jesus: "I can promise you this. If you had faith no larger than a mustard seed, you could tell this mountain to move from here to there. And it would. Everything would be possible for you." Reverend Willis was not all bad. He was not even half bad. He was pure good, the opposite of her. That was why he was a man of the cloth and she was what she was. A counter. A checker. A bringer of disasters.

They searched the field behind a fishing shack, and Paisley thought she spied a promising sparrow, but it turned out to be a LeConte's sparrow (*Ammospiza leconteii*), another secretive bird that spent its time in tall grasses and made a cup-shaped nest there. An amateur could easily mistake one for the other.

Each discovery of a grasshopper sparrow or a LeConte's sparrow made Paisley's heart skip, but faith wasn't getting her very far. As dusk descended, Rory rode alongside Paisley back to Mildred's farm, where they parted ways, having gained nothing.

In the evening, when there were no distractions, the demons came to play. She repeated over and over the moment she'd revealed to Garnet and the schoolyard what was happening with her parents. How had she been so dumb? She deserved her mother's punishment. Paisley counted to push the bad feelings away, but with the darkness all around, counting didn't work. That night, after Hu was safely snoring at eight o'clock or so, she pulled on her rubber boots and went tramping across the farm to resume her search for the Henslow's sparrow. She combed the fields all around Mildred's property, but there was no trace of the bird with the nothing song.

By the end of the night, she fell into a pattern of eights and was trapped there: eight steps to the next destination; eight steps thereafter; eight efforts to find the bird; eight pinches of her thigh, very, very hard; eight chews at a time to eat the piece of fruit she'd stolen from the kitchen, counting up and down on her fingers—one, two, three, four, five, six, seven, eight. Over and over. She did not find the bird and she did not get a wink of sleep, and when 4:00 a.m. rolled around, she left her wet boots by the back door, tiptoed up into bed, and slipped under the covers just before her father rose for milking.

At breakfast, she said she was under the weather and needed to go back to bed.

"Suit yourself, Paisley," said Hu. "You're a big girl now. You can do what you want after washing up. Besides, I've got bigger problems. The milk pump's acting up again, and who knows if we can get someone over from the mainland to fix it."

"Sick and tired of that milker," Mildred clucked. "Been a curse since we installed it."

Hu wandered out the back door. Paisley was exhausted but knew this was her moment to take action. She hadn't found the bird, but she could move forward with her plan anyway.

"You must just dream of being able to let all this go," said Paisley, running water to do the dishes, pouring in the detergent, and watching bubbles appear as if by magic. "Being able to go to auction any old time you want."

"My true calling," said Mildred, drifting toward the dining table, which was covered in her latest purchases.

"That's for sure," said Paisley. "Look at all the wonderful things you've found."

"I know," said Mildred. "Come see what I bought."

Paisley dried her hands, said eight sorries in her mind, and did as she was told.

"This crystal decanter. Feel how heavy it is and yet how delicate the neck is, too. See the cut glass? That's real beauty, isn't it? Careful now, don't drop it. It cost me a whole— Well, you go ahead and guess how much it cost me."

Paisley knew the rules of this game: never guess too low. "Thirty dollars?"

"You must be joking! I'd never spend thirty. Don't you know me better than that? Go ahead, guess again."

"Twenty?"

Mildred scoffed.

"Fifteen?"

"Eight-fifty! Eight dollars and fifty cents. Can you believe it? It's real Baccarat crystal. That's French for très, très expensive."

Paisley was appropriately impressed. She asked about the other items displayed on the lace tablecloth. Mildred took her through the details of a genuine dough box from the 1850s; the owners had thought it was an inconsequential piece and so let it go for almost nothing, but Mildred knew it was probably worth in the vicinity of eight hundred dollars or more. And did Paisley know that in this dough box a peck of flour would have been stored to make bread—which was about seven gallons. Seven gallons of flour, could she imagine? Mildred showed her a paper bag of ancient handwrought fence-post nails and some kind of kitchen implement neither she nor Paisley could identify. Good for urban antiquers; you could charge them an arm and a leg for those sorts of things. They thought them rustic and quaint.

Mildred clucked over her purchases like a hen about to lay an egg. Paisley oohed and aahed, which made Mildred even happier.

"You really are good at finding treasures," said Paisley.

Mildred lit a cigarette. She inhaled deeply and lifted her chin so she blew the smoke up toward the chandelier. "Paisley, you make me blush. But I must say, you're wise beyond your years. I am gifted at auctions, it's true. And I'm just waiting for the right time to leave farming behind and go into auctions full-time."

"What makes it the right time?" asked Paisley.

"The right *thing*," said Mildred. "All of life is captured in the things we have. Important people have important things. Important moments are captured in important things. And that's all worth money."

"And so you need really important things to open your store?"

"Exactly. There are a couple of stores in Kingston that buy my items on consignment. But when I open my antique store, I won't just be making part of the profit, I'll make it all. Shouldn't I make all the profit?"

"You should," said Paisley.

"And all the glory."

"All of it," said Paisley. She went in for the kill. "I just might have a really precious thing that I could give you—so you could open your store."

"Oh?" Mildred said, cigarette in one hand, crystal stopper in the other. "What do you mean by precious?"

"You know," said Paisley. "Really, really precious. Like, for example, I'm into birding, right?"

As it turned out, Mildred hadn't particularly noticed. Never mind. Paisley explained about birding, and how passionate people were about it, and how the birders who had seen the rarest birds were famous. As in, movie-star famous.

"Curious," mused Mildred, polishing Sir John A.'s ashtray with her apron and taking a drag on her cigarette.

"But I've never been a famous birder," said Paisley, "because I've never seen a rare—I mean a really rare—bird. And then"—she paused for effect, just as she'd watched Del do a thousand times, while Mildred held the smoke in her lungs a little longer than usual—"at the summer social, I heard two ladies from away talking about a bird. A very, very rare bird, seen right here on Amherst Island."

Mildred exhaled, eyebrows raised. "What's it called?"

"The Henslow's sparrow."

"A sparrow is a rare bird? They're just about the most common—"

"This one is. They thought it was extinct."

To be accurate, the Henslow's sparrow would be considered locally rare. But Mildred looked interested, so Paisley let the lie stand. In for a penny, in for a pound.

"What does that have to do with me?" Mildred asked.

"Well," said Paisley, "I have a birder's notebook that has a whole two pages on the Henslow's sparrow, with an original sketch and measurements and location of where it was sighted—on Amherst Island—and what its nest looked like and everything. The book is an antique. Written by a very famous person who lived around here."

"No one famous lived around here," said Mildred.

Paisley kept her eyes glued to the lace tablecloth and ever so slightly shrugged her shoulders. As in, *okay, if you say so*...like Del might have.

"Who?" Mildred couldn't resist. Paisley had her now.

Paisley lifted her gaze and looked Mildred in the eye. "Sir John—"

"Not Sir John A. MacDonald!" Mildred gasped.

Paisley nodded. "His initials are on the cover."

"Of the notebook?"

Paisley nodded again.

"Lord in Heaven," said Mildred, resting her cigarette on Sir John A.'s bulbous nose.

And then Paisley laid the foundation for her lies. How she'd followed in Mildred's footsteps, listening to her sage advice all this time about searching the boxes of leftover junk at farm auctions, and how she'd bought a musty old box of stuff for five bucks, only to find this treasure at the very bottom.

"You see?" Mildred said, proud as a peacock.

"I do," said Paisley.

"Why didn't you tell me?"

"I don't know," said Paisley. "I should have. Because I always knew I should give it to you. You're the one who knows what to do with it."

"True," said Mildred, and then she paused. "But why would you give it to me? As a birder, wouldn't you want to keep it? Or...are you wanting part of the profit?"

"Well, that's the thing." Perspiration collected in Paisley's armpits. "I know you've wanted to give my father the farm, after all these years of working it for you, and I've always been so impressed at what Reverend Willis would call a truly Godly act."

"I don't know about that," Mildred said.

"I do," said Paisley. "You giving my father the farm for all his work, his years and years of work"—she was speaking faster, tapping her index finger against her thumb, a run of eight, then another—"for taking care of the cows and fixing that milker over and over and for haying and raising the new barn a few years back and everything else he's done here. And you've been saying how fed up you are with farming and that this would be the perfect time, any day now, to give it to my dad, and I just think that you getting ready to give my father the farm is…fair. You know? You made this deal, a long time ago, and some people might have pretended they didn't make that deal, or would have pretended to forget, but you're not like that. You're known for your deeds and your actions. Like the Bible says, faith without works is dead."

A thin plume of Mildred's smoke drifted toward the faded curtains.

Bring it home, Paisley.

"I want to be just like you when I grow up," Paisley said. "And so even though I love birding—birding is my life, and I would give anything to keep this notebook that belonged to basically the founding father of Confederation—I love my dad more, and if you passed him your farm now, I'd give you the notebook, so you could open your store in Kingston. People would come from, you know, far and wide to see the notebook. There would be so much—"

"Buzz," said Mildred. The grandfather clock, a major auction purchase last summer, ticked quietly: *tick, tock, tick, tock.* The pendulum swung. A breeze came through the dining room window and made the lace curtains flap.

Mildred butted out her cigarette and took off her apron. "Let's go," she said. "I'd like to see this notebook right now."

But Paisley didn't move. "So when do you think you might tell my father? About the farm?"

"Well…" said Mildred.

Paisley stared at the tablecloth. Each lace flower had eight holes for petals. She wanted to be far from this moment, from Mildred. But she focused on the eight holes and waited.

Mildred considered. "I know he's been waiting a long time," she said, "and I can see you need the help, you and your dad. You need a fresh start, and I do, too. I've got enough collected.in the way of excellent antiques—there's even more at the back of the tractor shed, did you know? Boxes and boxes. And what with this one very precious thing, I can see making a go of it. So I think I'm ready. What do you say we get our boots on and go? I can drive."

"We don't have to go anywhere," said Paisley, trying to contain her excitement. "I've got it here."

"The ladies at the antique shop where I sell my pieces, they're not going to believe it. Sir John A.'s notebook. I don't mind telling you, that does not come along every day."

"No, it doesn't," said Paisley, intoxicated by guilt and happiness.

Way to go, Del would say. *Take the bull by the horns. Even when her name is Mildred Mickie.*

NOW

Of course, she still had to deal with Garnet. Mr. Bertram's Alzheimer's had not improved and he'd been moved to a palliative care facility in Kingston. Garnet was the only one familiar with Paisley's file. He offered to pick her up at the Kingston train station and drive her to the island, given she didn't have a vehicle of her own. That was friendly.

Suspiciously friendly.

Paisley opened several boxes and could find no decent clothing. She dug out one pair of jeans that had never fit right and found that now, apparently, they did—one benefit of all the stress, at least. The jeans weren't her style really; a salesgirl had insisted she buy them one Boxing Day sale because they showed off her "great ass."

She packed Hu's old parachute bag with Amherst Island papers, documents, maps, her father's expired passports and driver's licences, anything she'd kept related to back then, including Eudie's box of letters, and, of course, her birding stuff, and carried it with her on the train to Kingston. She brought it all along in case...in case she needed it for the lawyers. Or in case they bulldozed Dale Manor pre-emptively. She was numb with indecision about the letters, about the house, about Garnet, about what she should do this minute, and the next, and the next. No amount of counting took away the doubt.

Garnet was there on the platform, as promised. This time he was much more casual: faded jeans, suede boots, a bulky Irish cable sweater over a white T-shirt.

"Hey."

Her mouth was dry. "Hey." She followed him to the parking lot.

"My car's just over here. Insanely warm, isn't it? I'm overdressed."

He held the door open for her, then came around to the driver's side. Before he got in, he pulled the thick sweater over his head. The T-shirt rode up a bit, and Paisley saw the definition of the bone above his right hip and the muscles on the side of his torso. She felt out of it, like everything was happening in slow.motion. She gripped the car door handle for support.

THEN

Hu grinned from ear to ear as their truck flew along the road toward the ferry. Paisley dared to grin, too.

"Yes!" he exclaimed again, and Paisley burst out laughing. "Imagine, Paise, imagine how different our lives'll be in just two months. Two months it's going to take Mildred to move to her daughter's in Kingston, and the farm will be mine. Finally, finally. I just can't believe it."

"Me neither," said Paisley, and that was the truth. She had to pinch herself hard that she had done this very brave thing. Yes, she'd told a lie about the notebook's provenance. But Mildred Mickie had bought it. Paisley pinched her thigh harder to punish herself. Thing was, though, Mildred had always said the farm was going to be theirs. Paisley had just sped that along.

She looked out at the fields where cows grazed lazily, swishing at flies with their tails. It all looked different. She felt more a part of it now. The island was theirs, a kingdom—a very small kingdom, but a kingdom nonetheless. She imagined what it would be like to wander about the Mickie farm as if it were hers. She imagined the farm doubling in size, with several farmhands, not just Stanley but others, too, making it more profitable than ever. Eudie would be so impressed with Hu and his business sense that she would promise never to kiss Reverend Willis ever again, and it would all work out perfectly. Paisley liked perfectly. It was a mathematical problem that had the same number on either side of the equal sign, like this:

$$x = x$$

A very satisfying image to behold.

"What should we do?" Paisley said. "I mean, right now?"

"I dunno, but something good. What do you think?"

She had six ideas at once: dinner in Napanee at Wong's Chinese and Canadian Food; anything you wanted at the

Paper and Supplies store; ordering a new outfit from the Sears catalogue window in Bath; tickets to the movies with an extra-large bag of popcorn sopping with butter; a bowl of milk for every barn cat; a great book to read with Hu on Mildred's wraparound porch. Their wraparound porch.

Paisley felt instant guilt at not including Eudie in this list. Churlish child, only ever thinking of herself. Eudie had once made her look that up: *churlish*. It meant sullen or ill-bred. Paisley said four eights to undo her churlishness and amended her list: Hu, Paisley, and *Eudie*, enjoying chicken balls smothered in bright red sweet-and-sour sauce at Wong's.

"So?"

"I don't know, Dad, you choose."

"I say Wong's." The ferry was in sight, about halfway across the Bay of Quinte. Hu patted his pants pocket. "Rats. Left my wallet at Mildred's."

He pulled a U-turn and sped back up the Stella 40 Foot and across the third concession. "We'll still make this ferry, don't you worry," he said.

They pulled back into the Mickie farm. Mildred's truck was gone—Stanley must be out, running an errand—but Eudie's car was parked in its spot in the driveway. The smiles disappeared from their faces.

Hu strode inside. Paisley followed. No one was in the kitchen. Two applesauce cakes sat on a wire rack, cooling.

"Eudie?" Hu called out tentatively.

They heard a smash. Hu broke into a run, Paisley right on his heels.

The dining room and parlour floors were covered in shattered crystal and china. Mildred stood, terrified, her back to a wall. Eudie stood amid the shards—in one hand a Royal Doulton china lady in a purple hoop skirt selling balloons, in the other a dagger-like piece of crystal—her hands bloody, eyes wild.

"Eudie!" said Hu. He tried to approach.

"Stop!" She threatened him with the crystal.

"What's going on?"

"The bitch has been killing the cats!"

"What? Eudie, for God's sake—"

"I came here to drop a letter to Paisley. I was in love with Arden. She made him take a leave from the island, and I wanted her to know why that was her fault."

Mildred's eyes widened at that one.

"So I drove over here, but the damn mailbox was taped shut. I had a letter to deliver. I'm allowed to have my thoughts, so I marched up to the house to give it to Paisley directly, make sure she hears my opinion on things. I have opinions on things! But the house was empty, so I went to the barn. And Mildred was out there, cooking the cats. I mean, Jesus Christ."

"The cats are wild, Eudora," said Mildred. "Pests!"

"Paisley came to me plenty of times after her visits to this awful place and asked me, 'Mum, where have they gone, all the barn cats I just named?' And I always said, 'The fields, Paisley, the fields, because that's where barn cats go when they disappear.' That's the only answer I could think of. I grew up with cats. I'd save them from the alley behind our house and nurse them back to health and then find them a home or even keep them—at one time I had five—and, of course, there was always my special cat, France. And those cats stuck right by me, so yes, it's different here on an island, cats come and go. I told Paisley that. Barn cats are wild and you can't keep a wild thing in. They're not meant to be tamed. But they weren't disappearing at all. She's been killing them."

"This is absurd," said Mildred. "Eudora, put down the Royal Doulton. She belongs to me."

"You don't deserve her," said Eudie. She threw the figurine to the floor. The lady's purple hoop skirt broke into several pieces. Her balloons shattered.

Mildred cried out like a wounded animal. "Hu, do something!"

Eudie grabbed a small stack of antique teacups and saucers, pink posies delicately painted over the lips, and threw them to the floor. "Go ahead, Mildred," she said. "Tell them about the cats."

Mildred seemed so weak and frail, standing there, her pastel floral blouse tucked into elastic pants under a worn apron.

"The cats, Mildred, and what you're doing with the rain barrel and the barbecue."

Mildred's lip quivered, which made her chin pucker in an unattractive way. Kids looked sad when they cried, thought Paisley. Adults looked pathetic.

"I was dealing with a farm problem."

Eudie swept every last dish off the dining room table. Cups, saucers, oval vegetable dishes, ornate candy dishes, the Sir John A. MacDonald ashtray, all to smithereens.

"The barbecue!"

"I didn't want to have to take them to the dump," said Mildred. "Or leave them in the manure pile where someone might see them."

"Oh Jesus," said Hu.

He understood. Paisley wished she did. She was having trouble taking it all in. She couldn't imagine what the farm cats had to do with the barbecue, which was famous for being where Mildred cooked her homemade sausages and hamburgers for family reunions and picnics.

Hu turned to Paisley. "Go up to your room."

"Your room?" said Eudie. "She doesn't live here, Hubert. Don't let her live in this place. Mildred's been cooking the cats, for God's sake—those poor little cats." She choked on her own words.

Paisley felt the strength drain from her extremities.

Eudie walked over the shards, *crunch*, *crunch*, as she headed for Paisley. Hu grabbed at her, and Eudie lashed out at him. The glass she was holding caught his cheek and drew blood. They fought. His face was a grimace. She spat and screamed, thick tongue hanging out, bloody hands scratching at anything within reach.

Paisley turned and fled outside. She ran across the tall grasses to the barn door.

1 2 3 4 5 6 7 8

Into the barn and through the milking parlour, past a dozen cows, their tails swishing, past the medium-size calf pens, to the back pen, the empty pen. But there wasn't a cat to be found, not a one, so she retraced her steps, out the barn door and around the barn, fast, like the wind.

Please, God. Please.

1 2 3 4

There it was, the barbecue, made from an oil drum cut lengthwise, the metal grill off to the side, small wisps of smoke still rising up into the air. And next to it, near the rain barrel, a half-open garbage bag and a cage—the kind you use to catch raccoons—holding a pile of wet barn cats. Limp bodies, necks flopped at unnatural angles.

5 6 7 8

One tiny kitten, burned to a crisp, lay right on the fire in the barbecue. Beneath it, a tall pile of ashes in the drum, mixed with bones.

Paisley lay still under the afghan. She watched a spider crawl through the August light, up the wall, and into a corner, to wait patiently for its prey. It was both impressive and dangerous. Spiders were not insects but arachnids: insects had three pairs of legs and three body segments, whereas spiders had eight legs and two body segments.

1 2 3 4 5 6 7 8

What else had eight legs? Scorpions, also arachnids. Four legs? Mammals—but not all. Human beings once walked on all fours.

The cluster flies in the window were quiet now; they always were at night. Flies were insects and, like all insects, had three parts to their bodies—a head, thorax, and abdomen—and six legs.

Cats had four legs.

Two legs: human beings, yes; birds; kangaroos and meerkats—but only to lift themselves and sniff the wind. Otherwise, meerkats and kangaroos had four.

The cats.

Paisley pulled the cover up to her eyeballs. How to stop the thoughts? Hu's bed was empty; he was downstairs talking to Mildred. Del had already taken Eudie back to their house. Paisley was to do her math puzzles, read a book, and put herself to bed.

She listened to the sound of glass being swept up and voices.

"Just unacceptable..." said Mildred. Her voice was tight, like a stretched elastic band.

"I know," said Hu. "So sorry...not herself."

"I take care of my farm!"

More crystal and china being swept up—tinkling like a wind chime.

"I know, Mildred."

"My Royal Doulton lady. My crystal decanter!"

"...repay you for the damage."

"No way...the farm..."

The sweeping stopped.

"The farm?" Hu's voice tight now, too.

Paisley strained to hear Mildred's answer. Nothing, too low. Then she heard the door slam. She threw off the afghan and ran to the window to see Hu get into his truck and drive off.

Paisley was alone with a lady who drowned and cooked cats, one spider, and a bevy of flies.

She counted flies in the window (twenty-eight), the squares in her blanket (sixty-four), the circles in the rag rug. She wasn't sure they each counted as a separate circle, given it was all the same braided rag sewn together, but...

Forty-seven. An uneven number.

Where was her father?

She counted again.

NOW

They took the Bath Road west toward the Amherst Island ferry. The houses along the waterfront had changed. No longer the 1970s split-levels from Paisley's childhood, they were bigger, more opulent, with landscaped gardens, circular driveways, and SUVs parked out front. Tulips and crocuses dotted flower beds.

"Things are different," said Paisley.

"Yeah," said Garnet. "When was the last time you were around?"

"I was eighteen. So…1986?"

"In all those years, you've never come back?"

"There wasn't really a point."

"I suppose not."

She turned back to the window. She wasn't interested in going over her history. Their history.

"Do you go back?" she asked.

"Not really. Except for funerals, that sort of thing."

"Who's died?"

"Who hasn't is more the question. This year and last year alone, Cory Fancy…Prue Bellechamps, Able Notham… Rory Whit. Remember him? Weren't you two friends?"

"Yup," said Paisley. "He was good to me. Stuck with me through thick and thin. We used to— He patrolled the roads, you know, kept the island safe, at least in his mind. So we walked together. And I was a birder, so…"

Too much information. Stop opening your stupid mouth. This was the kind of thing Garnet used to crucify her for.

"I remember."

She waited for the axe to fall. It didn't.

"You were saying?"

Was this safe?

1 2 3 4 5 6 7 8

"We were birders together. We went birding."

"Ever find any good birds?"

"Nope."

They were nearing the ferry dock.

"How'd he die?" she said.

"Silo gas got him, I think. They printed his obit in the Kingston paper."

"I'm sorry I didn't know. I would have written his parents. I...I'm sure I look like an awful person."

"I don't think so," said Garnet. "I think everyone understood the circumstances around your—you know—departure."

Circumstances. Now there was a lawyer's word for crap.

"So you're a lawyer," she said.

"I know, it's nuts. Even I wouldn't have guessed. I was destined for jail for sure."

Paisley nodded just enough so he'd know she'd heard, but not enough so he'd think she was agreeing with him.

"Very polite of you not to comment," he said. "I was a disaster. Everyone knew it: me, my parents, the teachers, you for sure. Back then, I was a shit disturber of monumental proportions. I actually hold a PhD in shit disturbing. Not sure you were aware."

Paisley stole a look at him. He stole a look back.

"At least you accomplished something," she said.

Garnet chuckled.

"I have my PhD in..."

"Fretting?"

She laughed. "Fretting, yes. Back then, I was a junior achiever. Now I'm actually the Fretter Laureate of the Commonwealth, though I don't like to flaunt it."

"How considerate of you."

"I also hold a master's in being considerate."

"That it? Doesn't sound like you're applying yourself."

He turned into the parking lot for the three-thirty ferry. The boat was disgorging cars from the island. Those waiting in line to board had already started their engines.

"How is it that islanders always arrive within two minutes of the ferry, no matter where they're coming from?"

"It's a very good question, actually," he said. "I should put it on my CV under special skills."

"Yeah. Shit-disturbing lawyer who can get to the ferry on time. You'll have the opposing counsel trembling in their boots." They smiled at each other. Paisley instantly regretted it. Don't let him in too much.

Guided by the deckhand, Garnet parked on the ferry deck, leaving only an inch between his licence plate and the bumper of a pickup truck in front of him. The truck bore a decal that read *Farmers Feed Cities*. They took the stairs to the ferry's upper level.

On the upper deck, a breeze came off the bay and she gave up trying to make her hair behave. Garnet didn't seem to mind the wind against his bare arms. He had a tattoo on his right bicep in the shape of Ireland. Another island, and, if she thought about it, one that also looked a little like a squid, but less so than Amherst Island. She hadn't felt that breeze for a long time and willed herself to enjoy it rather than feel awkward about the silence between them. They looked out and around and avoided eye contact.

"What do you do in Toronto?" he asked. "For a living, I mean?"

"I work at the ornithological archives."

"Ah, because you're a birder. Do you like it?"

"I do. It's probably not enough, but, you know."

"In what sense?"

"In the grand sense of 'making something of myself.'"

"Oh, that old chestnut. I think that's overrated."

"Do you like being a lawyer?"

"Nope. Mostly hate it, actually."

"You must make good money."

"Sure, but it just accumulates in my bank account. I don't own a house, I don't have expensive pastimes, and my parents are gone, so I don't have anyone to spend it on really. Being a lawyer is mostly about pushing paper. And arguing with people. If that's what you'd call making something of myself."

"Winning cases, that's not something?"

"I suppose. But not much of it is meaningful. You take care of a file, finish it up, and you turn around and you're facing a stack of files just like that one. A magical stack of not very interesting files that just keeps replenishing itself."

"What else would you do if you had a chance?" she asked.

"The million-dollar question."

A herring gull (*Larus argentatus*) coasted effortlessly by on a gust of wind. Gulls were known to stamp their feet in a group to imitate rainfall, which would bring earthworms to the surface. Or drop mollusks onto rocks from up high to break open their shells. They were both smart and carefree. Carefree sounded pretty good to Paisley right about now.

"I've thought about going back to Ireland, although it's a little late for my esteemed football career."

"I might be responsible for that," said Paisley. "You didn't go that summer because of me."

"I didn't go that summer because of *me*," he said, looking at her straight-on.

She broke his gaze and looked down to a thin ledge on the boat's side where people had thrown pennies. They glinted in the sun, and the thick grey-blue water rushed past them.

"So if not soccer, what would you do in Ireland?"

"I could pass the bar there, although it would take time. I could do sports law, but that would still be pushing paper. I could offer legal advice for some kind of youth agency. Or...I don't know. I could...insert great idea here. I think of things and then talk myself out of them. I'm a bit stuck."

"I have no idea how that feels." She could tell they were both smiling without looking at him. "Does your family still own land there?"

"Some. A few uncles and aunts. They'd probably take pity on me until they found out—"

"—what a shit disturber you are."

He patted his heart in a mockery of cinematic romance. "Aww. You get me."

Paisley looked out the front of the ferry to the island. The dock. The farms and houses on the north shore. A silo.

"How's your brother?" Paisley asked.

"Shawn? I visit him in the Kingston Pen every Wednesday and Sunday."

"Oh, no."

"Oh, yes. Around the time I scared myself straight, Shawn fell in with a gang, got into B and E's, some bad shit. His common sense meter was broken. So when he got in with those new guys, and he didn't have me around to tell him where the line was and when not to cross it, he took the fall. He has three years left. I'm not sure he'll ever get out, actually. He may just be better in there, with the right people telling him what to do."

"I'm sorry."

"Yeah, me too. I didn't help him when I could have. One of my many regrets."

"We could start our own gang," said Paisley. "The gang of regrets."

"I'd have to be the leader."

"No way," said Paisley. "I'd fight you for it." She paused. Too risky? "I take it back," she said. "I'd never in a thousand years fight you for anything."

"I don't know," he said. "I think, after all these years, you might give me a run for my money."

"Maybe I'd settle for second-in-command."

"Are there dues for this gang of regrets? This…"

"Gang of regrets and sorrows?"

"This gang of regrets, sorrows, and apologies."

"Gang of a long list of very bad things."

"Pithy," he said. "I was actually going to add 'eloquence' to our gang name, but that's a bit over the top."

This trip was not going the way she'd thought it would.

THEN

Paisley awoke to find the other bed still empty and the window buzzing with flies. They weren't very bright, buzzing up and down the same closed windowpane all day long, looking for a way out. Even if you lifted the sash right up, they still almost never made it to freedom. Why, if given the choice, didn't they leave, fly away, go somewhere else where there was food and safety? Why did they stay in the same place, moving an inch or two up, and an inch or two down, never ever going anywhere?

Paisley dressed and tiptoed down the stairs (fourteen). She stepped up onto the first step and back down again (sixteen, a better number). Her dad wasn't there. Maybe he had gone home to check on Eudie. Maybe they'd talked all night and worked things out. Maybe he'd cared for her wounds and she'd apologized for smashing all of Mildred's things. The living and dining rooms looked better now—less cluttered—though Paisley decided not to share that thought.

The kitchen was empty, but a bowl of porridge was on the table. Paisley assumed it was hers.

What if it wasn't? Maybe it was Mildred's.

It wasn't Stan's. He ate at four, before chores. And he preferred molasses on toast to porridge, being originally from Newfoundland. That much Paisley knew.

Should she eat it?

She sat in the chair in front of the porridge for a good five minutes. She counted squares on the tablecloth beneath its protective thick plastic sheet.

The auction clock *tick*, *tock*ed from the hallway. The pendulum swung slowly. Mildred loved that clock. Paisley was glad it had survived.

Twenty-five squares up the side of the table by...fifty-three along the length of it. That equalled...

Should she eat the porridge?

Where was everyone?

How would she get to camp? It was week two, arts and crafts.

Mildred came in the back door. "That breakfast is for you, Paisley. Eat up, then I'll drive you to camp."

The porridge was stone cold and too salty. A little skin had formed over its hilly regions, no brown sugar in sight. Paisley ate it all anyway. Then she went out to the car.

The bench seat in Mildred's station wagon had a spring that jabbed into Paisley's bum; she bore every pothole and bump with a cringe. Between them, on the vinyl upholstery, was something in a plastic bag. They passed Rory on the road, out for his first walk of the day. He waved. They waved back.

"I'm sorry about yesterday," said Mildred, staring up the road as she drove. "That's nothing for a child to see."

Paisley nodded.

"You may think I'm horrible," said Mildred, "but I've opened my doors to you and your father. I always had a sense about him, what a good man he was, so I offered him a job. I cooked him meals, he tended the farm... It's been a good arrangement. Because after Mr. Mickie died, I was all alone."

Paisley stared at her feet. A piece of plywood under them covered a hole where the floor had rusted out. Around its edges, she could see road speeding along under the car.

"I know what I'm talking about," Mildred said. "You're only a child. You haven't lived yet. You don't know how complicated life can be."

Paisley was pretty sure she did.

"What I do think you understand, I hope, is life on a farm, how it's important not to be overrun with wild things, wild animals, that might carry disease. That's all. I was tending to my farm."

Here's what Paisley knew: tending to your farm was one thing. Cruelty to small, beautiful, living, soft things was another.

"What you also won't understand, because you're so young and you haven't really lived, is that sometimes things change. Yes, you and I discussed an arrangement yesterday about the farm, but now all that's different. Things were said, horrible things I won't stand for. A person has her dignity. I'm going to keep my farm, see what it's worth on the open market, when I'm good and ready to sell."

Paisley went numb. They pulled up at the school just as Mr. Chadwick rang the bell. The kids streamed inside.

"Hurry up now," said Mildred. "You don't want to be late on top of everything else. Oh, and here." She passed Paisley the plastic bag. "It's Sir John A.'s notebook. It wouldn't be right for me to keep it."

Paisley took the notebook and pried herself from the vinyl seat. If Del were in this situation, she'd take her own sweet time. So Paisley left the car door open as she put the notebook in her knapsack and zipped it back up, collected her lunch bag, then retied one shoelace and the other, as Mildred looked on impatiently, fingers tapping the steering wheel.

"For God's sake, Paisley, are you slow? No wonder you and Rory get along."

Paisley slammed the car door. A small act of rebellion but one nonetheless.

Camp offered no solace. Arts and crafts seemed inane. Paisley's mind was elsewhere, everywhere, nowhere. Mr. Chadwick sensed something was wrong and offered to face her in chess. She declined, though it had pleased her many times before to checkmate him. She wasn't in the mood.

Garnet wasn't there, playing hooky no doubt, and Shawn had no courage without his leader. Sonya made a couple of attempts to strike up a conversation—thinly veiled efforts to drill for personal information—but Paisley found a way out each time. She counted eights and counted eights and counted eights some more.

After camp, no one came for her. Shawn told a couple of boys that Garnet was at the volunteer fire station helping to build a new outhouse because he'd been caught painting cocks and balls on the island's yellow fire truck. Shawn said he thought he'd wander over and rub it in a little. Paisley was sure that'd earn him a beating from his brother. Shawn seemed a little like a cluster fly: none too bright.

The girls with braids whispered about Paisley for a while but then scurried home for an early dinner because it was a 4-H night, and all girls with braids did 4-H. Eventually, Paisley was left alone. She read through June's notebook, and then, when her father still hadn't shown up, she started walking down the school's driveway.

On the way back to the farm, Paisley counted every step. She estimated that the walk might be around seven thousand steps or more, hard to tell.

"Paisley, honey, get in."

It was Hu in the truck. He was wearing the same clothes as yesterday. His shirt still had Eudie's blood on the front. Paisley wondered who else had seen it. What had they thought? A nosebleed? A bar fight? She climbed in.

"You didn't have to walk," Hu said. "I was coming to get you."

"Oh."

"I stayed at Walter's last night, in Napanee. I'm sorry I didn't call to let you know."

His breath smelled of liquor and onions. Spicy. He had stubble on his cheeks and neck. He pulled back onto the road, gathering speed as they headed up the Stella 40 Foot.

"Are we going to Walter's tonight?"

"No, honey, there's no room for two, plus it's too far from camp, isn't it?" He coughed up phlegmy bits and spat out the window.

"So where are we staying then?"

Hu turned onto the third concession. They passed Ethel's place—Ethel who played bridge with Del and Eudie. She was out weeding her vegetable garden and waved, then watched the truck pass. When one of the bridge women saw anything, interpreted anything, it got around. It wouldn't be long now. The bridge ladies would be first, church second, the Women's Association after.

"I'm working a few things out," said Hu. "I need a little time."

"Time for what?"

"For everything."

"So where are we staying?"

"I'm going to leave you with Mildred for a short while, Paisley—"

"No. Please, Dad. I'll be good, you won't even notice I'm there."

"She's a good lady."

Paisley was praying not to cry. Please don't make me one more thing my dad needs to take care of. Please let me be invisible. Please don't make me stay by myself with a cat killer.

"I have no choice, Paisley. Walt lives in a one-bedroom apartment. I'm on the couch. Where would you sleep?"

"So let's both sleep at Mildred's."

Or at Walter's. Her on the floor, in the bathtub, quiet as a mouse.

"Mildred's changed her mind about the farm. I need to find work and a place for us to live." At the bottom of the driveway, he pulled to the side of the road. Not even one foot, one wheel, on Mildred Mickie's property.

"I can help you look."

"It's grown-up work."

"I'm grown-up. I can read the newspaper for apartments and job ads."

"Mildred's a good cook, at least, Paisley. She'll feed you while I'm sorting us out. Your mum's not right. She needs time to get better, so I think you know you can't stay at our place. Now, off you go. I'll be back soon."

One sob escaped.

"Get out, Paisley, please. Don't make this any harder than it is."

"I want to stay with you. You can't make me go!"

"Don't you think I'm upset, too?" Hu yelled. "Don't you think I've worked my whole life for this farm, and spent every last bit of energy making your mother happy? I can't take this now, Paisley. You have to be strong. I need to figure things out."

"No, I can be with you. I'll be so quiet, it'll be like—"

Hu got out of his side and walked around the truck. He was crying, too, but trying to cover it up. He opened Paisley's door. She reached for the steering wheel and held on tight. He got her by the waist and yanked, pulling so hard her hip bones hurt. He carried her, flailing about and crying, and deposited her on the driveway on all fours. Paisley scrambled back toward the truck, gravel cutting into her knees.

"Please don't leave me, Dad, please!"

Hu picked her up and deposited her farther from the truck. "Stay there."

Then he walked back to the truck for her knapsack, dropped it on the ground, shut the passenger door, got in the driver's side, and peeled away. He didn't look back. Like she wasn't even there. Like she didn't exist.

NOW

The ferry pulled up to the island dock and squeezed the massive tires that cushioned the side. The deckhand threw the hawser onto the bollard and the passengers got back into their cars to unload.

The island looked exactly the same to Paisley. As they pulled off the ferry, an old guy in overalls was changing the plastic letters on the sign at the dock. It read, *AI Men's League Auction, May 17, $1 hot dogz* and *Fish Fry @ School, May 22 c/o Rec Committee*.

At the four-way stop, a car raced past them to get into the ferry lineup. A truck looking a little worse for wear was parked outside the Country Store.

"Uh-oh. Rush hour on Amherst Island," said Garnet. They could see, to the right, that the public school had a fresh coat of paint. The Canadian flag outside its front doors flapped in the wind.

"I have acid reflux just looking at that place," said Garnet.

"Me too."

"Because of me, I'd wager."

"Tell me something I don't know."

He laughed, so she laughed, too. For once it seemed easy to talk about the pain of her youth.

Garnet turned east on Front Road and continued past tiny Centennial Park, past clumps of fragrant purple and white lilac bushes.

"I meant to ask," he said. "Did you find another apartment in Toronto?"

"I did."

"Great. Where?"

Her mind drew a blank. He noted the pause.

"Not that you need to tell me," he said. "But I should have a forwarding address—the firm should, I mean—in case we have paperwork to send you."

"I'll send it along when I have it." Oh God.

"Haven't you moved yet? I thought the eviction was May 15."

"It is."

He drove. Here it was. The moment she revealed how well and truly fucked she was.

"I haven't found another place. I lied. I don't have another apartment."

Garnet took this in stride. "Seems like a good time to check out your mother's house then."

"Right."

One step at a time.

"Maybe you can live here," he said. "And if not, you can put it on the market and buy something in Toronto."

"My thinking, too," she said.

See? He'd had the same idea. This was going to work out.

"And in the meantime, I'll just crash on a friend's couch." As if.

"Cool," he said. "You'll sign the paperwork, I'll hand over the keys, and we can make the five o'clock boat if you like."

They drove in silence. Islanders were out waking up their gardens, gently pulling the piles of last year's leaves away from the daffodils, pruning the bushes for new spring growth. Gardeners looked up from their work and waved at the car, a few squinting as if trying to recognize them. Garnet and Paisley both waved back on instinct.

In one field, a horse grazed, its tail swishing. In another, beef cattle stood in the warm sunshine.

They turned into her family's driveway. Her breath caught in her throat. Garnet drove down the bumpy lane full of potholes and crowded in on both sides by dense lilac bushes.

He pulled up in the tall grass and turned off the engine.

They stared out the windshield at the property. It was wildly overgrown. Hu's shed was almost completely collapsed. The house was the definition of ramshackle. All the windows were broken. The roof was down to tar paper in places, and moss covered what few shingles were left. The porch was rotten; she could count several broken planks of wood. The back door stood wide open.

"Maybe we don't need the keys," said Garnet.

Paisley was incapable of moving.

"You okay?"

"I'd say not really, no."

"Why don't I take a look around? Okay?"

She nodded.

Garnet got out of the car and made his way to the back porch. He picked where to step so his foot wouldn't go through the rotten wood, approached the open door, and disappeared inside.

Paisley counted a set of eight. Get a grip, she told herself. Get a fucking grip. Eudie isn't here, it's just you. You're an adult. You can do this.

What was she going to do? This property had been her last chance. A part of her had thought she might be able to live here. She had under a week before Dale Manor would be torn down. Her apartment was still full of things. She had nowhere to go. She had nothing. And yet, maybe there was freedom in nothing. You couldn't get any lower, could you? This was it, the proverbial rock bottom. The be-all and end-all. What they talked about: the big test.

A dragonfly landed on the windshield. It had a bright green thorax. A green darner. Paisley knew a little about them only because they migrated, like birds. Odd. Small, seemingly insignificant beings with tiny, tiny brains but big enough instinct to migrate from one place to another to survive. She'd heard you could see flocks of them at Sand-banks, not too far from here—Prince Edward County. A flock of dragonflies? That seemed like the wrong word to use. A swarm? A hovering?

Garnet reappeared.

"No lions, tigers, or bears," he said from the doorway. "Not even cats."

"No cats?"

"Not a one. Little shits got the house and didn't even have the decency to stay."

Get out of the car, Paisley told herself.

Garnet stepped off the porch and strolled back to her. His movements were smooth, as if he didn't want to startle her.

"What do you figure?" he said, standing by her car door.

"I haven't quite... I don't know actually. Please don't make fun."

"I won't. I'd like to think I've learned my lesson." He picked a few bright yellow dandelions. "We don't actually have to do anything. I can spring for a Creamsicle at the store and we can hang out at the dock until the five o'clock comes. Or we can wait around here awhile longer—see if I can make one of those dandelion crowns."

"Don't you have to get back to work?"

"I took the day. You're one of our most important clients."

She smiled despite herself. "I'd like to see if I can get out of the car. I just need...a moment."

"Sure."

Garnet pulled his sweater out of the back, grabbed a blanket from the trunk, and stomped on a circular area of grass until it was flattened.

"Look, Ma, a crop circle!" he said. He put down the blanket, pulled off his boots, rolled up his sweater to make a pillow, and lay down, picking another dandelion nearby and twirling it between his fingers.

A male red-winged blackbird (*Agelaius phoeniceus*) flew past, showing off its sleek black plumage and bright-red-and-yellow epaulettes. Paisley could hear the waves lapping out of sight at the shore...a motorboat passing...cars driving along Front Road. Every time her thoughts flitted back to Eudie or Hu, she tapped out a series of eight on the dashboard. It was almost hot in the car. Summer hot. She heard nothing from Garnet for quite a while. The silence made her a little braver, and she eventually coaxed herself out of the car.

There. That wasn't so bad.

The house truly was a wreck. She looked at Garnet stretched out on the blanket. His T-shirt wasn't tucked in. She could see his flat midriff. He seemed like a person who was wholly comfortable in his skin. She had never once felt like that.

"You asleep?"

"Nope," he said, languid. "I'm inspecting the inside of my eyelids. You should give it a try."

He cracked open one eye and patted the blanket.

Paisley thought, oh what the hell. This was already the strangest day in recent memory. She sat beside him. He passed her the wilted dandelion. She couldn't bring herself to lie down.

"I don't think I can live here," she said.

"Nope. So what are you going to do?"

She had no answer. He didn't press. Time passed. She listened. He dozed.

Off in the distance, she heard the engine surge of the departing ferry.

"I think we missed the five o'clock," she said.

"Yes."

"I hope I'm not wasting your time."

"Because what I really want is to be back in the office, reading through pages and pages of contracts. It's true: this is a hardship."

Not even one cat on the property. Garnet was right. They were little ungrateful shits.

"So why'd you choose law?"

"Hmm. I was caught doing something stupid, and my parents by then had given up on me and walked away. So I represented myself and got off."

"Enterprising."

"Yeah, all that smart retort business of my misspent youth turned out to be good for something." He propped himself up on an elbow. "The next time I screwed up—something that really could have landed me in jail for a significant stretch—I defended myself again, and got off that time, too. But as I was leaving the courtroom, I flipped the bird at the prosecution. And the judge saw it. So he called me up to the bench, and he gave me the old fork-in-the-road speech. Except he added one thing. He said I wasn't going to believe him, but he was me when he was eighteen. Cocky, out to prove himself, a glib ass-hole. And then he robbed a variety store and everything changed. The arresting cop told him he was smart enough to beat the less-than-stellar upbringing he had and help others do it, too. And so he did. He became a lawyer and then a judge. He said to me, 'Prove there isn't just one of me in the world. Do it to flip me the bird, too, if you must. But for God's sake, do it.'"

"And you did."

"Yeah. Only I didn't do anything nearly as cool as criminal law. I stuck to family. You know, estates, wills, divorces—all the tedious stuff."

"And no soccer career in Ireland either."

"Nah. I managed to sabotage that while we were still kids. I like to make it hard on myself. What about you, in the Big Smoke?"

"Not much to report," said Paisley. "I moved away, as you know. Found an apartment. Went to University of Toronto, took me seven years to get my ornithology degree. I took classes part-time while I worked at the archives. Minded my own business, mostly. Wanted to travel and see big things, but I didn't have the courage to go alone... You know. I like to make it hard on myself."

He smiled.

"And as you can imagine," she said, "I'm a bit of a hand-ful, so I...just kept going. And here we are."

He said nothing for a second. Then he asked, "How's the counting?"

"We all have our things."

"Not I."

She laughed.

The counting and checking—plus losing her place in Toronto and the state of affairs here on the island—was out in the open. She didn't have anything else to hide. She was suddenly overcome with fatigue and lay down herself. He passed her the rolled-up sweater. She closed her eyes.

THEN

The next few nights in the blue bedroom, Paisley watched the spider catch a fly, cover it in silk, suck its blood, leave its carcass trapped in its web, then disappear and not return.

Paisley killed all the cluster flies by crushing them with the hunched feet of a porcelain squirrel figurine pilfered from the apothecary case Mildred had styled on the landing. She kept the case locked, but Paisley had seen where she hid the key. After Paisley had killed all seventy-eight cluster flies, she brushed them out onto the porch roof below and replaced the squirrel in the case, cluster-fly guts stuck to its paws.

She peed her bed one night but told no one. She stuffed the sheets into a big hole in the plaster and lathe that Mildred had hidden behind the dresser. Then she slept in Hu's bed. She slept better there.

She stole baking from the deep freeze while Mildred collected eggs before breakfast.

Arts and crafts trickled by. Paisley got out of the schoolyard as soon as possible so she couldn't be cornered and grilled about who her mother was sleeping with. She spent her afternoons walking up and down the roads with Rory, listening to his Brylcreem song or his booming version of "O Canada." He'd sing and she'd tap her thumb and index finger to the rhythm. They made quite a pair. Thank God for Rory.

When Rory wasn't around, Paisley would hover at the end of Mildred's lane, near the mailbox, waiting for Hu to come home. Counting, making deals with God—none of it summoned Hu down the gravel road, the truck kicking up dust behind it. In the evenings, she alphabetized Mildred's auction LPs. She was well into the P's. Elvis had his own section: *Blue Hawaii*, *Elvis Is Back!*, *Separate Ways*, and *How Great Thou Art*. Look at that. Elvis had an entire album named after her favourite hymn.

At dinner (Daisy's mother again, from the deep freeze—tough, but with lots of gravy), Stanley asked if Paisley wanted to play Scrabble. She declined. Then he asked if she would like to help milk the cows, but she said no thank you. She could never set foot in that barn again.

"Stop bothering the girl," said Mildred. "She's here on my good graces, but we don't have to entertain her."

"Just being pleasant," said Stanley. "There's no law against that, far as I know."

"Finish your food, Paisley, then help with the dishes. And then you can help Stan with the milking. Anyone who eats food at my table needs to pull their weight. Who knows when your father will be back, so let's at least use our time well until then."

Paisley hated Mildred. She tapped her index finger and thumb under the checked tablecloth and imagined that with each tap she was shooting the cold-hearted, greedy woman. Then she felt guilty about her evil thoughts and tapped eight more times to wipe the slate clean.

At the beginning of the third week of August, Hu appeared in the driveway. He thanked Mildred for taking care of his daughter but refused to make eye contact with her.

"Very nice of you," said Hu.

"Least I could do," said Mildred, sending them off with a dozen cranberry muffins.

Muffins, thought Paisley.

They drove back to Hu and Eudie's house to get some things. Hu had called ahead. Paisley studied him out of the corner of her eye. He had a short beard, a not-on-purpose beard, the kind Paisley imagined lumberjacks grew while in the bush. And his whiskers were silvery. She'd never noticed that before.

"I've found us an apartment in Amherstview. It's not much, but you have your own room. I painted it pink."

She hated pink but smiled anyway. She had a room.

They picked up Rory on the way, pinwheel in hand. Hu had asked him to help move some furniture.

"I'm strong, I can move furniture," said Rory, oblivious to the tension in the truck.

Outside the house, their stuff littered the lawn. Beside it sat Delilah in a lawn chair, smoking, shapely legs folded, one red heel sinking into the grass.

"That's a lot of things," Rory said.

"Sure is," said Hu, getting out of the truck. He eyed the Ratchford family dining table. Hu's grandfather had made it himself from a huge oak struck by lightning behind St. Andrew's. Scattered around it were Hu's worn recliner, the TV, old luggage, the rake and mower, books and magazines, the fishing tackle kit, a metal filing cabinet, framed photos of great aunts, paint cans and a large toolbox, Paisley's bed and stuffed toys, a few party dresses she'd outgrown, Hu's wooden shoeshine box, last year's Halloween doctor's lab coat with plastic stethoscope dangling from its pocket, and many garbage bags of clothes. What the neighbours must be saying now.

"Eudie's lost it," said Del, throwing her butt into the flower bed. "She's gone and taken everything out of the house, pretty much, as you can see, and she won't let anyone in except cats."

"Cats?"

"Meow, meow. Cats."

"Christ."

"I like cats," said Rory helpfully. "Paisley and I have barn cats, don't we, Paise?"

"Well, you've come to the right place then," said Del. "We've got 'em in spades."

In the window, a lazy calico cat eyed them between two curtains and squinted in the heat.

"Apparently, Eudie's been driving around the island picking them up from barns and fields. There are at least two dozen in there. It's quite a sight."

"Christ," Hu said again. He headed for the door.

"Don't," said Del, lighting another cigarette. "She needs some time, that's all. Told me she was the new patron saint of Amherst Island's cats, saving them from rain barrels and barbecues, and that I needed to back off. Completely crackers."

There was something vaguely exciting about having a mother go completely crackers. There was no telling what might happen next.

"We all have our moments, Hu," said Del. "Eudie's just as entitled as the rest of us. Oh, Paisley, this letter's for you."

Hu tried to intercept it, but Del yanked it from his grasp. "Now, Hu, you don't think I'm a fool, do you? I've read it. It's fine, and it's something a mother should be saying to her daughter. It's woman stuff. Let her have it."

Paisley slipped it into her pocket for later.

"Guess we'll take our things and try her in a few days," said Hu. "Should I call the doctor?"

"He was just here, and he got the big kiss-off, too. Maybe let her work it out. She says she's writing you a letter about it all."

"I bet she is."

"Paisley," said Del, "you hold tight there. Your mum's having a hard time, but you be patient. She'll spring back."

Paisley nodded. It seemed like the right thing to do.

"And she loves you," said Del, ruffling Paisley's hair. "She does."

Hu and Rory packed up the truck. Del asked for a ride back to Bath, since there was nothing to do here and she wanted off "this godforsaken rock." Rory headed back to the road to continue his mayoral walk.

"Thanks for helping, Rory," said Paisley.

"No problem, Paise. See you soon so we can count grosbeaks. Okay? Okay. Okay? Okay." He waved at her and headed up the road, pinwheel twirling.

They took the ferry back to the mainland. When they dropped Del off at the supermarket, Hu leaned out the window. "If there's anything I should know, Del, I can be reached at the plant. The apartment doesn't have a phone line yet."

Del gave a sigh.

There was only one plant in the area: the sanitation plant. It was the worst place you could work, thought Paisley. Hu must have been desperate to take a job there.

Paisley changed her mind. Having a mother go completely crackers was not exciting in the least.

NOW

When Paisley awoke, it was much later. Garnet was staring at her.

"You're tired," he said.

She sat up. "What time is it?"

"Gone seven. You had dreams. You talked."

"God. What did I say?"

"Mickie."

"Oh. Yeah. I had a dream about my dad working for Mildred. He was always there, working away, hoping she'd eventually give him the farm. Which she did—until my mother scuttled the deal."

"She had a knack for that sort of thing, didn't she?"

Paisley nodded and stretched. "Mind you, Mildred had just as much to do with it. I guess some things aren't meant to be."

So they'd missed that ferry and would have to wait another hour. Paisley felt cold.

"Use my sweater," he said, reading her mind.

"Sorry I held us up." She pulled it over her head. It was heavy. And scratchy.

"I started the nap thing. At least give credit where credit is due."

He put on his shoes and opened the car's trunk. He returned with a bag of groceries and tossed it onto the blanket. "I went shopping before I picked you up, so may I gallantly offer you a dinner of...let me see...Cheetos...Pop Tarts...Cap'n Crunch—but no milk, sorry—Ritz crackers... and Nutella."

"Curious assortment of food for an adult."

"It was all that shoplifting I used to do at the Stella Country Store. I developed a sweet tooth."

"It doesn't show." Paisley blushed as she realized what she'd said. She focused on inspecting the snacks.

"That's very kind. You too..." For the first time, his volubility seemed to fail him.

"Pop Tart or Cheetos?" Paisley asked.

"Tart me."

She tossed a foil pack his way. "Thanks for dinner," she said.

"Never say I did nothin' for ya."

"I have this house, thanks to you."

"It's a keeper."

"Might even make the cover of *House & Home*."

"What do you think you'll do with it?"

"I don't know. I'd written it off. Or forgotten about it. Or...blocked it from my consciousness. I don't know which. Never thought I'd own anything, but here we are. I'm rich, I tell you, rich!"

"I should scoop you up right away. Be a kept man."

Paisley guffawed at that one. "Actually, you're not that far off. I was with a guy once, a few years back. I met him at the archives, and, long story short, he dumped me for two reasons. One, he thought I was certifiable. He caught me counting and checking, of course."

"You should have kicked him to the curb right there."

"Oh, I did—eight times."

"Good one. And two?"

"Two, he'd mostly stuck around because he thought I was flush, what with my almost-Rosedale address."

"Tell me where he lives. I'll rough him up for you."

"Ha."

"Seriously."

She inspected his face, unsure what to think.

"No, no, I'm not serious," he said. "Sorry. I forget that irony doesn't work if you actually *were* that guy."

Paisley laughed but still felt uncertain. "I wouldn't want to be the agent of your demise," she said. "You know, be the reason you get sent to the slammer. One Mulligan there is enough, don't you think?"

"I do." Garnet finished his Pop Tart. "Want to catch the eight o'clock or hang around awhile longer?"

"What do you want to do?"

"I want to hang around awhile longer."

"Okay."

"Shall I start a fire?"

"God, no."

"Right. What was I thinking. Sorry I suggested it."

He went back into the trunk of his car and produced a six-pack of beer and a bottle of red wine. "I also hit the liquor store. Well, not *hit*. You want?"

She nodded, pointing to the wine.

They had no glasses, so she took a few sips right from the bottle. I have to be careful, she thought. She didn't want to make a fool of herself. Jesus. What was she doing here? She had no home. She had nothing to her name except a shack ready for demolition. A nothing life.

She took another swig. It gave her a bit of courage. "It's still like when I was a kid. Not just counting. Counting and checking," she said.

"Mm."

"Worrying about fire—wiring, electricals, leaving the stove on. A doubt about most things. Big things and little things. They actually call it the doubting disease. And so you come up with these rituals to ease the doubt."

"Do they work?"

"They do... Sometimes it takes longer than other times. Sometimes I don't count for a while. Months. Then it comes back. Then it calms down, sleeps a bit. It's very unpredictable."

"Sounds tiring."

"It is. I could have run a marathon with the same energy."

"Or ten."

"And there's a concern about people's safety." She was relieved to list all the things. To be transparent. "Just so you get the full picture. But I think that's about it. That's enough, isn't it? It's…very fucked up in here." She tapped her temple. "My brain works overtime. It invents stories. Creates patterns. Triangulates things that have nothing to do with each other. Will things get better if I count eight sets of eight? Will I prevent a fire if I touch each light switch and outlet eight times? Not likely. But I do it anyway."

"Don't believe everything your brain tells you."

"Wish I had that option. But it's mostly manageable. I'm very high-functioning."

"Clearly. So…no roaring bonfire to toast our Pop Tarts then." They were silent for a moment. In the absence of talk, she suddenly felt very vulnerable. "I don't know why we're even talking about this."

"We don't have to."

It had gotten dark. She'd forgotten how dark it got on the island.

"Why are we getting along?"

He laughed a bit. Or exhaled. She heard it, but she couldn't quite see his face. Was this a joke?

She stood up, uncomfortable. Exposed. Here she was with the man who had always been the most dangerous person for miles. Now she was being asked to trust that he had changed. She wanted to believe it.

"We going?" He got up, too.

"Maybe. I don't know."

"Okay."

He could feel the shift. Her emotions splayed out in the darkness.

"I can tell you why I think we're getting along," he said.

"We're not," Paisley said. "Not really." An alarm bell rang between her ears. "You're being nice, and I'm getting sucked in. I can't trust that. And I don't want any pity either. I don't need it. I got enough of that when I was a teenager— and by the way, it didn't help me one bit."

"Understood."

She stepped toward the car and opened the door. The interior light turned on. She could see his face and tried to read it. His jawline. His eyes. The way he held himself. "Or maybe you're just messing with me the way you used to. And that would be colossally crappy."

"It would. It would, in fact, make me Shitballs Mulligan, I believe, to have Del tell it."

"Are you Shitballs Mulligan?"

"I was, but I'm not anymore."

She eyed him.

"Can we sit down again?"

"I don't know." She took off his sweater in a sudden movement. "I think I have to leave."

THEN

Hu wanted Paisley to continue with week three of summer camp. She didn't want to. He needed her to go because he had shifts at the plant every day. She begged him to let her stay alone. She would behave. She was old enough—there was no reason to worry. Reluctantly, needing to work, he agreed. She didn't tell him about her nerves or her counting or her fear of fire or not sleeping right, or that she hadn't had a good poop since they'd moved to the mainland because she was worried about someone in the house next door—which was closer than any neighbour she'd had before—seeing her on the toilet. Hu didn't have blinds in the bathroom, and neither did the neighbours. She'd seen the man—he was Italian, she thought—in his bathroom shaving, and his fat wife, in her bra and big underpants, plucking hairs from her upper lip and chin in the mirror. If Paisley could see them, it was logical that they could see her, so she'd hold her poop and try to use the bathroom only after midnight with the light off. Her gut was as hard as a rock.

One Saturday, the Italian neighbours had a pig roast. The man dug a pit in his backyard and stoked the coals all morning. They built a temporary wood frame and stapled a huge tarp onto it as an awning, and the lady scrubbed down their tile patio with a brush and soapy water. People streamed in all morning, bringing dishes and homemade wine and talking in Italian. Having that many people around with an open, frequently unmonitored fire made Paisley anxious, and no amount of counting calmed her nerves, so when Hu got ready to head to the plant for his Saturday afternoon shift, she begged to come.

Hu was the second man in charge, which Paisley thought sounded quite good, but Wilson Matthews, the supervisor, was what Del would have called "a piece of work." Wilson, who was at least ten years younger than Hu, wore his hair long in front and longer in the back. The St. Andrew's Sunday-school teacher called boys with long hair hippies, and said that all hippies wanted to do was lie around all day and mooch off the government.

Wilson pulled a small purple hairbrush from the back pocket of his tight jeans and brushed his hair in the glass covering a portrait of the Queen. "Nice to meet you, Paisley. How's tricks?"

"Fine, thank you."

"Cup of Nescafé?"

"No, thank you."

"See, from a managerial point of view, offering free coffee to staff and their family members in the staff lounge makes for a tight-knit team."

Paisley hadn't been aware they were in the staff lounge. Only two people worked each shift, three shifts per day. In the fall, Hu's shift would allow him to drop Paisley off at school in the morning and pick her up in the afternoon. It was perfect, at least as far as timing went. She could see why he'd taken the job. And in addition to this being the lounge, it was also the one and only office. It held two large desks on its faded lime-green-and-yellow linoleum floor, and a map of the plant and its fire exits pinned to the fake wood panelling.

"So, you like it on the mainland?"

"Yes, just fine, thanks." Paisley didn't know any adults interested in talking to a kid except Rory. And Rory was different.

"I'll be out of here any day now, then your dad will get a promotion to supervisor. From a managerial point of view, a promotion in your first year on the job isn't bad at all."

Paisley looked at Hu. He smiled, set a pair of big yellow gloves on the edge of his desk, and tucked his coveralls into his boots.

"I'm taking plumbing in Kingston," said Wilson. "I'm apprenticing with a guy who's got too much work on his hands. Plumbers make big money, it's a well-known fact. This guy has a three-bedroom house and a car and a boat. He works for himself. See, that's the key. None of this working-for-the-man stuff."

Paisley looked at the desks again. There were only two. Where did the man sit?

"Mind you," said Wilson, examining the straightness of his part, "I'm not saying this isn't a plum job. It is. And there's no shame in supporting yourself or your family, no matter where you work. These guys I used to know when I went to Odessa Secondary, before I left in Grade 11, they'd see me in the bar and give me trouble—once they waited in the bar parking lot until I was getting into my car and they yelled, 'Shit for brains!'—excuse my French—and you can imagine what they launched my way."

Wilson went back to brushing his hair.

"Thing is, I was bringing in more money than all of them put together, because here's a nugget: not everyone wants to deal with other people's crap. But if you set your mind, focus on a goal, and don't waver—like a horse with blinders on, I see it as—then you can achieve your dreams. Whether that's with other people's shit or not."

"Think I'll take Paisley on my rounds," said Hu.

"Sorry, Hu. Shoulda watched my language there," Wilson said, sticking his comb back in his pocket. "I'm off to the main plant." And then to Paisley: "That's the hub for the county, where my boss Grant works. Me and Grant got manager-to-supervisor stuff to discuss. I'll be back after lunch."

Grant. He must be the man. Paisley was glad to have one mystery solved.

Hu offered to leave Paisley in the office to read, but she was worried Wilson might return, so she asked to come along.

She wondered if it would smell like you-know-what. She'd been amazed coming up the drive that the sanitation plant didn't look or smell like she'd thought. It was located behind a big public park that was filled with giant oak trees and beds of flowers. People rode by on their bikes, ladies walked their strollers, a bunch of kids were playing baseball on the diamond. And then they'd arrived at the fenced-in area marked *Ernestown Sanitation Station—Keep Out*.

Back outside, Hu and Paisley approached a shed. Hu went in and pulled big rubber waders over his boots and picked up a rake and pail.

He took her to a flat area where water was streaming over small cement steps. "People's used water—we call that raw—flows down the hill into our system, where it comes in through a tube and through a maze, and then the water tumbles over these little ledges in waterfalls. Our morning job is to pick away at all the big stuff that hasn't been weeded out by now."

"Like what?"

"Well, ladies' bathroom stuff. Cigarette wrappers, dental floss, the things people throw in their toilets without thinking." Hu waded into the water, picking up gunk with his rake and dumping it into the pail. Water trickled out through holes in the bottom. "It only takes me about a half-hour," he said, "so just occupy yourself, sweetheart."

Paisley could only think of how she wanted to be running around the park with her dad—or even Eudie, though Eudie had always said that taking kids to a park made her want to die of boredom. She preferred baking a pie or reading a book or some such. Plus, there were only really two parks on Amherst Island: Centennial Park, which was tiny, and one at the schoolyard, off Front Road, in the other direction. The school's swings and jungle gym were rusty. And the schoolyard reminded Paisley of Garnet and Shawn. Come to think of it, she didn't love going to the park either.

Paisley sat on a rock and wished she hadn't left her book in the office. She pulled out the letter from Eudie that Del passed her and opened it.

> *Dear Paisley,*
>
> *You are thirteen, which must feel very old to you, but I can certainly say that you were slow in the proper sense of the word because you have not yet gotten your menstrual period. You're an anxious one and sometimes that can delay things. Or maybe you have something medically wrong with you. If you don't get your period soon, you should get Del to book you an appointment with the GP in Kingston.*

It was true. She suspected every other girl in her grade had gotten her period a long time ago, and sometimes she got these pains in her right or left side, which the health movies at school said might be ovulation, but nothing ever arrived. The health movies said that stress could prevent your period from coming, like Eudie said, so she'd also tried to forget about it.

> *Unless you have gotten your period since you've been at Mildred's. But Mildred will be useless at helping you, so I'm going to tell you a few things. If you get your period, you should go to Del and Noble's supermarket. Make sure you talk to Del because it will be too awkward with Noble, for obvious reasons. She'll get you some maxi-pads and some pain relief of some kind. Take two immediately, that always seems to help me—then get the hot water bottle and hunker down—it's*

only the first two days that are bad, usually. Hopefully you're not one of the unlucky ones with cramps the whole way through. Make sure you wash your underwear right away because of the stains. Take a really hot bath, that's another way to help the cramps. Wait until the water cools down, and then throw your underpants in the water with you. It's important to wait until the water's cool because hot water sets blood stains. Then wash them by hand with soap and scrubbing, bleach for bad stains, but don't bring that into the bath, do that over the sink and don't let your skin touch it. Don't wear white, obviously, that week—but then you wouldn't wear white anyway because as I've told you before, white makes everyone look larger, especially across the rump.

And for God's sake, if you've started menstruating, don't spend any time with boys, don't let them get their way. Or you'll end up pregnant and marrying some farmer, and your life will be over.

I'm sorry I can't be there, but I'm doing important things right now and I need time. You're better off with your father anyway.

Mum

PS: The adhesive on those maxi-pads goes on the underwear, facing down—I'm being clear because sometimes you're thick about these things. If you put the adhesive pointing up, it'll stick to your pubic hair, and won't that be painful. If you have any trouble,

> *maybe Del can demonstrate, but make sure*
> *she takes you upstairs into the apartment so*
> *you have some privacy. It'd be just like Del*
> *to think it was all a big joke and show you*
> *right there in the hygiene products aisle.*

Paisley gazed at her father, knee deep in water, eddies swirling around his waders. He lifted up the rake. In its tines was a brownish bloated maxi-pad, triple its normal size. He flicked it into the bucket. Paisley folded her letter carefully and put it back in her pocket.

"Anything you want to talk about?" he asked, letting water drip out the bucket holes.

"No thanks." Periods sounded like a dirty, ugly business. Paisley hoped to never get hers.

"Your mother's getting better soon, you know," he said. "Then you can talk to her about all the things that maybe we can't."

He focused on scraping again. All that people let disappear down their toilets, down their sinks, out of sight, gone. Trapped by Hu's rake.

"Although of course we can talk about anything," he said, "even if you don't think you could. That's what I mean."

Something was caught in the rake's tines. Paisley thought it was a dead brown rat. No, it was some bloated thing with a string hanging out the back. Hu caught her looking. He hit the rake hard on the side of the bucket and the thing fell off with a *splot*.

"The fellow who had this job before me was a mechanic," said Hu. "But it got so that he couldn't stand the smell of diesel anymore, so he gave up being a mechanic and worked here. Fifteen years he worked at the plant, day in, day out, doing this job, until he couldn't stand the smell here either. He said it made his head pound. So now he's home resting. Only, his wife has to work nights at the hospital laundry, because she's afraid they'll lose the house. So he's got time off, but he's no happier. Your mother can't support us, and I looked and looked, and this is what I found. Life is not all glamour and sunshine. We do what we have to do, Paisley. There's no shame in it."

"Can you stand the smell?"

"So far."

She loved him. The solidness of him. "Me too."

I can help him, she thought. And I can help Eudie with the cats, and maybe that will make her better.

"Do you ever find something exciting?" asked Paisley.

"Not so far, but I haven't been here long. Wilson says sometimes there's lost earrings, trinkets, coins. Last week I found a keychain with a naked-lady fob on it." He smiled. "I gave it to Wilson."

He continued to search. All he found out of the ordinary was a toy train, a hairnet, four rusty bolts, and a rotting fish head. Paisley worried she might disappoint Hu by throwing up. She turned to the sky and watched the clouds float by. She hoped Eudie's cats weren't pooing or peeing in her room, marking their territory. Cats would poop or pee anywhere if they were nervous enough.

When the water had gone through the maze and over the waterfalls, it flowed through big tanks into water pits. Eventually all that was left in the tanks was sludge. While Hu was occupied pumping chlorine gas into the water pits to kill any bacteria, a big tanker truck arrived to drain the sludge from the tanks and haul it away to spray on farmers' fields. Never on crops for human consumption, Hu told her, just animal-feed crops. The driver of the tanker heaved himself out from behind the steering wheel. His belly hung way over his belt buckle, and Paisley could see the crack of his bum and the big sweat stains under his armpits. He nodded at Hu, did his job without conversation, and left, but not before holding his thumb against one nostril, blowing a long string of snot onto the grass, wiping off the last bit with his hand and flicking it away.

Hu had to clean out what was left. He turned off the stream of water down one side of the maze so it could drain, while the other side continued to flow. Then he backed up a John Deere lawn tractor with a trailer hitched to it, which they used to collect "grit."

"What's grit?" asked Paisley.

"Nothing. It's not the real name for it. It's what it rhymes with, but never you mind about that. Do you want to go back and sit in the office, pumpkin? The next part is a little stinky."

Hu straddled the maze, his feet on the grates on either side of it, and started shovelling. The water did an amazing job of containing the smell, but once you broke the surface of the sludge, the reek that came off it was worse than anything Paisley had smelled. Worse than any smell she'd made herself, or any barn she'd been in. Hu shovelled quickly into the trailer. Paisley pulled her shirt over her nose but could still smell it. Then Hu dry-heaved, and that made Paisley vomit right on the grate. She wished she'd been stronger, for his sake, but she couldn't help it. She let go entirely.

Hu took Paisley to the office and put a wet face cloth on her forehead. The air was all right in the office, but the smell on Hu's coveralls made Paisley retch some more, though there was nothing left to come up but water. He told her to stay put—he only needed a few minutes to finish—but she held on to him and wouldn't let him go. She counted, fast, over and over, in groups of eight. This time he didn't push her off like he did at the bottom of Mrs. Mickie's drive. He let her hold on to him. He refolded the face cloth so the coolest part was on her forehead and hummed a hymn. Eventually, he stopped humming, but Paisley kept counting, low, under her breath. She knew he didn't know how to make it stop. Neither did she.

NOW

"Paisley?"

"Yes?"

"Are we okay?"

"Probably."

She was still holding the car's passenger door open. Waiting to move, but not capable yet. The car's dome light shone on individual blades of tall grass by her legs.

"I get that you can't trust me. For the record, I am nothing like what I was. Or...I'm the same person, but I learned from my mistakes. And I made a lot of mistakes."

1 2 3 4 5 6 7 8

"Are you counting? I can see your fingers tapping."

"Yes, I'm counting, Garnet. Jesus. Can't a person have a bit of privacy?"

"Sure." He turned his back.

That made her laugh a bit. "I'm stressed, that's all."

"Understood. Go ahead. Don't mind me. I have all the time in the world."

She counted seven more sets of eight until the moment abated. "Sorry. It's embarrassing, really. Like wearing your underwear on the outside."

"I can wait."

"I'm done."

He turned around. Shoved his hands in his pockets.

"Were you trying to set me on fire that day?" she asked on impulse. "In the shed?"

"God, no. I wanted to scare you. I wanted you to hurt as much as I was hurting—not physically harm you. Ever. I would never do that. It was more a 'misery loves company' thing. I was horrified when the wind turned. And terrified."

"I felt pretty much the same, so you succeeded."

"Too bad it didn't occur to me how similar we were. I could have saved us both a world of grief."

"I don't think you could have saved me."

"Maybe not. But maybe I could have saved me. I seem to have to make plenty of mistakes before I fly right."

The car light threw interesting shadows on his face. His Adam's apple. His kind eyes. Her fear dissipated.

"Do you want to go then?"

She considered. "Maybe not yet."

She closed the car door. It went very dark now. Some lights on the island, in the distance. And from far-off Kingston across the water. She moved back to the blanket and sat down. Took another swig of the wine and passed him the bottle. He took it as an invitation to join and sat down with her.

"Did you know that in my bag there's a shoebox of letters from my mother?"

"The ones I sent?"

"Yeah. I've been avoiding looking at them. I thought I might know what to do with them at my mother's house. But I don't."

"What's in them?"

"Don't know. It can't be anything good."

"So why read them?"

"I don't know that either. There might be something important. I can't just throw them out. Maybe there's a...a safety deposit box number in there. Okay, probably not. But she wanted me to read them, and I've just always done that—done what she wanted. My mother told me things, and I believed her. Even as she lost her mind, I believed her—that I could do nothing right, that I was responsible for everything, especially the bad things."

"We are, after all, the two founding members of the gang of regrets, sorrows...and..."

"A long list of very bad things."

"One, two, three, four..." offered Garnet.

"Are you making fun?"

"No, just joining in."

"I haven't ever had anyone count with me."

"Can I try?"

"Are you kidding?"

"No."

Paisley paused. "Okay."

They counted in unison.

1 2 3 4 5 6 7 8

Paisley burst into laughter. "That is ridiculous," she said.

"You don't think I'm a good counter then?"

"I'd have to watch you over a period of time."

"What are the criteria?"

"You have to count well enough to make yourself feel safe, feel the switch in your head go off so you can breathe again. And what else? Save buildings from burning down and pre-empt other assorted disasters."

"So nothing too major. I might need practice," he said. "It seems like you've got the system down."

Paisley took a deep breath of Amherst Island air—she'd missed it—and gazed up. The stars were out. The sky was giant above them. "Can I have your sweater back?"

"Jesus, make up your mind," he said with fake exasperation. And then: "I'll trade it for the letters."

"What? No. They'd be terrible for you to read. You'd finally see how crazy the Ratchfords really are."

"I think we're now well acquainted with each other's imperfections." He walked to the car, got the bag, and passed it to her. Give me the letters, I'll give you the sweater."

"That's extortion."

"I do have extensive experience with the law," he said, "and you're right. This is what I propose. I'll go through them one by one. If there's something important, I'll read it out loud. If it's bullshit, I'll toss it into the fire I'm not allowed to make."

"I don't know."

"See, you're a complicated person; that's what makes you so fascinating. Your mother was another complicated person—and a complete wing nut. Those letters are the crap of life, something both you and I understand. I hope you think I'm man enough for the job."

He leaned in and put his hand on hers. It was warm. She could feel his breath on her cheek. He smelled of red wine and Pop Tarts. Intoxicating. She released her hold on the bag and let him take it. He passed her the sweater.

"I do think you're man enough," she said. "I'm pretty sure you're the only man for the job."

THEN

It was the first day of the last week of summer camp. Hu had insisted she go back because of what had happened at the plant, and he refused to leave Paisley alone. They stopped by Del's supermarket to buy sandwich ingredients for lunches—both Hu's and Paisley's.

Hu asked if there was any news about Eudie. Del glanced over her shoulder to the magazine racks, saw a lady from bridge, and took them out behind the supermarket, where, between the Dumpsters, there was a small patch of yellowed grass and a picnic bench littered with Coke bottles the employees used as ashtrays.

This past weekend, apparently, Eudie had trespassed onto Mildred Mickie's farm and stolen her barrel barbecue—the one Mildred had used to do in the cats—and tossed it into the Bay of Quinte. Cyrus from the ferry saw it floating by and fished it out for Mildred.

Del lit up and patted the bench beside her. "You know I treat you like you were my own, Paise," she said. "So I want to be honest with you."

While Del talked and smoked, Hu used his Swiss Army knife to make liverwurst and half green pepper sandwiches on Wonderbread. Eudie's excellent minced beef on homemade sourdough sandwiches were no longer.

"Your mother's going through more than a rough patch," said Del. "She's more like...in a...in a..."

"Hole?"

"Yeah. Like that. Your mother's always been two people: a real pistol, you know, a woman with fire in her belly, and also a scared girl with lots of dark thoughts she can't control."

Paisley and Del watched a starling peck at a garbage bag in one of the Dumpsters.

"It's like that," said Del, gesturing at the bird with her cigarette. "There's a bird in her head, feeding on the good thoughts until there's nothing left but scraps."

"That's a European starling," said Paisley. "*Sturnus vulgaris*. It's got a pretty advanced terrestrial feeding technique. It uses the open-bill method, sticking its bill into the ground or a garbage bag, then opening it to search for food. It's why the bird is so widespread."

"Uh-huh. Widespread's one way to describe it. We call those birds sky rats." Del took a drag. "But don't feel sad about your mum, Paisley. Life goes on, know what I mean? Think of life's opportunities. There's sunshine ahead."

The starling yanked a slimy brown banana peel out of the garbage and pecked at it.

"Do you need new socks?" Del said. "Yours are a little grubby. We have some in aisle one, near the melamine dish sets. Why not pick yourself out a couple of pairs?"

She stood up, took one last drag, and dropped her butt into a Coke bottle. It fizzled in the dark brown liquid. No chance of fire there. Probably.

Hu took Paisley to the ferry dock for the boat to the island. He passed over her lunch.

"See you after camp," he said. "Don't let that stuff Del said about your mum get to you."

How could she not? The ferry ropes were looped around the bollards three times. Seven cars came off the ferry. Paisley cast her eyes about in search of an eighth. She knew Hu needed her to go to camp. She didn't want him to worry about her on top of everything else. He had enough to worry about. "I'm fine."

"All right then."

Six people walked onto the ferry. Paisley looked around, hoping for more. Wait—one woman had a stroller with a baby. The baby made seven.

"Just enjoy yourself, and I'll meet you off the four o'clock boat. We'll go for Wong's."

She was already focused on walking over the ramp and onto the ferry to make it eight people. There. That was better.

Garnet was in the make your own comic book group, so Paisley chose the group creating children's picture books. The scandal of Paisley's mother sleeping with someone had only festered since she and her father had moved off the island. Garnet glared at her from across the classroom. Paisley focused on her project and counted eights as much as possible, tapping them out with a foot, with thumb to index finger, but nothing worked.

She wanted lunch period to come so she could escape Garnet and head off to visit Eudie. She'd hang around a bit. Eudie would see things could be normal, maybe consider accepting Hu and Paisley back in the house so Hu could give up his sanitation job. Paisley could help her father find another island farm to tend, and maybe eventually buy. It was a lot of maybes, but she could pull it off.

Paisley worked hard until first recess. Then, while everyone else was outside, she read up on health care for cats from the library trolley. She had company: Garnet was kept inside for backtalk. Shortly after they'd started writing that morning, he'd stood up to ask Miss Montgomery if he could take a piss. Miss Montgomery pretended not to have heard, so Garnet upped the ante.

"I said—"as he cast an eye around to make sure everyone was listening"—can I take a piss?"

"Garnet," she said, "you may go to the bathroom when nature calls, but 'piss' is neither polite nor correct. It is not 'take a piss,' it is 'urinate.'"

"Urinate," he responded, "but if you had better tits you'd be a ten."

The kids exploded with laughter. The younger kids didn't all get the joke but laughed anyway. Paisley was both scandalized and impressed. It took Miss Montgomery a full ten minutes to restore order.

Garnet was sent home. He gathered his things and walked to the front of the class, whispering to Paisley on the way, "Montgomery may only be an eight, but your melons make you a solid nine," which made her feel gross, bullied, and attractive all at once.

Garnet's parents couldn't come immediately to collect him, so Miss Montgomery made him sit in a chair in the corner, facing the wall.

"While you wait for your parents, you'd do well to behave," she said. "And I hope that in the meantime you don't need to urinate."

Paisley tried to concentrate on *The Big World of Cats*, while Garnet sat in the corner, jiggling his knee, picking his nose, and wiping his finger on the blackboard. One advantage to Garnet was that he pulled attention from Paisley.

At lunch, Paisley felt nauseated about visiting her mother, and at the same time strangely disconnected from it, maybe because she'd started to see her from the outside like everyone else. Paisley headed out.

Sonya approached her just outside the front doors. "We're double-dutching in the parking lot." She flipped a blond braid over her shoulder. "Want to join?"

Paisley did. Oh, she did! But she was determined. "Are you skipping tomorrow?" she asked Sonya, hopeful.

"Probably." Sonya was suddenly uninterested and already heading over to the other girls. They were scrunching their socks down to their ankles; they were tucking in their shirts; they were pulling out skipping ropes and untangling them.

Paisley had missed her chance.

Sonya stopped halfway. "I saw your mum on the Emerald 40 Foot yesterday, near my uncle Albert's. I kinda wondered who she was visiting. Any ideas?"

"Really?" said Paisley. It didn't even come close to answering Sonya's question, but not a single other response occurred to her in that moment.

"Really," said Sonya. "Who's she, you know, hanging out with?"

Paisley shrugged—what else was she going to do?—and Sonya, disappointed she couldn't own the island's hot gossip, turned and added herself to a double dutch without missing a beat.

Paisley ran. If she could see her mother, even for a short visit, she could make it back in time to skip with the girls.

On the way home, she saw two barn swallows. They were the most common species of swallow around the globe. Little known fact: the barn swallow is the national bird of Estonia. Paisley's eyes darted to the fields on either side of the road. No Henslow's sparrows to report. Of course not. Finding one of those was impossible. Something that good could never happen to a girl like Paisley Ratchford. She passed other birds but was distracted by the desire to count eights and to avoid other kids returning home for lunch. She kept her head down but felt their eyes on her nevertheless.

A girl called Marguerite interrupted Paisley's counting—never a good thing. Marguerite weighed half as much as Paisley but was a force to be reckoned with. She wore a blouse to school every day, never a T-shirt. Her hair was perfectly parted down the middle with a ponytail above each ear, little clips pinning down every stray hair, slick and smooth. Marguerite's mother was a hairdresser who ran a salon from their summer kitchen. A sandwich board at the side door read *Haircuts by Sally, at It's Best*. Sally had two lilac porcelain hair-salon sinks by her stand-up freezer and a hair dryer that lowered over your head so you couldn't hear what the lady in the next chair was talking about, though you could be fairly sure it was you.

Sally knew all the island gossip, was quite happily the hub of it, and Marguerite wiled her afternoons away eavesdropping, saving whatever she heard, big or small, to be used as ammunition.

"Hey, Paisley, who's your mum with? Give you a dollar if you tell."

Just like Sonya.

"I can't talk, Marguerite, I'm expected home for lunch." Which she wasn't.

"If you don't tell, I'll only find out anyway."

"I have to go."

Marguerite looked at her through squinty eyes. "You're a nothing, can't you see that? You count for nothing. The only way to be someone is to be interesting. This is your chance."

Count for nothing, thought Paisley. The irony.

"Didn't you hear me? Who is your mother with? I'll find out, I swear."

Then leave me alone, thought Paisley. She broke into a run for her driveway.

"You're a nothing!" screamed Marguerite.

Paisley paused at the door, breathless and sweaty, to gather her courage. Down at the shore, the ferry engines reverberated. A car raced along the road past her driveway to make the boat—it would probably be the last car on the twelve o'clock. Dust settled behind it. A rabbit hopped out of the lilac bushes, saw Paisley, and disappeared in one bound. A butterfly flitted by.

Quiet.

Then some mewing, very faint. The screen door was slightly ajar. A cat wandered out, brushing up against Paisley's legs. Another cat stared at her from just inside. And behind it were at least five or six others, variously engaged in grooming, sleeping, quietly observing.

Paisley let her heart return to a normal rate. She didn't want her voice to be wobbly or scared. "Mum?"

No answer.

She stepped tentatively into the house. It was a disaster. There were cats everywhere. Dozens of them, mewing and purring.

Eudie was cleaning up cat food from the kitchen linoleum.

"Mum?"

"Paisley?"

The cats looked up.

"Paisley, leave."

"But—"

Eudie was dishevelled and dirty like the men who lived on the streets near the Kingston Pen. Halfway between jail and freedom. She shooed Paisley away with the backs of her hands. "Hurry back to camp now."

"But, Mum—"

"Paisley, go. I'm working on something. I don't know when it will be over."

"I can help. I'm good at projects."

"This one isn't for you. Run along." Eudie's hair was oily. Her shirt had stains on it. Her feet were bare.

"But I came all this way," said Paisley, "and I know about cats."

"You have camp."

"I can be sick."

"You have your father. These cats have me. I'm saving them. I don't need you to do that."

Eudie pushed her out the screen door and shut it.

"But I could help," said Paisley.

"You're not listening! You don't belong here," Eudie said. "All I've ever been on this godforsaken island is a meal service, a maid, an indentured slave—if you don't know what that means, look it up, use your brain! So I'm putting myself first for once. Doing what I think is right."

"Please?" Paisley hated to beg. She knew it was futile.

"Go away!"

Out on the back porch, Paisley listened to another butterfly flap its wings clear as anything, each up-down discernable from the last. They came in groups of eight, so easy to count.

1 2 3 4 5 6 7 8

And while nature quietly rearranged itself into numbers, Paisley mimicked the pattern, counting her steps back to school in eights, too. Nice and tidy.

In the schoolyard, the girls had joined the boys in a game of murder ball. No one took notice of Paisley.

She passed Garnet's dad's truck parked out front. Garnet was already at the school doors. "C'mere you little shit," Mr. Mulligan yelled at him. "Get in the goddamned truck!"

Paisley kept her eyes down and approached the entrance. She ignored Garnet as she touched the door handle eight times, then tried to pull it open on the ninth, which ruined the whole thing. Garnet had his foot right in front of the door so it wouldn't open.

"Who's your mum fucking?" he said to Paisley in a low voice.

"Garnet Mulligan, so help me God, if I have to come over there!" Paisley needed to count again. She needed to touch the door handle seven times and pull it open on the eighth.

"Don't make me squeeze it out of you."

"Reverend Willis," she said, like it was someone else speaking the words. "The Reverend Arden Willis."

"Garnet, if you don't want a life of hard labour, you'll get your arse into this truck!"

Paisley wanted to tell him it was over—it was over between her mother and the reverend. The reverend had figured out what was right, even if her mother hadn't. But maybe that didn't matter.

Before she could say anything, Garnet removed his foot from the door and walked to the truck.

Paisley touched the door handle seven times, pulled it open on the eighth, and scooted inside, making sure the door didn't touch any other part of her body to ruin the number.

The school, and its dark, cool corridors, swallowed her whole.

NOW

Garnet ripped the first letter into little pieces.

"What'd it say?" Paisley asked.

"None of your business."

He opened the next letter. Paisley got up. She paced. She came back. He ripped it up, too.

"What about that one?" she asked.

"I beg you. Let me make a fire," he said. "Because I can see you angling for the pieces. You want to reconstruct them and their stupid secrets, which will force me to eat them, and I'd rather toss them in a small, contained, well-supervised campfire."

"Not on your life."

"I've set my fair share of fires, and—I've—"

"What could you possibly say that will convince me?"

"I won't run away this time?"

She glared at him.

"Too soon?"

"Too soon. And no way."

"Please."

"No."

He read the next letter. He ripped up that one, too. "Your mother didn't have a lot good to say."

"No, she did not."

"So why the curiosity?"

"I don't know. Self-flagellation, I guess. I'm very good at that."

"Get in line."

"I suppose it's all that's left of her. I don't want to miss something important."

"I'll make sure you get the important bits. I just haven't found any yet."

Paisley lay back down on the blanket and gazed up at the

stars. "Can I talk while you read?" she asked.

"Talk away."

"I remember something funny about you."

"Funny as in ha-ha, or funny as in weird, fucked up, bizarre? Because if it's the latter, I'm not sure I want to hear."

"It's more like ha-ha and a little bizarre."

"Well, great. Then shoot. I can hardly wait."

"I think I was maybe fifteen...sixteen even? I fell on a stick once, do you remember?"

"Did I throw you onto said stick?"

"No, no violent act on your part. Unusually."

"Go on," said Garnet, ripping up another letter.

"We already lived on the mainland. I was back visiting Rory, birding with him in the cemetery. I fell on a stick and practically poked my eye out."

"Oh...yes. I do remember that. Do we need to talk about this?"

"It was red and bloody."

"Stop."

"But suddenly you were there."

"Shawn and I were smoking up behind the drive shed. I was high. I was not in control of my actions. Can we move on?"

"I was stumbling around, and there you were, and I was terrified. I didn't want to face you alone. I didn't know Shawn was there. That would have made it worse."

"Like I said, he was behind the drive shed. Very, very high."

"So we eyed one another from a distance," said Paisley, "or, rather, I really only looked at you through one eye; the other was a mess. I hoped you hadn't seen me, but you did, and there was nowhere to run. And you would for sure outrun me if I tried."

"I remember. Vaguely. I think I've blocked it out. I have a weird thing about eyeballs—mushy parts of the body.

Mangled mushy parts. Not my thing."

"I looked for Rory," said Paisley. "He'd gone looking for a bird in the bushes... And there you were coming up to me, and I knew I was screwed."

"Did I say something asshole-ish?"

"You said, 'What's your problem?' And I said nothing. I'm pretty sure I just stared at the ground. You were in work pants and a T-shirt with the sleeves cut off. I remember wondering what happened to the sleeves."

"I cut them off to look cool," said Garnet. "I was pretty proud of my guns. Shawn and I would do chin-ups in the barn—compete. I'd always whip his ass, and that'd piss him off, which made me even happier."

"I remember wondering, is that what they call a muscle shirt? Because Garnet has muscles."

He laughed. "I would have been very pleased to hear your thoughts on that at the time."

"So you said, 'How come you're not looking at me?' You know—cocky."

"My trademark."

"Everything was so screwed up in my life at that point. I was living with my father, my mother was living with her cats, my counting and checking was off the charts, and so I had a little death wish, right in that moment. I thought, what more could happen? We'd had a few intersections, and somehow I'd survived all of them."

"What a jerk I was."

"True, but I'm getting free legal work now out of it, so maybe in the end I'm the winner."

"Accurate—pretty clever of you, actually. So you thought you had nothing to fear."

"Which made no sense, if you think about it, given—"

"The fact that I'd almost set you on fire?"

"Exactly. So you said, 'Look at me,' and I did. I'd forgotten about my bleeding eye, so when I turned to you, you froze."

"Mangled mushy parts. I told you."

"'Wow,' you said. 'Your eye.' 'Oh, yeah,' I said. 'I fell on a stick.' And you said, 'Right on a stick?' And I said, 'Pretty much.' You asked me if it hurt, and I told you not at first but it was hurting now. Then my eye started bleeding even more, and you basically keeled over, face first. Your muscly arms sort of flopped on the ground, and your legs went askew... You, this big, intimidating guy, just fainted dead away."

Garnet guffawed.

Paisley was having fun, unspooling her story like Del at her mother's old bridge parties. "I panicked. I poked you. You didn't move. So I shook you. I always think people are dying and it's my fault. So I heaved you onto your back and your arms flopped up and I saw your hairy underarms, which grossed me out, so I dropped you. I leaned right down to your face, and I yelled, 'Garnet!'"

Garnet doubled over. He was laughing so hard he was crying. "And I woke up," he said, gasping for breath, "and I opened my eyes, but your face was right by mine, and I got a close-up of your horror-show eye, and I fainted again."

"And that time, no amount of shaking woke you, so of course I was really, really sure you were dead, and it was all my fault, and God was going to finally get me for my sins. I didn't even think to find Shawn—or Rory, for that matter—and running for help would take too long, so I grabbed the pail by the drive shed and it was filled it with slimy old rainwater and I threw it right on your face. And that did the trick."

Garnet was heaving for air, laughing so hard no air was coming out.

"You know what's weird?" she said. "I'd seen you eat a caterpillar for five bucks in the schoolyard and do tons of other gross things on a dare, but it just seemed so odd that my eye would make you faint."

"So you see, you're not the only odd duck," Garnet said.

He offered her the wine bottle. After a moment, he said, "I think I might have given you as much attention as I did—unfortunately for you—because I liked you."

"Oh, come on."

"No, seriously. You were fucked up; I was fucked up more."

"Not possible."

"And now I find myself interested," he said, "because you know who I am, more than anyone else."

"I know you don't do mushy parts."

He looked at her briefly. "We get along—I do think we're getting along—because we're sort of the same. We are...I hope I'm not overstepping my bounds...damaged goods. Everyone I've ever tried to be with, my whole adult life, has been very normal. And they end up thinking I'm for the 'As Is' rack, yeah? And I finally realized, you know what? I am. I am firmly on the 'As Is' rack. I am not for all markets, as Shakespeare said."

"Wow. Shakespeare."

"I know, I know, me, quoting the bard. Impressive, yes?"

"Yes. Well, I'm not for all markets either. But before that...did you say you're interested in me?"

"I did."

She swallowed a big gulp of wine. "Why?"

"Because you're a thoroughbred."

"A what?"

"A thoroughbred. Wild. Unpredictable. Something special. I think you heard me the first time though."

Paisley was speechless.

"I'm going to finish these letters now."

"Okay." She paused for a moment. "Or maybe the letters could wait."

THEN

In September, Paisley moved to the high school on the mainland, in Napanee. Garnet and Shawn Mulligan were sent to a school in Kingston with a stricter principal. Their parents thought he might set their boys straight, but, from what Paisley heard through the grapevine, that wasn't the case.

The high school in Napanee was, of course, much bigger than the island school. All the kids came from surrounding areas on the island and mainland, and Paisley hoped that without the Mulligans to single her out it would be easier to blend in. Which was true at first—until a kid in her Grade 9 home room had food poisoning after Thanksgiving and projectile-vomited on her, which caused her to count out loud in front of all her classmates. Then, in February, Eudie sent Paisley five rage-filled letters on the same day about what a horrible person she was to have ruined their lives, which brought on some counting again, this time in class; the teacher witnessed it. On the Grade 9 graduation overnight camping trip, the bonfire for marshmallows sparked a small fire that was entirely extinguished by Paisley's science and geography teachers, who were chaperones on the trip, but not before it caused an OCD meltdown that kept both teachers up most of the night supervising Paisley as she counted eights and surveyed the campsite inch by inch for wayward embers that might start a forest fire.

She was referred by the guidance counsellor to Mr. Webb's special class at the start of Grade 10. She was allowed to come and go as she pleased between her regular class and the Specials, depending how she felt on any given day. Which was good, because there was a stigma if you were there full-time. Not that the popular, racy, cool girls like Fidelity and Cherie in the regular classroom thought twice about Paisley. But she still liked to be near them, to eavesdrop on their lives, so different from hers, and dream that one day she might fit in with them, even if only a little.

It was a motley crew of kids in the Special Room. Even though she didn't wear a helmet like Bruce Meyers, and wasn't hyper like Veronica Pearson (Veronica couldn't focus on one thing for one minute if her life depended on it), Paisley liked it there. Eight was still her special number and provided temporary relief from anything that set her off. And it was true, her nervous pastimes had grown. She was quite afraid of fire and the myriad ways it could materialize in any given building: faulty fire alarms, poor electrical wiring, children playing with matches, a stove left on. She'd also developed a "sorry" tic; that is, she found herself apologizing for everything. Sometimes she had to apologize in a series of eights, which got under people's skin. It was a sort of cleansing ritual, and only when she'd apologized enough, or checked the outlets and stove knobs enough times to feel she was good and safe again, could she move on with her day.

Sometimes things at home set her off. Hu might have had a worse day than usual at the plant and not want to talk, which made Paisley feel bad or guilty and led to a ritual of checking. She'd check the stove and the outlets, then she'd knock a paper or magazine off the table on purpose so she could apologize, and when Hu finally pried his eyes away from the TV to state categorically that it was all right, no problem, Paisley could move on. Sometimes he'd just put his big farmer's hand on her head and let it rest there, without saying a word. A soothing thing. A loving thing. Like in the movies when a priest laid a hand on a congregant's head to absolve sins. They'd do this ritual, Hu and Paisley, in silence. Then, after a minute, he'd go back to the TV, and she'd feel calmer. Apart from that, Hu seemed resigned to his inability to help. He didn't understand the counting, the checking, the apologizing. How could he? She didn't blame him for that. She barely understood it herself, except that these things made her feel calm and organized. They couldn't be escaped, not even if she'd wanted to escape them. So while she moved through rooms in their apartment, counting eights, he'd sit in his La-Z-Boy and watch either the CBC or one of the other couple fuzzy channels—whatever was on—and then he'd fall asleep. It was exhausting for both of them.

But there were good days, too. Days when Paisley fit in like a normal person, did ordinary high school stuff. A blur of tiny typical moments no one would ever remark upon or remember. She studied, took tests, sold tickets for a swim fundraiser, became vice-president of the math club, helped with the yearbook. But on bad days, Paisley went to the Specials. She and the regular class teacher worked out a little signal: Paisley tapped index finger to thumb on her raised hand—and she'd slip out the back and settle in at her special class desk with whatever homework or lesson unit she was working on. Her regular classmates barely noticed. They didn't care. All the better.

Paisley was doing her Grade 13 practice math exam when Delilah appeared at the special class door. Bruce Meyers had launched a book across the room, and Del ducked just in time to miss getting walloped. The book hit the corner of the door jamb, broke its spine, and split in two.

"Jesus H!" said Del. She spied the teacher. "Can I steal Paisley for a sec?"

Mr. Webb was glad to release Paisley so he could deal with Bruce.

Paisley went out into the corridor with Del. Paisley could feel her fingers tingling. Something must be wrong. Del never came to her school.

"See they've got you in with the crazies," said Del. She lit up, her hands trembling as she held the flame to her cigarette.

Paisley worried the match might fall and set the school on fire. "I don't think you can smoke here, Del. It's a school, remember?"

"Honey," said Del, "today I can smoke anywhere. Now brace yourself, because... Shit, who made me the responsible one? Listen. Your dad...he just up and...and...he's dead. I'm sorry. They found him face down in that muck at work. It's really goddamn awful."

Up the hall, the principal hovered near the stairwell, looking uncomfortable.

"They're pretty sure it was a heart attack."

Paisley had a crushing desire to count something, but she didn't want to count in front of the principal. Or Del.

Del took another drag. Paisley touched thumb to finger in a sequence of eights. No one would notice. And if they did, how could they hold it against her?

"The good news is," said Del, blowing smoke up to the ceiling, "if it's the job that killed him, you'll get compensation for that."

Paisley looked for Del's match. She had dropped it to the floor. There it was. It seemed to be out, but Paisley picked it up anyway and closed her fist over it. It was cold. The school would not burn down.

"I'll need my knapsack," she said.

NOW

Paisley awoke first. She was in the passenger seat, covered in the blanket. Garnet was in the driver's seat, still asleep. It wasn't true that his body was the same; he was leaner than before. Desk job, she assumed, as opposed to farmer's son with chores to do. He'd lost the muscles from all that manual work. But he also had a bit of swagger, like a rock star. It was shocking that he would be interested in her. And maybe, honestly, he wasn't. Maybe this was a one-night stand—the end of it. She'd get the keys to Eudie's house and sign the papers, they'd say their goodbyes at the train station, and that would be the last she'd see of him. She tested out that thought to see how it felt. Not enough information to make a decision yet.

She got out of the car and stretched. The house looked just as desolate as it had the day before, but less frightening in the morning sun. She walked through the tall, dewy grass to the porch, then to the door, and then moved inside. She could do this.

The place was a wreck, frozen in time, the same wallpaper and furniture as when Paisley had been young. It was sparse—of course, Hu had taken half the furniture to their apartment on the mainland—but the counters where Eudie had baked were there, the Arborite kitchen table was there, the old yellowed recipes for lattice apple pie and winter squash soup were still taped to the kitchen window.

The house reeked of mould, ancient urine, and feces. Even after the cats had long ago disappeared, other animals—mice, raccoons, squirrels—had made their homes there. Birds had nested above the kitchen cabinets, and the cracked, rotten counters were covered in droppings.

Upstairs, her parents' bedroom was no better. The furniture was covered in animal hair and a few small bones, either from some creature's meal or death. The bed was destroyed, used by animals for sleeping and who knew what else. Paisley's bedroom was empty—Hu had taken that furniture, too—but the sight of the four walls and little else was devastating. Paisley imagined Eudie living with that empty room—the evidence of a failed daughter. She wished she had done more for her mother. Wished she had made her proud; that she could have saved Eudie from a lifetime of small but crushing defeats. But was it that she had failed her mother—or was it the other way around? This was a new thought. Paisley, too, had suffered, and done so virtually alone. She suddenly felt furious. At her mother, at having to be an adult too soon, at the incredible mess of events that led her to this moment, at the four small, round indentations in the carpet where her bed had once been.

Paisley cried. She didn't feel thirty-nine; she felt thirteen.

She went back downstairs and, not ready to face Garnet yet, headed out the back door. It was half off its hinges, the screen door long ago shredded by animals. She stepped out onto the rotten back porch to catch her breath.

The land behind the house had been reduced to rough pasture, a damp field with tall grasses and messy wildflowers. There was a derelict car that someone, at some time, had set on fire. Piles of wet, mossy wood and a rusty, upturned claw-foot bathtub. A laundry basket on the back porch with tattered clothing still in it, even after all these years. It was all sad and wild, much like Eudie herself had been.

Paisley pulled her shirt up and wiped her face and snotty nose on the hem. Stop this, she thought. It's been too long to mourn, to feel so bereft and alone. She dropped her shirt and saw movement from the corner of her eye. A flutter. A bird was perched on a tall weed, not two feet from where she stood, inspecting her.

It was a Henslow's sparrow.

Impossible. Paisley refocused again. Salt stung her eyes.

No, no, it was, it was a Henslow's sparrow, right there, like a dream.

It was exactly as she had imagined it, exactly as the books had described it, exactly as June MacIntosh had sketched it in her notebook so long ago: a small, streaky brown bird. What birders called an uncommon but common-looking bird, "famously inconspicuous."

It cocked its head, looked at her, hopped off to a safe distance, then turned and looked at her again.

She barely breathed. She stood perfectly still.

The bird sang, and that, too, was just as she'd read it would sound: a nothing song. A simple, short, thin, two-syllable *tsi-lik*, *tsi-lik*, *tsi-lik*.

She couldn't believe it. The Henslow's sparrow was down to an infinitesimally small number in this region, practically nothing. And yet, as Paisley looked back over the unplowed, weedy field behind her mother's house, she realized this had become the perfect nesting ground for the bird.

"Paisley?" It was Garnet.

The Henslow's sparrow darted into the tall grass. This was its way; it almost never flew to escape danger, preferring to run off into dense cover. Paisley watched where it ran, the slight disturbance of the grass. If she walked over there, she might find an open bowl nest of loosely woven dry grasses, just off the ground. The Henslow's sparrow's nest was always well hidden, and any birder worth their salt would never, ever want to disturb it.

Garnet approached. "Morning," he said, looking in the direction of her gaze. "What do you see out there?"

"Possibility," said Paisley.

They folded the blanket and packed up. Paisley went to close her father's parachute bag and in it saw June's birding notebook beside hers. She showed Garnet June's sketch of the Henslow's sparrow. Last officially seen on the island on August 17, 1895, maybe in 1981 (only rumoured, never verified—Eden and Olive, the two ladies Paisley had met at the Summer Social, were terrible birders), and now, again, May 11, 2007.

Garnet didn't know anything about birding, but he was trying to understand the attraction, which she appreciated. He found June's life list tucked in the back of the notebook and pulled out a pen. "Why don't you add the bird to the list?" he asked.

"I couldn't."

"Why not?"

"It's not my list."

"Where's yours?"

"In my bag."

"Then write it down in there. But, for the record, I don't think June would mind. I think she'd be pleased. Just a tiny note in the margin on the Henslow's sparrow page."

"I'm a stick-to-the-rules kinda girl. Birders don't write on other birders' lists. Pass me Eudie's letters."

"These torn-up bits? No way. They're not worth keeping."

"Well, you can't litter." Paisley said. "give them here and we'll throw them out on the ferry."

Garnet refused to give them back. He was sure Paisley would piece them together and read their contents. Instead, he dug a hole and buried them. A pleasing sort of ritual.

"A fire would've been better," he said.

"On what planet?" said Paisley.

He proposed picking up some bread, peanut butter, and jam at the store and taking a drive around the island before catching the ferry. Paisley agreed, but as he held the car door open for her, she hesitated.

"I think I might have forgotten something inside."

"Oh, yeah? What?"

"I'm not sure, just...I'd just like to check."

"Your bag is in the trunk. You didn't have anything else, did you?"

"I know, but I'll just check. It'll only take me two seconds."

She headed for the house.

"Hey, you. Strange girl," he said. "What's going on?"

"Oh God, Garnet, I'm worried about the stove, okay? I just want to check it and then I'll be able to come."

"Oh."

"It's nothing, really. It's just a small thing, it won't take a second."

"But you never used the stove."

"No."

"So there's no way it could be on."

"No," said Paisley, "but I might have bumped it. And then, you know, an element is on and there's a gust of wind through that open door, and it blows a piece of paper onto the stovetop. And a fire starts. Then it burns down the house, and this brush outside, it catches fire, too. Before you know it, the Henslow's sparrow is burned to a crisp, the whole island's on fire, and four hundred people are dead, charred to nothingness, and it's all my fault because I didn't take the thirty seconds I could have taken to check it. See?"

"Absolutely."

"I just need to fix the doubt. I know it seems funny to you, but—"

"It doesn't seem funny to me."

"I had a shrink for a while. In Toronto. He called it paren-tification. Very scientific."

"Not the other thing?"

"Well, yes, that, and you're kind to put the OCD so delicately, but parentification was how some kids get through absentee parenting by parenting themselves. My mother was, as you know...complicated. The kind of person who made everything about her. And my dad was pretty great, when he was around, but he did spend most of his time on the farm rather than with us. When he finally tuned in, it was too late. You're a kid, and no one's watching you, so you find a set of rules to parent yourself. Like counting light switches and checking stove elements. I thought I could escape this little visit with a shred of dignity, but I guess not. Here's an official close-up view of a nut bar. Please enjoy."

"What if I checked?" Garnet asked.

"I don't understand."

"What if I took it on, to check for you? That would absolve you of it."

"More penance for your misspent youth?"

"Nah, just practicality. If you have to check, it might go on for a long time, right?"

"Well..."

"It might go on all day. No offence."

"None taken. It would likely be eight times. But if anything went wrong, I'd have to start again. Those are the rules."

"So if I check, then we can get to our PB and J faster, right, and I can call work and say you needed more time, so I won't be coming in just yet?"

"You have to swear to God you'll really check."

"Swear to God. Let's get this done. I'm starving."

He went inside. She spied on him through the broken windows. He was really and truly doing it.

THEN

Del took Paisley from school to the apartment in Amherstview to gather her things. They picked out a suit and a tie for Hu—not hard, given he only had one good suit—and a shirt to press. Underwear and socks. In the top dresser drawer, Del found Hu's watch, inscribed on the back with *First Prize, Holsteins, Napanee Fair, 1953*, and his wedding ring. On second thought, Del gave these last two items to Paisley. "They won't do anyone any good six feet under. Put them somewhere special."

Paisley, numb, packed a bag. Del said Paisley would stay with her and Noble until she was sorted out. So they filled two suitcases: one for a dead man, one for an eighteen-year-old with an unknown future.

In the middle of it all sat the worn La-Z-Boy. The newsprint monthly *Properties for Sale, Amherst Island*, lay on one threadbare arm, the jumbo math puzzle book Hu and Paisley did together on the other. He'd read her the problem and check in the back to see if she'd gotten it right.

"I'll get that minister from the Presbyterian Church in Amherstview to do the funeral. What do you think, Paisley? No, wait, don't answer that. It's just...yes, Hu'd want to be buried on the island, but it's too ridiculous to have that lout Reverend Willis do the service, isn't it? I wouldn't be surprised if that made poor Hu pop right out of his cedar box and deck the guy—one swift right hook, you know, right across the bow, as Noble puts it. You're the one who got the disaster rolling, Arden. It's your fault."

Paisley felt it was hers. She got the disaster rolling. But no matter now. She said nothing.

Del pulled open the fridge in the galley kitchen. Paisley touched the La-Z-Boy arm eight times, then did a quick check of all the outlets.

"We'll want to bury him in St. Andrew's cemetery," Del went on, a little softer this time, "on the island, with his folks. So I'll have to call Arden about that one. No fear, Paisley, I'll be as frosty as the polar cap. I'm his worst nightmare. There's a cheese slice in here, you want it?" She emerged from the kitchen to catch Paisley counting and checking. "God, Paise, I can be coarse sometimes," she said. "Sorry. This is a tough time, and I'm here for you, okay, babe?"

Paisley nodded and shoved the puzzle book into her bag.

"Let's see," Del said, unwrapping the processed cheese slice and putting it between her lips. "Service on the mainland, interment on the island, reception at St. Andrew's.... Not likely. Maybe I can just take Arden aside and say no way on God's green earth can he be there. He has to be sick that day. Away. And if he says no, I'll deck him myself."

Paisley zipped up her suitcase and looked around the apartment. The sun was setting, bathing the room in orange-and-gold light. Through the rays, dust swirled and danced, settling and lifting again. She wondered if she had everything she needed. She wasn't sure. She also wasn't sure it mattered.

NOW

They had forty-five minutes before the next ferry. It was another warm morning, so they rolled down the car windows and let the air whoosh in. Soon enough, St. Andrew's came into view. Garnet pulled into the cemetery and slowly took the dirt drive around its perimeter.

It looked exactly the same as it had when Paisley was a child. The grass and flowers were well tended. They passed several parked cars. On one bumper, a sticker read, *If you're having trouble sleeping, don't count sheep, talk to the shepherd.*

"Do you talk to the shepherd?" Garnet asked.

"I stopped going to church after that business with my mother and the reverend," said Paisley. "And then, when everything else happened, I sort of stopped thinking about God altogether."

"Guess you would."

"I don't really blame either of them. God has a lot on His plate, and Arden was young and inexperienced. He had a handful with my mother, and it got away from him."

"Kind of sums up my youth here, too."

"You should've taken up counting."

"I'll take that under consideration," said Garnet.

From the church windows, the sound of the organ leading a choir floated over them.

> *Will your anchor hold in the storms of life,*
> *When the clouds unfold their wings of strife?*
> *When the strong tides lift, and the cables*
>   *strain,*
> *Will your anchor drift or firm remain?*
>
> *We have an anchor that keeps the soul*
> *Steadfast and sure while the billows roll,*

Fastened to the Rock which cannot move,
Grounded firm and deep in the Saviour's
love

"I appreciated what you did back there at the house," said Paisley. "Checking the stove for me. That was chivalrous."

"Chivalry is my middle name."

They drove along the third concession, which wound between farms and large oak trees. Cows eyed them idly and went back to chewing and shooing flies. The odd farmer waved without recognizing them. Paisley liked her anonymity. Suddenly they were passing Mildred Mickie's farm.

"Stop," she said.

A fading realty sign stood in the overgrown garden.

"How long has Mildred's place been for sale?"

"Long time," said Garnet. "She had a stroke, and her daughter brought her to the mainland and hired an attendant to look after her. I heard Mildred lost her speech and the use of her whole left side, so she just sat there surrounded by all the stuff she'd bought at those auctions and stared at the visitors who came by. She died not long after, and her daughter put the place up for sale. But, you know, farming's changed—there's even an emu farm here now—and so Mildred's old milking parlour isn't of use to anyone. I bet the place would go for a song. I've thought of buying it myself."

"You have? Would you farm?"

"Not a dairy farm—too hard a life. I wouldn't mind doing a bit of hobby farming though. And if I don't completely cave to a mid-life crisis and go back to Ireland, I wouldn't mind living here and commuting into Kingston. Haven't ever really said it out loud like that, actually." He looked around. "But coming back would be hard."

"I get it. All these places we can go but we don't. Or will. Or could."

"Exactly," he said.

"What do you miss about it there, if you don't mind me asking?"

"Ireland? My friends wouldn't really be around any-more...or they might be, but I haven't kept up with them, so it's not about that. It's more of a sense thing. The smell of the earth and the water. Moss everywhere, because it's so wet. Stone walls on the sides of the roads, ivy that grows on everything, the grey skies, how it could rain sideways, right in your face, soak you right through. Lots of people couldn't take it, how much it rained, but I loved it. It made me feel alive—cold and wet, maybe, but alive. And then when you got into someone's kitchen, and they cooked and laughed with you, there was pure warmth. Unbearably romantic, I know."

"You say that like it's a bad thing."

"More specifically, the Guinness is better over there."

"In what way?"

"Not as watery. Creamier for sure."

"That sounds like a very important reason to go back."

"You have no idea."

Paisley looked at the *For Sale* sign on Mildred's front lawn. "You have so many choices. You could stay here and be great at hobby farming. You could go to Ireland. You pulled yourself out of a hole and became a lawyer instead of going to jail. You got me the house that was rightfully mine. You can do anything."

His face did a little sensitive thing she'd never seen be-fore. A lip wobble. He looked like a kid. "No one's ever said that about me," he said.

"It's true."

"I know you work at the archives, but do you make ends meet, if you don't mind me asking?"

"Just. Pay is terrible, job is good. Good enough. I have the insurance money from my dad's death. It wasn't a ton, but it was something, and I invested it at the bank when I was eighteen. So I pull in something from that every month, too."

"Would you ever come back to live on the island?" he asked.

There were no whirligigs left on Mildred's lawn. Nothing spinning in Amherst Island's endless wind. But the wrap-around porch was solid and looked out over the farm, the lawn and the oak trees lining the third concession.

"I don't know."

THEN

The funeral service at Amherstview Presbyterian was nice enough. Farmers came from all over in their Sunday best. The entire island was there. Thieves would've had a field day with every house left unattended. The only ones not in church: Reverend Willis, on an invented trip to Toronto, and Eudie, who couldn't get it together to come, no matter how much Del begged.

Paisley had heard Del and Noble discussing it while getting dressed that morning: how Noble had sat outside Eudie's place for an hour until she screamed at him through the door, telling him she couldn't go. Noble, like everyone else, was secretly relieved. Lord knows what Eudie might have done had she been faced with Mildred Mickie, for one thing. Only a few had really gotten a good look at Eudie in years, actually. Maybe most of the people, said Del, were, in fact, not there for Hu at all, but to try to catch a glimpse of Eudie.

Del presided over the funeral as though it were a social event, wearing her best satin dress, a deep fuchsia number cut on the bias. She welcomed people at the door, complimenting the women on their outfits and the men on their wives' outfits.

The minister did an all right job, considering he hadn't known Hu at all. He had met with Del and Paisley beforehand and to gather a few facts: Hu had been born in 1938, the only son of Russell and Mabel Ratchford, well-known farmers of Amherst Island before Russell became manager of the quarry; Hu had farmed most of his life and had a real knack for it; he'd married Eudora, from Toronto; they'd had one child, Paisley—and his sincerest condolences went out to her, God was watching over her, God had a plan for her, even as she worked through her sadness. He left out the bits about the last years at a sanitation plant and having made the biggest mistake of his life marrying a lady who turned out to be nuttier than squirrel droppings.

Paisley had been to plenty of funerals, but never as the guest of honour. She sat perfectly still in the first pew, hands in the pockets of her navy blue dress—Del had picked it up for her. In each pocket, Paisley had placed eight pebbles, and she managed to get through the service looking composed by counting them. Several people complimented her on doing so well during such a difficult time. Paisley impressed even herself.

After the service, everyone got in their trucks and cars and drove slowly west along Bath Road to the Amherst Island ferry dock to catch the two-thirty. Lake Ontario lapped the shore. People stepped out of their front doors on both sides of the road, stopped mowing their lawns or washing their cars or scolding their bickering kids, to watch the procession. They lifted their hands to their foreheads to shield their eyes from the sun to get a better view of those first few cars. Was it someone they knew? Likely it was.

Cars driving in the opposite direction slowed to match the speed of the funeral procession. And as they neared the Amherst Island ferry dock, cars driving toward them came to a complete stop, halting traffic on the main thoroughfare altogether. Drivers got out of their cars and stood solemnly on the roadway, engines running. They took off their Massey Ferguson mesh caps and stood there, honouring the dead. If they hadn't heard who'd passed, they soon would.

Paisley was proud it took a whole ferry to get them all to the island—a strange sentiment for a sad day. She watched Cyrus line up the trucks and cars on the ferry deck, nice and neat.

"Don't you worry, Miss Paisley," said Cyrus. "I'll get everyone over on time. Sorry for your loss." Then he turned and with deft gestures squeezed in car after car within a hair's breadth of each other.

On the ride across, Paisley looked over the side at the water sliding under the ferry and wondered what was to become of her. She could stay in Amherstview by herself, couldn't she? She was eighteen, of age. Lots of people her age had already quit school to help on their family farms.

She counted the eight pebbles in each of her two pockets. She wished desperately that Hu were there, his big arms ready to comfort her. His hand on her head. His accepting silence. But the pebbles weren't doing the trick.

The wind played with the ferry in the divide between mainland and island. It whipped this way and that way. Funeral hairdos were teased up, up, and away. Ladies pulled out chiffon headscarves to batten down hot-roller hatches. Most ducked into their cars while the men stayed out, talking about Hu and what a crying shame it all was.

Del fished in her purse for her lipstick while she prattled on in the front seat about whether the party wieners in the cooler would last until the interment was over or whether she should drop them off first for the reception at Prue's, whether Noble liked the toothpicks she'd chosen, with the little multicoloured plastic tufts on the top, whether they were too festive for such an occasion.

"Will it be okay?" Paisley said.

Del twisted around, her upper lip refreshed, the same shade as her dress. "It'll be okay, Paise."

"Will it be okay?" she asked again. Stupid.

Del looked at her like she was losing it. "Yes, yes, fine, we'll get through this together."

"Will it be okay, will it be okay, will it be okay—"

Noble turned around, too. He and Del looked at Paisley like a spider had just crawled out of her mouth. What was happening?

"Five, six, seven—"

"Lord save us all," said Del. "It runs in the family."

NOW

They continued along the third concession and up the Emerald 40 Foot to the village of Emerald. Then they doubled back to the Stella 40 Foot and drove down to the South Shore Road. They parked the car on the tight shoulder and walked down through the brush to the abandoned rocky beach.

"Seriously, where are you going to live? Inquiring minds want to know."

"I'll send up a flare when I have an answer," Paisley said.

"What about all your Toronto stuff?"

"That's what storage lockers are for."

"Can't live in a storage locker," said Garnet.

"Noted."

The lake was choppy, as always, and the waves came crashing in, over and over, in a steady, soothing rhythm.

Paisley took off her shoes and dipped her toes in the water. Garnet did, too.

"I used to skinny-dip here with my brother," said Garnet. "Most kids used the ferry dock or the public dock off of Stella Bay, but if Shawn and I went there, it always ended in a scuffle. It was exhausting."

"Why?"

"It's like anything. More turns into more."

She understood that. "When you're fully into the counting—or maybe when the counting is into you—more makes more. You do another round of eight, you're waiting for the release in your head, but if the conditions aren't just right, you have to go another round. The water's good, isn't it?"

"It is. It's cool." He skipped a rock over the choppy water.

"Six skips. Very impressive."

"A professional stone skipper was my backup career of choice," said Garnet. "You know, if the footballer situation didn't work out, of course. Some of the most honourable pursuits. You?"

"You'll laugh."

"Could it possibly be funnier than professional stone skipper?"

"Not really. I wanted to be a bird artist. Then a zoopraxographer, someone who studies the movement of birds. Then nothing short of a world-renowned birder. But even better, someone who travels great distances to look for important birds. Otherwise known as a twitcher."

He looked at her with amusement. "And?"

"And it's a long, stupid story."

"For every stupid story you have, I have two."

Paisley tried a stone. It skipped once and sank. "I thought I would sally forth on exotic expeditions to catch sight of extremely rare birds and tick them off a big list. I'd travel to France. It's not the best for birding, but my mother used to talk about it. She'd always wanted to get to Paris and never did, and so as a kid I dreamt of birding in France. They have lots of forests there, at least. I pictured myself creeping along the forest floor, evading the chasseurs, the hunters, who loathe twitchers, and I'd drink red wine and cheese and tick birds off my list to my heart's delight. And maybe I'd even have a bird named after me. Some Latin version of my name. You know, *Paisleyum ratchfordium*."

He nodded and skipped another stone.

"Instead, I've spent my life working at the ornithological archives in Toronto, cataloguing other people's lists," said Paisley. "I'm a birder who has failed to ever see a rare bird with her own eyes. A twitcher who has gone nowhere. One of those underperforming twitchers who've dipped out."

"Dipped out."

"Which is what they say when you've missed seeing a bird you were hoping to see."

"But that's not true," said Garnet. "You saw a Henslow's sparrow."

"Holy shit, you're right."

"Besides, maybe your dream didn't mean you should go somewhere exotic and lead an exotic life. Maybe your dream meant you were exotic just as you were."

"Ha. I highly doubt it." But she did love the idea that he might find her exotic.

"So being a birder, or a twitcher, is like being a member of an exclusive club. That has its own vocabulary."

"Totally," said Paisley. "Like, you might call someone who is pretty new to birdwatching and doesn't really know what they're doing a dude."

"That'd be me."

"I wouldn't call you that. Because it's not necessarily the nicest thing to say about people. And there are acronyms. Like, LBJ in the UK means little brown job—a songbird that's sort of the same shade of brown as a hundred others and is hard to identify."

"Like your Henslow's sparrow?"

"You jest. I could recognize on those beauties a mile away. Maybe others couldn't, but..."

"You're just that good."

She eyed him to see if he was joking. He wasn't. "Mind you, the LBJ might be registered in your notebook as BVD—better view desired—which means you had an obstructed view, and you couldn't get close enough, or really enjoy the bird in all its beauty. But my Henslow's sparrow I saw up close and personal, so that doesn't pertain to me. And a CMF means a cosmic mind fucker—"

"Seriously?"

"—meaning something so good, your brain is blown."

"Again, the Henslow's sparrow."

"Definitely a CMF. And there's the crippler, which is a British term for a bird that was such a CMF, you had trouble moving on."

He laughed at that one. "So you've seen an LBJ that was not BVD but unquestionably a CMF. Could there be anything better." He took off his shirt. "Speaking of dipped out, I'm gonna take a dip right now. Avert your eyes if you must...although it's nothing you haven't already seen."

"It's not even mid-May, you can't be serious," she said.

"I am one hundred percent serious. It doesn't have to be long, but it must be done."

He pulled off his pants and underwear. She couldn't have averted her eyes if she'd wanted to. This whole situation was another CMF, if she thought about it. And other than the Henslow's sparrow—nope—nothing else could be better.

"Join me." He tossed his clothes onto a rock. His taut, muscular white ass was a sight to behold.

"Aren't you afraid someone will see?" she said.

"Nah." He came up to Paisley, buck-naked, and kissed her. "Being afraid takes too much effort."

He let his hands wander down to her waist and they found their way under her shirt. She kissed him back and he pulled her shirt up and over her head.

"People will see."

"Let them." He slid his hands around her back, undoing her bra. "After all, you're *Paisleyum ratchfordium*. You have amazing talents, to catch birds—"

"Not catch them. Observe them and record them and know everything about them."

"To observe birds and record them and know everything about them. But I have come to realize that you are also a rare bird, and that I have a strong desire to observe you and record you and know everything about you."

THEN

As the ferry pulled up at island side, Del tied her own chiffon scarf around her hairdo and braved the wind to have an impromptu meeting with Prue through the window of her Olds. Noble rolled up his window so Paisley couldn't hear, but Del had to yell over the wind, so Paisley heard them anyway.

"To think Eudie's going to miss her own husband's funeral!" Del yelled.

"Plus that she'd abandon her only daughter in her hour of need!" Prue yelled back.

"I need to talk to her," Del yelled. "Can I have your car to do it? Noble needs to take Paisley to the cemetery."

"Guess it's the least we can do for Hu," said Prue. "Now, there's a man—solid as the day is long, who was never rewarded for his efforts. I mean, imagine having to go from Mildred's farm that should have been his, to broken promises, to shovelling—"

"Other people's shit for a living?" said Del.

It's called grit, thought Paisley.

Noble, who knew that Paisley was hearing it all, stared straight ahead.

So Prue lent her car to Del. Prue got into someone else's, Del got into hers, and Cyrus expertly disgorged the ferry's passengers.

The cars made their way to St. Andrew's cemetery. The flower beds around the cemetery's old crypt door were full of red and white flowers. Paisley counted seventy-three people around her father's grave. Even the owners of the Country Store were there, which meant the store was closed. It was never closed. Everyone she knew from school was there, in dresses and suits. All the men were clean-shaven, hair slicked down. Stanley was there, stiff and pressed, alongside Mildred Mickie, who wept uncontrollably.

The minister from Amherstview started in. Del had not returned. Paisley wondered what the holdup was. She could tell Noble was wondering the same thing. Noble, now in sole charge of Paisley, had a tissue in his hand, positioned right where Paisley could see it should she need it.

The minister finished his bit and the men lowered the coffin into the ground. Everyone formed a line and walked past Paisley, and either shook her hand or hugged her. Through all of it, she kept her left hand on the pebbles in her pocket. Mildred moved forward in the line, and Paisley watched her start to hyperventilate like the juniors in the schoolyard did when they scraped their knees. Stanley took a cranberry loaf from Mildred's hands and passed it to Paisley, then pulled Mildred gently to the side and patted her on the back while she made the shoulder of his good suit wet and snotty.

The reception was at Prue's house, put on by the St. Andrew's Women's Association. They had agreed with Del: it would be inappropriate to hold the reception in the church fellowship hall. So everyone got back into their cars, and off the procession went again. Noble and Paisley were the last to leave. Del hadn't showed. Noble suggested they go past Eudie's to check up on them both.

"The sandwiches oughta be good," Noble said as he drove. "And those party wieners Del loves."

He suddenly took his foot off the gas. Paisley saw what he saw: Prue's Oldsmobile parked on the road's shoulder. Noble pulled up behind it and got out. They were at the quarry; the gate slammed open and shut in the wind.

"Stay here," said Noble. He walked through the gate and disappeared down the gravel road that led to the pit.

Paisley studied her new dress. It was a summer dress made of dark blue eyelet cotton. Del had said that anyone eighteen or under didn't have to wear black. The fabric pulled tight across her breasts, always her problem area. Del had also bought her a cardigan and showed her how to do up the first five buttons to cover that trouble spot. But the dress looked beautiful. Graceful even. It felt strange to look her nicest at her father's funeral. He was dead. Amazing how you could forget something like that for even a moment.

She could wear this dress to the Grade 13 formal. There was talk of girls going in a big group, the ones who didn't have a date. She could add herself to them. They wouldn't reject her. Her father had just died.

Paisley sat in the car and listened to the wind, a cow moo, and, farther off, the water lap the shore. A fly buzzed around the inside of the windshield, trapped despite the two open windows.

Where was everyone?

Her stomach rumbled. The Saran Wrap would be off the sandwiches by now. She got out of the car and headed for the gate. *Clop*, *clop*, *clop*—her shoes and their tiny heels were terrible for walking on gravel. She wouldn't wear these to the formal, though the colour matched the dress perfectly. She would wear stilettos like Del's. Maybe they had the same foot size and she could borrow a pair.

Paisley found herself at the edge of the quarry, a jagged, gaping hole in the middle of the island. Del sat on a big stone slab in her tight fuchsia dress, smoking a king-size extra-long cigarette. Noble stood nearby, arms dangling awkwardly at his sides.

At the bottom of the pit was Eudie's body, sprawled and face down, one arm caught beneath her body, the other splayed at an odd angle out of the socket. Black dress, black pumps, one still on, one off to the side amid the rubble.

When the men came to help Noble retrieve Eudie's body from the bottom of the quarry, Paisley overheard James Mulligan: "And there are the three."

Del hadn't known what they were talking about. James said it was an old Irish saying about funerals coming in threes. "Three?" said Del. "What three?"

"Well," said James, "them cats, Hu, and now Eudie. Three."

NOW

Garnet and Paisley had missed the ferry. It was becoming a running joke.

They let the sun dry their bodies, got dressed, and drove farther along the South Shore Road, all the way to the eastern end of the island. Then they turned north again on the Lower 40 Foot, stopping at a large property on the eastern tip of the island. Garnet pulled up on the gravel easement just outside the fence, lined with tree swallow birdhouses (*Tachycineta bicolor*). At the corner, there were several multi-compartment purple martin (*Progne subis*) houses, too. They settled on the hood of the car and gazed out across the fields. He said that it was a nature reserve run by the Kingston Field Naturalists, in action since 1986, five years after Paisley moved to the mainland.

"I grew up thinking those folk were the coolest people alive," said Paisley. "They'd come by ferry with their binoculars and notebooks and maps. They knew everything there was to know about birds. And now they have their own reserve here."

"Where I lost my virginity," Garnet said.

"Way off topic, but okay," said Paisley. "How old were you?"

"Fifteen. You?"

"Older."

"Ah."

"With?" she asked.

"Not worth mentioning, I don't think."

"The event or the girl?"

"Both—at least at the time. The girl I'm sure has become a far better human than I," Garnet said.

"You were kind of a dick back then."

"Harsh yet true."

"My first time was less than stellar, too," said Paisley. "It takes a great force of will to focus on the events at hand when you're worried about a place spontaneously bursting into flames."

He nodded, quiet. Not judging her. Listening.

"I just...I figure here, with you, I won't bother doing my normal routine of overthinking and worrying and not saying anything or, if I do say something, not saying what I really mean, because you already know the worst of it all, and we'll probably never see each other again."

"Probably."

They gazed out at the reserve.

"So many birds to see here," said Paisley, "and all over Amherst Island. There are short-eared owls and long-eared owls. Oh, and great horned owls—they keep the island's vole population in check. In the fall and late winter, there are snowy owls, saw-whet owls, and even boreal owls, which I bet you've never seen."

"How much older?"

Paisley looked at him.

"I'm just asking."

"I had a ton of shit to get over. But I practised a lot in my head."

"It worked for you."

She smiled. "So. The short-eared owl. *Asio flammeus* to its fans, meaning flaming or the colour of fire."

"Of course *Paisleyum ratchfordium* speaks Latin. Be still my beating heart."

"All the cool kids know Latin. And it gets you extra points at bird trivia pub night. The short-eared owl's not really the colour of fire, but it has mottled tawny or brown plumage with stripes on its tail and wings. And yellow-orange eyes surrounded by thick black rings that makes it look like it's wearing mascara. And little tufts of feathers on the sides of its head that look like mammalian ears.

They might not be visible at first, but it displays the tufts when it defends itself."

"Tell me more," said Garnet.

"It lives in open areas like this—grasslands, marshes, and tundra. It eats voles, too. It's a wonder the vole species can survive, to be honest, with all the owls going after them."

"The voles must be fornicating all day," Garnet said. "Not a bad way to go. Get laid 24-7, then, wham, one day an owl swoops down and you're gone. But you've lived a very, very good life."

"And the short-eared owl is monogamous. They generally lay four to seven eggs at a time, and there is one brood a year. They nest on the ground, just like the Henslow's sparrow in the field behind my mother's house."

"Your house."

"My house. Right."

Paisley watched the purple martins doing aerial acrobatics to catch insects, their iridescent plumage catching the light.

"That's a purple martin," she said. "Their flocks can be so huge that when they take off en masse, they can actually register on Doppler radar. They start small, and the radar ring gets bigger and bigger until the birds disperse and it disappears."

"You're such a bird nerd. It's very hot."

That was about the best compliment she'd ever received. "You know..."

"Yeah?"

"I might leave the house, my house, as is."

"How come?"

"Well, that Henslow's sparrow... Like I said, it's a rare bird. I can't tell you how astonishing it is to have found it there. I spent all that time looking for it as a kid because I thought it could be the answer to all my problems."

"Was it?"

"Of course not. Things got much, much worse, and finding a Henslow's sparrow, which I never did, would not have stopped any of it. But that was typical of me back then—grasping at straws, looking for any kind of solution to my problems. Kind of like the counting and checking, if I think about it."

"Does knowing that make it something you could let go?"

"I don't know. Maybe eventually, one day. That's something to look forward to, at least."

"You are remarkable," Garnet said. "You have this shitty past and were subjected to some not very spectacular parenting, and you overcame it."

"The same could be said of you."

They sat in silence for a moment as the sun beat down.

"So you'd leave the house to the Henslow's sparrow?"

"You must really think we Ratchford women are off our rockers. First my mother leaves her house to cats, then you fight to get it back for me, and now I tell you I'm thinking of leaving it to a bird."

"It does sound a little out there. If you do that, you don't have anywhere to go. What's your plan?"

"I don't know. Birds that migrate know where to go on instinct. But then every once in a while something forces a change to their migratory pattern. And I guess that's what's happening to me."

"It's not some abstract thing happening in the distant future though. It's happening in a couple of days."

"Being untouched has made that place the perfect habitat for the Henslow's sparrow. I could observe it—try to help it re-establish itself on the island. Even report in to the field naturalists here."

"Honestly, Paisley, you know so much about the birds on the island, if you wanted to move back, I'm sure these Kingston Naturalists folk would give you a job."

"Does anyone ever give someone a job, just like that?"

"Not really. But they'd be lucky to have you."

She should have been terrified. Given all the uncertainty. And the degree to which she had practised being terrified. But this time she wasn't.

THEN

Eudie's letter, which Del had found pinned to the Ratchford house front door, said she'd left a will with a lawyer. Paisley decided to wear the navy blue eyelet dress to the lawyer's office. Eudie would have approved. Del wore a smart pantsuit, dressed up with chunky jewellery, high-heel boots, and hot pink lipstick that clashed with her hair colour. Noble wore corduroy pants and a shirt and tie. The same tie he wore to the funeral.

The lawyer's office was two flights above an army surplus store in downtown Kingston, in a nice old limestone building. On the oak-panelled walls hung faded prints of fly-fishing anglers. On top of one cabinet was a shellacked swordfish.

The lawyer, John Bertram, read the will to Del, Noble, and Paisley, as well as an accompanying letter. The will itself was very short; the letter, not so much. It went on for pages, and the lawyer spoke in code to Del and Noble about wanting to "refer only to the relevant bits," to which Del responded, "Finally someone other than me has to read the non-relevant bits. Good."

The bits in question essentially said this: Eudie had owned a beloved cat in Toronto, which had left her with an affection for felines that was impossible to quantify. As a result, she felt responsible for Amherst Island's cats, given the fact that no one else seemed to be. At present, she had twenty-seven cats and fourteen kittens in the house, all in need of shelter. Therefore, she was leaving the house to them, and neither Paisley nor Del was allowed on the property. No one was.

The lawyer confirmed that Eudie had no other assets except a small bank account, and they would forward a cheque for the balance to Paisley shortly. Also, Paisley would be receiving Hu's insurance from the sanitation plant. It wasn't much, but it was something, and if she placed it in an annuity—Mr. Bertram could help her with that—it would last until she died, probably allowing her to meet modest living costs but not much more.

So what did Paisley want to do now? asked Mr. Bertram. Was she going to live with Del and Noble?

Paisley looked over to Del.

Del searched her purse for another cigarette, though the one in her hand was only half-finished. "I'm sure you've got other plans, Paisley," she said into her purse.

Paisley's mind was blank, so she said nothing.

"And if you don't," said Del, finding her pack and removing a cigarette with trembling hands, "you'll get some. You're all but done high school. You're eighteen. Who doesn't have plans when they're eighteen? I know I've got plans, and I'm a lot older. It's time for us all to spread our wings and fly."

John Bertram looked at the fish on the cabinet. Noble looked at his corduroy pants. Del took a deep drag on her cigarette.

In one fell swoop, Paisley had lost every single thing that was familiar to her, and no amount of counting and checking or apologizing was going to change that.

NOW

Paisley and Garnet caught the two o'clock ferry. They stood on the boat's open upper deck, where it was sunny and windy, and she watched Amherst Island get smaller and smaller. The island didn't hold such terrible memories anymore. Better ones were sneaking in at every opportunity.

They were both famished when they reached the mainland, so Garnet drove to the Bath supermarket. As they pulled into the parking lot, Paisley suddenly felt sick.

"You coming in?"

"Is this still Del's store?"

He nodded.

"Then, no thanks. I don't feel like seeing her."

Garnet got out of the car. He promised something vaguely more substantial than Pop Tarts.

Paisley waited in stillness, like she'd be invisible if she didn't move. The shops in Bath had changed; flower baskets hung from the street lights.

The car was airless. Garnet had taken the car keys in with him, and it wasn't possible to lower the windows. She got out of the car and stretched. She probably looked like a disaster—she'd gotten laid several times, she'd swum in the lake, she'd slept in a car, and was wearing the same clothes as yesterday. And yet she felt good.

"Paisley?"

She turned and saw a woman at the picnic table by the Dumpster, smoking.

It was Delilah. As always, her hair was up, and it was still red—absurdly red, given her age. She no longer looked glamorous; it looked like she was trying too hard. She wore a tight pair of jeans, high heels, and a silky blouse undone one button too far. She had chunky rings on almost every finger. Not the movie star Paisley remembered.

"It's you! Paisley Ratchford. Well, holy shit."

It didn't make sense, but Paisley felt afraid. She was an adult now, she had nothing to fear from Del—not that she ever had. And yet here they were again.

"Yes, it's me," Paisley said. "How are you, Del?"

"Well, I'm still here, aren't I?" She took a drag on her cigarette. "How the hell are you?"

"Just fine, thanks."

They observed each other. "I would have written," said Del, "but I didn't have your address. Are you still in Toronto?"

"I am, mostly."

"Mostly?"

Paisley shrugged.

"Well, aren't we mysterious. And what are you doing in Toronto, mostly?"

Paisley observed her warily. Unsure whether to keep talking and what to say if she did. "A bit of this and that."

"Ah. So you're in Toronto, mostly, doing a bit of this and that. In other words, same old, same old. I've got some of that happening here, too."

"You still own the store, that's something."

"True. Although Noble divorced me about a decade ago and made off with a tramp half my age from Montreal. Left me holding the bag, and I just haven't quite gotten up the gumption to, you know, move on."

Paisley nodded.

"I've got plans, but..." She trailed off, took another drag on her cigarette, and butted out. "I used to talk a good line, didn't I? All my options. Talked about the big world out there."

"It takes some of us longer than others." Paisley heard what that sounded like and added, "I'm referring to myself, of course."

"Of course."

There was that sarcasm Paisley had found so enticing as a child. So cosmopolitan.

Del strolled over. She still walked well in high heels, like a beauty queen at a pageant. But as she came closer, Paisley could see the wrinkles. The weariness.

"Can't throw stones in glass houses, can we? I used to go on and on to your mum about how she should get out, get the hell out of here before the place did her in. But it's not really the place that does us in, is it."

"You can change that." Paisley was meaning to be helpful, but Del shot her a glance.

"Don't lecture me, Paisley."

"I'm not—"

"Yes, you are." She guffawed. "I mean, come on. You? Lecture me? The Amherst Island crazy girl? What a joke."

Paisley's knees trembled. She considered one set of eight to set things right. "I—I didn't mean to offend you."

"Yes you did." Del was now on the other side of the car. "Just angling for that chance to condescend, to get one over on me. Do you know what I did for your family? Do you know what I did for you?"

"In the end, sweet fuck all." Garnet stood behind Paisley, holding a bag of groceries.

"Garnet?" Del looked at him, agog.

Garnet opened the trunk, threw in the food, and slammed it shut. He came around the car to Paisley's side and wrapped his arm around her waist, pulled her to him, and kissed her deep and strong. Del just about fainted. So did Paisley.

"Let's go," he whispered.

Without releasing Paisley's waist, he pulled her to the car and opened the passenger door. Her knees were weak, but she got in. He closed the door after her and strode around the vehicle.

"See ya, Del," he said as he got in. "Have a great day." Then he put the car into reverse, screeched back ten feet, and tore out of the parking lot.

Paisley didn't look back.

The platform at the Kingston train station was awash in sunlight. They sat on a bench and ate sandwiches from the food Garnet had bought. Paisley had signed all the paperwork for the house, the keys were in her bag. The train would be there any minute. She stood up and looked down the track. No sign of it yet.

"Well..." She had no idea what to say.

"Well."

"Thank you for all you've done. With the house."

"No problem."

"And...with other things. Like Del."

Garnet nodded slowly. He shoved his hands in his pockets. The train appeared, gliding toward the station.

"So, what are you going to do about your apartment? The eviction?"

"I'm not too sure what I'm going to do...but for once I don't feel panicked, so that's a start."

"Stay."

"Are you kidding?"

"No. I can help with your stuff in Toronto—we can put it in storage. Or pack it up. Or maybe bring it here."

"Okay...and what would I do here?"

"Take care of that sparrow. It needs you. Talk to those Kingston bird people. They might need you, too. And maybe...maybe I need you."

"You?" Paisley laughed. "Why?"

The train pulled in.

"Because you're strange and interesting and exotic, like I said, and you don't quite know where you want to be, and that feels a lot like me. And because I think I could help with your counting and checking. I think you could help me too."

"Well, what about you? Still a lawyer? Or are you buying Mildred's farm? Or are you moving back to Ireland?"

"Yes."

She laughed.

"I don't know either. But you could help me try to figure it out. And stay sane."

"That makes no sense. I'm the craziest person I know."

"So life will never be boring. I'm not saying I know what's going to happen tomorrow—but today this is what I'm asking. Please stay."

The conductor blew the whistle.

No one disembarked. No one boarded. A moment of stasis. Garnet looked at Paisley. Paisley looked at Garnet.

"One...two...three," counted Paisley.

The conductor blew the whistle one last time.

"Four...five...six," said Garnet.

The doors closed.

"Seven...eight," said Paisley.

The train pulled slowly out of the station.

They headed back to the car.

"So where are we going?" she said.

ACKNOWLEDGEMENTS

I am indebted to Dolly Reisman and Tracy O'Hara, my first writers' circle. We shared a ballsy dare to write forty pages of material with which to apply to the Ontario and Toronto Arts Councils. Those pages miraculously earned funding from both, and I thank them for their early and much-needed financial support.

I used some of that funding to go through the Humber School for Writers (twice), where I received important mentorship from Antanas Sileika and Richard Scrimger.

Nathan Whitlock then helped reimagine the book's structure—and though there was gnashing of teeth on my part, he never took it personally and it was the right thing to do.

Along the way, many people helped with research, including Steffen Reinhart, Adam Poel, and Joanne O'Sullivan, as well as ornithologists and birders Elizabeth Kellogg, Cheryl Anderson, David Okines, and Chris Grooms.

People from Amherst Island have helped so much, especially the Caughey and Forester families, and my in-laws, Nancy and Zander Dunn, who lived there for many years and introduced me to the wonders of the place and its community.

I am particularly indebted to my readers and fact-checkers, Paul Mackenzie from the Kingston Field Naturalists and Jill and Lori Caughey from Amherst Island.

Alex Schultz, a truly great editor, helped bring the book home with his insights into the story and the area, and with his sense of humour. I could not believe my good luck when I learned that not only did he live in Prince Edward County and could see Amherst Island from his deck, but also that, at the age of thirteen, he had been a card-carrying member of the Young Ornithologists' Club in Ireland. I knew I had found the right editor.

I also thank Invisible Publishing, who have brought the book to fruition in ways I never could have imagined. I learned so much from both publishers Leigh Nash, who edited the book, and Norm Nehmetallah, who released it into the world.

Carl Lyons was key to helping me overcome much of the OCD I suffered from in my youth.

And finally, I have Kirk to thank: my husband, my life-long partner, and my first reader, always. He was key to closing the book on an old and tired history, and helped me write a new chapter with our marriage, and our children, Findley and Emmett. For those gifts and so many more, I dedicate this book to him.

INVISIBLE PUBLISHING produces fine Canadian literature for those who enjoy such things. As an independent, not-for-profit publisher, our work includes building communities that sustain and encourage engaging, literary, and current writing.

Invisible Publishing has been in operation for over a decade. We released our first fiction titles in the spring of 2007, and our catalogue has come to include works of graphic fiction and nonfiction, pop culture biographies, experimental poetry, and prose.

We are committed to publishing diverse voices and experiences. In acknowledging historical and systemic barriers, and the limits of our existing catalogue, we strongly encourage writers from LGBTQ2SIA+ communities, Indigenous writers, and writers of colour to submit their work.

Invisible Publishing is also home to the Bibliophonic series of music books and the Throwback series of CanLit reissues.

If you'd like to know more, please get in touch: info@invisiblepublishing.com